LOST OASIS

LOST OASIS

A Novel

By R LAWSON GAMBLE

Zack Tolliver, FBI, Series Book Eight

R Lawson Gamble Books Imprint
Rich Gamble Associates
Los Alamos, CA

For Annie

Thank you ex-neighbor but always friend Craig, who rides my rough drafts as in a paper boat in an ocean storm, all the while tossed by inconsistencies, flooded with abandoned articles, confused by fact fogged with fiction, guided only by the erratic compass of the author's intent, yet somehow always finding a safe harbor.

"…We make guilty of our disasters the sun, the moon, and the stars, as if we were villains by necessity…"
Wm. Shakespeare (King Lear)

CHAPTER ONE

"Your kind have ever been a puzzle to me, White Man," Eagle Feather said, stopping to glance back where the wash widened and merged in the shimmering distance. "Why would anyone come here?"

Heat radiated from underfoot and rebounded off the stone walls on either side of the wash. Sparse snatches of creosote, palo verde, and ocotillo, like stubby whiskers on an old man's chin, were scattered across the dry bed. Runnels from recent storms carved wide ruts in the sand, and the terraces between them were sprinkled with small stones rounded from eons of tumbling. Every living thing in the breathlessly still air of the wash seemed to gasp. It was as if the two men had walked into a giant baker's oven.

"Gold, silver, iron ore, jade." Zack Tolliver wiped the sweat from under his eyes.

Ahead, the dry bed narrowed, its banks grew and became canyon walls, their sheer surfaces built from massive sandstone boulders tumbled one upon the other as if a giant child had stacked balls of play-dough. Zack had to agree that only the most fanatical and stubborn of men would pursue wealth underlying such a wasteland. He knew that native peoples had lived comfortably in this desert environment for centuries, but during the heat of mid-summer they were smart enough to move to cooler places.

"And the one we track now?" Eagle Feather asked. "What brought him here?"

Zack took a mouthful of water, wiped his lips, and returned the bottle to his belt. "That's a good question." He glanced around at the immensity of his surroundings. "When they told me this man disappeared from the face of the earth, I was surprised. Now it begins to feel possible."

"Many people disappear in the desert each year," Eagle Feather said.

"True enough, and for many reasons. Some don't want to be found. Some are novices and come unprepared. But the person we seek is a scientist with all the latest devices, including a SAT phone and GPS locater, I'm told." He shrugged his pack higher on his shoulders and tightened the straps.

"Why did they assign you to this case?"

Zack grinned. "You mean us? My boss volunteered me."

Eagle Feather nodded his understanding and turned to lead on.

Zack grinned to himself. There was no need to explain more. Eagle Feather knew Zack's boss, Supervisory Agent Janice Hooper. She was a mighty force in her own right, belying her diminutive and attractive appearance. She was responsible for the special investigative branch Zack now headed, the Special Cases Branch, a unit dedicated to investigating crimes that defied normal FBI protocols and approaches, crimes that occurred in seemingly impossible and irrational circumstances. At this point in time, the

LOST OASIS

Special Cases Branch consisted of one agent—Zack himself.

Janice understood that Zack's impressive record of successes with difficult cases in Navajo Land came from his belief that once one eliminates every other possibility, whatever remains, however improbable, must be the truth. His application of this ideology in cases involving Navajo mysticism and superstition had brought him to metaphysical places where other more traditionally minded agents balked. She sensed a need for this approach within the conservative ranks of the FBI and grasped the initiative to create this new branch and to convince Zack, at the time a disillusioned and conflicted man, to take charge of it. In so doing, she had re-energized both man and organization.

Agents facing extraordinary or unusually strange cases could now opt to seek the assistance of this special branch, but as yet few of the cases brought to him had merited Zack's involvement, in his opinion. But if Janice Hooper called and asked Zack to take a case, as she had done this time, he took it. Zack's first call usually went to his Navajo friend and mentor Eagle Feather, whom he hired as his "special consultant". The arrangement served both men well.

Zack had texted Eagle Feather two days prior, asking his friend to meet him here near Joshua Tree National Park and directed him to the junction of Pinto Basin Road and Black Eagle Mine Road. They had met there and driving in tandem, passed through the boundary gate of the National Park and onto private land following an old mine road toward the Eagle Mountains. They left Eagle Feather's truck at a wide bajada and drove on with the Jeep following ruts north through the deep sand mix. The quasi road they followed stopped two miles later at a deep, narrow gully. Here was the place officials had found the missing man's abandoned Land Rover. The vehicle had since been taken away.

Eagle Feather, a renowned tracker, studied the signs, no easy task due to the numerous footprints left by previous investigators. Regardless, he was able to isolate the scientist's footprints and conclude he had left the vehicle voluntarily with a full pack.

Seeing this, Zack and Eagle Feather loaded overnight supplies in their own backpacks and followed the frenzy of footprints northward up the gradually sloping wash. They were now several hours into the search.

The sandstone walls continued to narrow, the bajada became a canyon with a spongy gravelly mix underfoot, making heavy work of walking. Footprints lost definition here. Eagle Feather's progress slowed as he stopped to study even the slightest of impressions.

Eventually, the canyon walls fell away again. The dry bed steepened, narrowing to a hundred feet in width with undercut sandbanks. They were forced to find ways around and over stone piles, more than once disturbing rattlesnakes resting in the cool shade beneath ledges.

As they gained altitude, the sun's rays became hotter, but the occasional breeze cooled their sweaty bodies. Zack paused for another sip of water. He glanced at the thermometer function on his watch.

"It's 108 degrees," he said.

"I was better off not knowing that." Eagle Feather studied a steep slope of sand and loose stone that loomed above them. It was shaped like the prow of a boat. It was the spot where the dry bed divided, with flow entering from either side.

Zack didn't need his sharp-eyed friend to tell him where they were headed next. A line of disturbed sand was visible all the way up the face of the slope. Zack sighed. "I'll say this for him, he was determined."

"His course is direct as if he was following compass headings to a specific point." Eagle Feather turned to Zack. "Do you know what he was after?"

"No. All I know is the man was hired to consult for an energy company interested in creating hydroelectric power from abandoned iron mine pits somehow. But that is far from here. Something else sidetracked him up this way. Nobody seems to know what."

"You spoke of valuable minerals."

Zack nodded. "Well, the possibility of gold brought prospectors to this region a hundred years ago. Why not now?"

"What do you know about this missing man?"

"The report said he is a foremost expert in hydrology, specifically hydroelectric power generation and storage. He was hired by the EverSun Company."

"Then the man wandered over here and went missing. Why is the FBI involved?"

"The company feared he had been abducted. Apparently, what's in his head is quite valuable."

"Company secrets?"

"Even national secrets, possibly."

"And again, why you?"

Zack grinned, looked at his friend. "The stuff we are good at. Ghosts. Aliens. Take your pick. He vanished without a trace. This entire area was thoroughly searched by teams of dogs, helicopters, satellites, you name it, all at great expense, all yielding nothing. We are their last resort."

"Such a situation is not new," Eagle Feather commented as he turned and started up the slope.

When the land beyond the high bank came into view, Zack realized they had come to a plateau, flat as a table, a kind of place not uncommon in the Mojave desert where a subsoil layer of sandstone outlasted the surrounding landscape against the eroding forces of wind and floodwaters. Beyond it, the ridges and peaks of the Eagle Mountain range rose to touch a burnished blue sky. But for a tracker, the beauty of the scene was lost. The hard surface of the mesa left barely a trace.

Zack waited while Eagle Feather went to a knee to inspect the ground. The tracker took his time, moving forward inch by inch. Caught up in the inner dialogue of his sign reading, he no longer seemed to notice his companion or the sun beating down.

LOST OASIS

As Zack looked beyond them across the mesa, he saw a strange object shimmering in the far distance, its shape distorted by the desert heat. It appeared to be nestled against the foothills, a tall needle-like object silhouetted against the sky. He pointed it out to the Eagle Feather.

The Navajo stood and stretched. He peered at the object. "We will find out what it is. The tracks lead in that direction," he said. They walked on.

As they came closer they could see it was a pillar of rock, thick at the base, narrowing near the top. They began to see yellow police tape and red marker flags.

The pillar and its immediate surroundings were remarkable enough to be a destination unto itself, it seemed to Zack. Ancient palm stumps and rotting leaves surrounded a graduated concavity that one time contained water. Beyond the area, an arroyo cut into the hillside.

"This was once an oasis," Zack said. "This rock pillar would have been surrounded by palm trees. It must have been a lovely spot."

Footprints in the sandy ground showed where officials had wandered. The pillar itself was four feet in diameter and composed of black stone material, tapering to a shelf after which the rock finger pointed skyward. It appeared worn and broken near the top as if it once had reached higher.

"I know of several oases similar to this one in the area," Zack said. "There is one not many miles from here called Lost Palms Oasis."

"This one is very lost," Eagle Feather said.

Zack grinned. He studied the ground. "These isolated patches of vegetation are usually found where there has been seismic activity. Cracks open in the earth, an aquifer is breached, and a spring pops up in the middle of the desert."

"There is no water here anymore," Eagle Feather said.

"No, it hasn't been an oasis for a long time," Zack said. He studied the base of the stone pillar. "These small pockets in the stone might have been created by human hands, and this black area might be from smoke."

"This could be a sacred place," Eagle Feather said.

Zack gazed up at the tower. "At one time this pillar must have been significantly taller."

"It is strange how it rises from the earth."

"Yes, like a giant arrow or spear landed here," Zack said. "It is a curiosity." He put his hands on his hips and looked around. "But the question remains, what happened to our scientist?"

Eagle Feather shrugged. "Yes. It is time to get to work." The two men began a minute inspection of the ground surrounding the stone pillar.

Before very long, Eagle Feather announced, "The scientist did not travel beyond this point."

"That doesn't leave many options."

Eagle Feather shrugged. "I cannot tell you where he went, but I can tell you where he did not go. He did not go beyond this place."

"Did he go back?"

"No, he did not go back."

Zack looked up. "Balloon? Jet pack? Hovering helicopter?"

Eagle Feather raised an amused eyebrow, shrugged again.

Zack took a sip of water from his bottle, passed it to Eagle Feather. "As head of the department of last resort in the FBI, the pet project of one Supervisory Agent Janet Hooper, I can officially inform you we are expected to find an answer where everyone else has failed. What shall we say happened to this scientist?"

Eagle Feather stared at the horizon, then looked at Zack. "My choice is an alien abduction," he said.

CHAPTER TWO

They camped under an overhang near the edge of the arroyo. Eagle Feather's tiny gas stove hissed comfortably at its task of boiling a pot of water. Their camp was dry, but the water-skin Zack had packed in was sufficient for their needs. The view from their camp encompassed the mesa they had crossed and the barren hills beyond, now tinted pink with afterglow. As hot as it had been that day, the desert air was cooling rapidly now as the sun set, and Zack was glad for the cup of hot chocolate he wrapped in his hands.

"What now, White Man?" Eagle Feather asked. He cast a glance up from the stove he tended.

"We learned nothing today to add to what we already knew. The man disappeared next to a strange rock in the middle of a wide-open expanse and left no trace. That pretty much sums it up, doesn't it?"

"Pretty much," the Navajo said.

"We know the company that hired this guy, the EverSun Energy Company, utilized every man and device possible to locate him after he went missing. We know all the usual law enforcement, including the FBI, were called in, to no avail. I think we can assume this entire mountain has been minutely scrutinized by man, dog, drone, and satellite. I see no point in repeating the effort."

Eagle Feather cocked an eyebrow. "But you have a plan."

Zack nodded. "Not a plan so much as a process. I want
to know more about this mountain, about the EverSun
Energy Company, about this missing scientist."

"He has a name?"

Zack pulled out his smartphone and checked his notes.
"His name is Dr. Carl Scheidecker. He served on the
United States Department of Energy Advisory Board
before coming to EverSun to work on their special solar
energy storage project. He has lots of classified
information stored in his brain that many other countries
would love to access. I want to learn who he is, all about
his family, his hobbies, his marriage, everything. Who is his
best friend, who has he spoken to lately, what calls has he
made, what caused him to make this long arduous hike up
here?"

"Has not the FBI already done all that?"

Zack shook his head. "I'm sure they have, but I need to
ask my questions, hear it for myself. I also want to know
more about this company. What is this project about? How
do you create hydroelectric power in the middle of the
desert, anyway?"

As the sun set, the cold settled over them, but Zack's
sleeping bag was toasty. He lay a long time with his eyes
open exalting in the brilliant display of stars, so sharp and
clear it felt as if he could reach a hand up and grab a few.
He didn't remember dozing off.

A rolling motion beneath him awakened him. It felt as
if he were sharing a waterbed. The ground itself was
moving, he realized, like a gentle ocean swell, back and

forth, and his stomach went along with it. He had been sleeping with his head on its side and his ear to the ground and he heard a deep rumbling in the earth below. He began to count the seconds and reached ten before the motion stopped. He turned to look at the shadow that was Eagle Feather in his sleeping bag.

"Earthquake," his friend muttered sleepily, without moving.

Zack lay pondering the event until sleep took him once more.

In the sharp morning light, after coffee and granola bars, they once again examined the strange stone and last signs left by Dr. Scheidecker. After that, they hiked out. They had learned nothing more.

Zack dropped Eagle Feather at his truck, noticing how its weathered red paint and rust spots blended peculiarly well with the surrounding desert as if desiring to camouflage itself. He waited to be sure the old truck started before driving off. When he reached the paved park road, he turned north. The park speed limit was fifty-five miles per hour, the day just heating up, so Zack left his window open to enjoy the breeze and more clearly view the play of light and shadow on the spectacular terrain. An unaccustomed rattling sound intruded into his consciousness beyond the louder rush of the wind. He focused on it. It was a fluttering noise as if some plastic had come loose under the vehicle. He sighed, decided he'd better pull over now, and fix the problem rather than risk a bigger repair later on.

At the next turnoff, he stopped and left the engine running while he peered under the vehicle on the driver's side where the noise seemed to have originated. At first glance, he did not understand what he was seeing, but seconds later he was covered in sweat that had nothing to do with the sun's heat. He jumped up, reached into the vehicle, turned it off, and removed the key, then walked swiftly away from the Jeep. At a safe distance, he made a phone call.

An answer came after three rings. "Supervisory Agent Janice Hooper speaking. Hello, Zack."

"Janice, please call the bomb unit closest to Joshua Tree National Park and dispatch them to the south end of Pinto Basin Road about mile twenty at"—he paused a second to glance at the sign—"the Colorado Desert Landscape Information turnoff."

She responded quickly, her voice crisp. "Stay on the line."

Zack listened impatiently to bland jazz music.

Three minutes later, Janice was back. "ETA forty minutes. You are pretty much in the middle of nowhere, Zack. What have you got there?"

"I have a metal cylinder attached to the underside of the driver's side of the Jeep. It has a threaded end-cap like a pipe bomb. I didn't hang around to see more."

"Is the Jeep running?"

"No, I turned it off."

"Okay, did you see anything that looked like a timer?"

"Nothing obvious."

"Maybe it's speed sensitive." She sounded hopeful.

"That would be good."

"Listen, Zack, no hero stuff. Just stay away from the vehicle until the unit arrives. Is anyone else there?"

"No, just me. I'll keep other cars away."

Zack hung up and immediately texted Eagle Feather. He didn't think the bomber would target his friend. No one could have known about him. Regardless, he left a message describing what was happening and suggesting Eagle Feather inspect his vehicle.

Fifteen minutes later a park ranger arrived and set up roadblocks at either side of the turnoff. A half-hour after that, Zack heard a siren and a white van with a Riverside Sheriff's Department logo roared around the corner. The vehicle parked at the roadblock and a uniformed policeman spoke to the ranger before walking briskly over to Zack.

"Agent Tolliver?"

Zack nodded.

"Sheriff's Deputy Hagen. Is that the vehicle with the suspicious item?"

"Yes, that's my Jeep. The metal cylinder is directly under the driver's seat."

"Okay. The Hazardous Device Team is en route. If you'll just remain a safe distance away, we'll inspect it shortly."

LOST OASIS

The officer went back to the roadway to help with traffic. By now, several cars were stopped in either direction, the curious tourists kept in their cars by the ranger. In another ten minutes, a flatbed truck trundled up and stopped near the entrance to the pullout. It carried a vehicle resembling a small cement truck and an even stranger vehicle with a factory-like robotic arm.

Zack watched with interest as a man in a protective suit used a small control board to guide the robotic vehicle off the truck and into the parking area toward Zack's Jeep. Once it arrived on the driver's side, it extended its arm beneath the vehicle and held it there. The man at the control studied his panel intently. A few minutes later the robot retracted the arm and backed away. Zack saw that the cylinder was in its grasp. The robot wheeled around and returned to the flatbed truck, rode up the ramp, and inserted the cylinder in the bomb detonator barrel of the cement mixer.

The suited man strode over to Zack.

"Officer Mahey," he said, shaking Zack's hand. "Looks like somebody doesn't like you. What we seem to have here is an explosive device meant to detonate once the exhaust pipe running under your seat reached a certain temperature. Very simple idea. The bomb is fused to an igniter wrapped in plastic wrap. Once the exhaust pipe heats enough, it melts the plastic and ignites the fuse. Lucky you didn't drive very far."

Zack thanked the officer. His knees felt a little weak as he considered how close it had been.

"We'll disassemble the bomb and send the materials to the FBI lab for analysis," Mahey said. "Have a nice day."

Zack's phone rang. It was Janice Hooper.

"I just had a call from the sheriff," Agent Hooper said. "You had a very close call."

"Lucky it was a nice morning and my window was open."

"We'll have the bomb analyzed to see what we can learn," Hooper said.

"It could be our first lead to Scheidecker's disappearance," Zack suggested. "Apparently someone wanted to stop my investigation before it even got started."

"What have you learned?"

"Nothing. That's the strange part. No need to knock me off. I haven't learned a thing."

After agreeing to keep his boss posted, Zack walked back to the Jeep. This time he gave it a thorough inspection before starting it up. His phone rang again. This time it was Eagle Feather.

"White Man, you answered your phone, so I assume the bomb did not kill you."

Zack chuckled. "And you are speaking to me, so I assume your truck did not blow up, either."

"I saw your message and pulled over. I gave the truck a good look underneath. I found a lot of things I did not know were there, but no bomb."

"Clearly, someone is well informed."

"An FBI leak?"

"Unlikely. Local law enforcement was also involved in the investigation. That's a lot of people, potentially. It's a place to start, though."

Zack started up the Jeep and drove away. By now the temperature had kicked into the nineties. He closed his window and put on the AC, thinking what might have happened had he done so earlier.

They had reservations at the Joshua Tree Best Western in Yucca Valley. He headed there now. He would need a telephone and the internet to get started.

Janice Hooper had said she would find who among the local police could have had information about Zack's arrival, but admitted it would likely be too large a group to narrow down much. Zack decided to leave that angle with her for now, and concentrate on the EverSun Energy Company. He went to the internet.

EverSun, he learned, was the world's largest operator of solar and wind farms. A company with revenues approaching $17 billion, they had invested heavily in lobbying and campaign contributions to sway California lawmakers toward their proposed project at Eagle Mountain. A bill was before the California Senate which mandated California build energy projects that could store large amounts of power for long periods by a specific date. The EverSun project would utilize huge abandoned iron mine pits left by Kaiser Steel. The proposed technology involved flooding the vast open pits, using solar power to pump the water uphill to another storage pit. When the sun goes down, the water is released back, and the resulting flow turns a turbine that generates electricity. The result is a readily available mega source of electric power 24/7. All of the bill's co-authors had received campaign funds from EverSun. The bill's other supporters included organized labor groups that would benefit from the project.

Zack saw controversy with the project even before he began digging into it. The company proposed to use California's most vital substance, water, to create its most vital utility, electricity. They intended to do it in a place surrounded on three sides by protected, fragile ecosystems while extracting groundwater from an over-allocated and sensitive basin. Although Bill 772 was recently moved to the inactive file, Zack well knew such a bill could be quickly reactivated, piggybacked on a more urgent bill, and passed before opponents were even aware of the voting. It was like Russian Roulette, he mused—an active bullet hidden among the empty chambers. While the principle involved in the project seemed basic on the face of it, Zack knew it would require much technical knowhow and a huge labor force.

He turned his research toward Dr. Carl Scheidecker himself. He found the man had an undergraduate degree in Mechanical Engineering, a PhD. in Aero and Hydro Dynamics, and his learned work included "Topographical Measurement of Water Waves at a Matrix of Measure Points", "Particle Image Velocimetry for Microscale Blood Flow Measurement", "Pumped Storage Plants in the Future Power Supply Systems", and "Pumped Storage

Plants - Status and Perspectives", among others. He was currently Professor of Renewable Electricity Generation at Münster University of Applied Sciences. In 2012 he had attended the SETIS expert workshop on the assessment of the potential of pumped hydropower storage where he lectured on "Identification of Potential PHS Sites in Large Areas based on a Multi-Criteria GIS-Model".

Zack shook his head in wonder. The man certainly knew how liquids flowed. But what had caused him to wander off to the lost oasis? The strange stone where his tracks led was fully ten miles away from his project. More to the point, who was ready to kill Zack just to prevent him from investigating the scientist's disappearance?

Zack's stomach gnawed. He looked at his watch and was surprised to see it was well past lunchtime. He grabbed his wallet, locked the room, and walked down the street to Castenada's Mexican Food where he ordered a California Burrito to go. The smells wafting from the warm bag heightened his anticipation on his walk back. He unlocked his door, entered the room, and went to the tiny refrigerator where he found a can of apple juice. After placing the burrito and apple juice on a small table he pulled up a chair. The burrito was partway to his mouth when his phone rang.

Zack answered. He heard the honeyed voice of Janice Hooper.

"Hi, Zack. The lab has begun a preliminary examination of the bomb taken from your Jeep. And surprise, surprise, we have a clear thumbprint."

Zack was taken aback. "Well, that was certainly careless. Have you identified it?"

"Yes, we have. The print belongs to one Dr. Carl Scheidecker, the missing man."

CHAPTER THREE

Eagle Feather turned left on Pinto Basin Road and followed it south over the Interstate 10 bridge, where it became Box Canyon Road, headed toward Mecca and the Salton Sea. His destination was Thermal, the home of Ida Martinez, Tribal Chairperson of the Torres-Martinez branch of the Agua Caliente Band of Cahuilla Indians. Eagle Feather had met her during an investigation in Palm Springs and they had remained good friends.

The concrete walk of her modest home was surrounded by a huge variety of desert plantings, some unfamiliar even to Eagle Feather. Ida met him on the front stoop. He followed her inside. The house, as always, smelled of fresh baking. Ida led him to her sitting room and left him there while she went to pour fresh lemonade.

"I happen to have baked a batch of oatmeal cookies and I'd like your opinion," she said when she returned.

"I will test one for you," Eagle Feather said.

She set the plate of cookies in easy reach and handed him a glass of lemonade. "It is so good to see you," she said, watching Eagle Feather bite into a soft warm cookie. "What new mystery brings you to these parts?"

Eagle Feather held up a finger to wait. He finished chewing with deliberate slowness. "On a scale of one to five this cookie is a six," he said, his tone solemn.

Ida smiled broadly.

He continued her thought. "It is always good to see you as well. And your cookies," He washed down the cookie with some lemonade. "Yes, I have come here with Agent Tolliver and we do have another mystery to solve."

"Oh, how wonderful," Ida said, clasping her hands together in delight. "I do love a good mystery."

Eagle Feather chewed some, sipped some, and then spoke. "We have lost an important scientist. He wandered into the Eagle Mountains east of Joshua National Park and disappeared. We tracked him yesterday and again this morning and could not find him. His tracks simply disappeared. I have no explanation."

Ida looked at him in surprise. "If even you couldn't track him, he must truly have disappeared."

"I do not exclude a paranormal possibility. But to understand it, if such a thing happened, I need to understand the place where it occurred."

Ida stood and walked to a bookshelf. She searched titles for a moment before removing a spiral-bound book of maps. She returned to her seat, asking, "Where in the Eagle Mountains is this place?"

"I can give you longitude and latitude." Eagle Feather check his phone notes and dictated them to her.

Ida flipped open the booklet, found a page, and moved her finger across it. "Here." She leaned toward Eagle Feather with the map, her finger at the location. "This is the coordinate. It's a mile or so west of Eagle Tank, one of a few dependable springs in the area known to my people.

At least it was dependable until Kaiser Steel began digging huge pits in the area."

"Has that effected the spring?"

"I'm told the water is no longer as clear as it once was. Precautions are necessary before drinking it."

"What about the precise area of the coordinates? What is that area? This flat land here." Eagle Feather placed a finger on the map.

"That is in the Great Wash. It is, obviously, quite a large one. I rode down it in a dune buggy at one time in my youth with several friends. We were caught by Kaiser security and escorted off the property."

Eagle Feather looked closely. "It seems to run along the park border."

Ida nodded. "They may even have used that wash to define the border. But the flat area you refer to, right there, is not familiar to me. But wait. Let me check something."

Ida went back to her bookshelf and searched again. This time she produced a very small book, more like a pamphlet. She walked back to her chair leafing through it. "Yes, I thought I remembered this." She looked at him "First a little anthropology lesson, if you don't mind. My people, the Cahuilla, inhabited mostly the area from the Colorado River to the San Jacinto plain outside of Riverside, including the southern portion of what is now Joshua Tree National Park. It was the Serrano people who first occupied the northern sections including what is now Twenty-Nine Palms. They occupied the Oasis of Mara there until a smallpox epidemic nearly wiped them out.

After that, they abandoned the area attributing their demise to evil spirits. When in 1867 warfare broke out between two Colorado River peoples, the Chemehuevi and the Mojave, the Chemehuevi people, led by Chief William Mike, were forced into the desert. They then occupied the Oasis of Mara, joining a Serrano band led by Chief Pine. After Willie Boy murdered Chief Mike and stole his daughter, the native people left the Oasis of Mara believing evil spirits inhabited the place. With relatives on the Torres Martinez Reservation, some Chemehuevi moved south to live here with the Cahuilla at the Torres Martinez Reservation. Over the years, the Chemehuevi maintained a close relationship with us."

She drew a breath, smiled at him. "Got it?" She turned to the book. "Now, this monologue was written by an archaeologist in 1912, and he appears to describe your area of interest as near as I can tell. He speaks of an obelisk. It stands, quote, "on a barren plain above the great wash formed by a division of sedimental flow, as if between two ancient rivers". He describes the obelisk as ten or twelve feet tall on a rounded base some five or six feet in diameter." She looked at Eagle Feather. "That sounds larger than the one you described."

"Yes. But a century of erosion might explain it."

"Indeed." She flipped a page. "He talks about finding artifacts on and around this pillar—baskets, pottery, animal bones, primitive tools. He attributes his finds to the Chemehuevi people, which seems likely."

"He seems to describe an altar, a place of ritual."

24

Ida nodded.

"Does he say anything else?"

Ida handed the booklet to Eagle Feather. "Not really. As you can see, this is just a reference to a site he labeled number forty-six among hundreds of other similar sites he describes very briefly."

Eagle Feather glanced at the booklet cover. The title was "Sites of Archaeological Interest along the Sonoran and Mojave Desert Transition Zone". He glanced at Ida. "Only you would own such a book."

She smiled. "I have a vested interest in everything concerning my people's origins, even tangentially."

"This David Ralston, the author; do you know anything about him?"

She shook her head. "The book was printed by the University of Southern California. You might start there."

After Eagle Feather's departure an hour later, he decided to call his friend Chief Dan Singletree of the Chemehuevi people to see what he might know about the eroded obelisk. Like Ida, Dan was interested in preserving his people's past.

Chief Dan lived on the Colorado Reservation along the shore of Lake Havasu with a couple hundred of his people. An old man now, he did not travel far from home. He answered after the first ring. They exchanged greetings and Eagle Feather explained his purpose.

"My friend, I am not personally familiar with the area you describe," Chief Dan said. "The Chemehuevi people who inhabited the Twenty-Nine Palms area were the

Shivawach band. I descend from the group now recognized as the Chemehuevi Indian Tribe of the Chemehuevi Reservation." He explained. "We are all considered Southern Paiutes, you see, but our people have always been solitary and less tribal than other peoples. These divisions were assigned by the mission in a somewhat arbitrary fashion depending upon the proximity of one family group to another. There is a reservation in Twenty-Nine Palms of the Shivawach people. You should contact George Madrigal. He is an old friend and has deep roots in the area."

Eagle Feather took down the number and called. It turned out George Madrigal was the manager at the Tortoise Rock Casino in Twenty-Nine Palms. He invited Eagle Feather to meet with him there. Eagle Feather glanced at his watch, arranged to meet George at four that afternoon, allowing two hours for travel and lunch. He'd grab a sandwich along the way.

Before he could pull back onto the highway, he noticed he had a message. It was from Zack Tolliver. It read, "Go home, Navajo. You are out of your depths."

Puzzled by this unlikely message, he called Zack. There was no answer, then the phone went to voice mail. Eagle Feather left a message to call him back, then drove on.

Half an hour later his phone buzzed. He pulled off the road to answer. It was Zack.

"Hey, Eagle Feather, what's up?"

"What do you mean, what's up, White Man?"

"Eagle Feather? You called me."

"After you messaged me to go home!"

"I didn't message you."

"Check your phone, White Man."

"Hang on." There was a pause. "I didn't send that."

"Your phone did. Where was your phone ten minutes ago?"

"Half an hour ago I went to get...Oh, wait! I left the phone in my room when I went to get a burrito. Someone must have—"

"Someone broke into your room while you were gone."

"Damn!"

"What's the security on your phone?"

"Facial recognition." Another pause. "Now that I think about it, I had it on to check some numbers just before I left. If someone broke in right away, they might have accessed it before security kicked in."

"Someone is keeping a very close eye on you."

"Yeah, way too close. I guess we better step up our personal security. And there's something else that's strange." Zack went on to tell Eagle Feather about the thumbprint found on the bomb that belonged to the missing scientist.

"How is that possible?"

"Either the man is not really missing, or he is missing but his thumb isn't with him." Zack paused. "Eagle Feather, I think we may be in real danger here. Where are you now?"

"On my way to the Tortoise Rock Casino in Twenty-Nine Palms."

"You should assume you are being tailed. Keep an eye on your six. Do not return to this hotel. I'll call you in a couple of hours."

Eagle Feather was attentive as he drove but didn't see any other vehicles on the small winding roads he traveled. He found the casino without any problem and knocked on the Casino Manager's door at precisely four pm. George Madrigal was short, barrel-chested, and wore a huge turquoise and pearl necklace with a Tortoise pendant suspended from it. His black silk shirt was open to expose a mat of chest hair.

He extended a hand to Eagle Feather. "I don't agree to see every stranger who calls me," he said, his words brusque. "But Chief Dan is a good friend and any friend of his..." He put both arms in the air to finish the thought.

"Chief Dan is a good man," Eagle Feather said.

Madrigal waved Eagle Feather into a leather chair near his shiny mahogany desk. "What can I do for Dan's friend?"

"I am a consultant for an investigator," Eagle Feather said. "Our interest is in some privately-owned property near the border of Joshua Tree National Park. I am interested in its history. Your people and the Serrano people inhabited that area. Dan thought you might be acquainted with it."

"Where, exactly?"

Eagle Feather took a copy of the map Ida had made for him from his pocket and showed it to Madrigal.

The manager glanced at it, glanced at Eagle Feather. He looked puzzled. "You are not the first to ask me about this place."

Eagle Feather raised an eyebrow.

"What is your interest?" Madrigal asked.

"We are investigating a disappearance."

Madrigal nodded. "Ah, the scientist from EverSun."

Eagle Feather nodded. "Who was the other interested party?"

"A certain Dr. Carl Scheidecker."

"The missing scientist."

"Yes."

"What was his interest?"

"He had become aware that it was a sacred place to our people and wanted to know why."

"Why?" Eagle Feather asked.

"Why he asked or why it was?"

"Both."

"He did not explain why he asked. I told him it was because it was a highly spiritual place." He gazed at Eagle Feather. "Have you been there?"

"Yes, I have."

Madrigal nodded. "Then you have seen the pillar, or what remains of it. Centuries ago, it stood much taller. On such a flat plain it was very distinctive. Because of the shallow depression in which it stands, it gave the impression a huge arrow had landed there as if shot from the bow of a giant. Occasionally there are strange rumblings and vibrations underfoot to add to the mystique."

"Do your people still visit the area?"

"Some believers, elders, shamans still do."

"You are aware it is the place where Scheidecker disappeared?"

Madrigal nodded. "I've heard so."

"Does this place have a name?"

"In our culture, we call it Ta'va Ma'ma'u, which loosely translated to English means Sun Woman or Woman from the Sun."

Eagle Feather thought about it. "Do you know why it was called that?"

"There is, of course, mythology connected to the place and it is known to shamans and spiritual people. Our band keeps one story, other bands seem to have their own, and the Serrano people have yet another. Long and short of it is, certain shamans have the power to summon intense heat. This is *tavan'nawigyah,* literally "calling the sun." In the old ways, the Sun Doctor *(tava-vuaganti)* specialized in the healing of sun-stroke victims. Probably the power to call for killing heat and the power to heal its effects were vested in the same person. It is believed the Sun Doctor could call upon the Sun Mother at this site to allow her powers to descend the pillar for the purpose of healing."

"If the place is so special to your people, why isn't it set apart in some way? Do you even own the land?"

Madrigal raised an eyebrow. "You are Native American, are you not?"

Eagle Feather nodded. "Yes, I am Navajo."

"You know, then, that the Native American concept of ownership of land is different from the Whites. In the Chemehuevi tradition, we own songs passed down to us by our parents and grandparents. These songs detail the land where we have always lived and through these songs, we understand it and celebrate it. Our land is recognized through our particular songs. It is as much spiritual ownership as physical ownership. We do not put up signs to declare ownership of land because it would draw unwanted attention and dispute. It suits us to leave such places unmarked and unnoticed and celebrate them in our hearts."

Eagle Feather understood the truth of his statement. "Let them come to the casino instead."

Madrigal smiled. "Exactly."

"Did the scientist Scheidecker tell you why he was interested in the site?"

Madrigal shook his head. "He did not."

There was a knock at the door and a young woman dressed in an orange polo shirt with a Tortoise Rock logo on it peered in, her face a question mark.

Eagle Feather used the interruption to stand. "I have taken enough of your time. You have been kind, Mr. Madrigal. Thank you."

Madrigal smiled and offered his hand. "Any friend of Dan's..."

He turned his attention to the young woman and Eagle Feather walked out. Along the narrow corridor outside the manager's office was a row of paintings and photographs of local scenes. One painting caught his eye and he stopped to study it. The scene was a many-hued orange to brown flatland stretching to folded purple hills in the far distance and in the center a slender rock pinnacle that seemed to reach up into the sky within a turmoil of roiling dark clouds. Descending the pinnacle as if floating along it was a beautiful black-haired native maiden with arms extended, her breasts bare, her body wrapped in a palm skirt. The maiden wore an expression of eternal calm and peace. Eagle Feather stood and let the image permeate him. When he finally walked on, it was with greater understanding.

CHAPTER FOUR

Right after Eagle Feather's call revealing his phone had been compromised, Zack called Supervisory Agent Janice Hooper and explained the situation in a few terse words, emphasizing the danger.

Janice did not hesitate. "Get out of that hotel now. I'll call back with directions."

Zack threw his loose clothing into his mostly packed suitcase, unplugged his computer and phone charger, tossed them in on top of his clothing, and closed the case. After a quick check, he left the room and walked down the corridor to the stairs. He left the building from the opposite side of the lobby area where he had parked his Jeep and approached it from outside.

After leaving the lot, he turned right on Twentynine Palms Highway, driving slower than the flow of traffic to watch for a tail. His phone rang. He answered using his Bluetooth gear.

"Yes, Janice."

"Zack, is your cell secure?"

"Yes, Janice. I had a technician check it before coming down here."

"Yet you left it in your room."

Zack remained silent, his best defense.

"However, I just had it checked remotely," Janice said. "You are still secure."

"You made your point."

"I hope so. Now we'll move on. Here's an address. Take all precautions not to be followed. It is 6200 Chula Vista Avenue."

Zack brought up the address on his GPS and at the next stoplight turned left onto Old Woman Springs Road. A couple of miles later the GPS took him off on a dirt road and through a network of rutted sand tracks. He parked in front of his destination, a small cabin surrounded by vegetation-covered hummocks. Joshua trees graced the entrance path. The door was of a heavy plank and was locked. Zack felt along the sill above it and found a key.

Inside smelled of cedar and dishwasher soap. He was in a living area with a couch and two wicker chairs. A counter set apart the small kitchen area. Doors opened to other rooms on his left and right where he could see beds.

Zack dropped his suitcase and walked back to the Jeep. He studied the road in the direction he'd come. He saw no dust to indicate he'd been followed, yet knowing a professional wouldn't be so careless. He turned on the GPS in the Jeep and studied the road network surrounding the cabin. He saw there were two ways in from the main roads, one to the west down the road he'd just come, and one to the east. There were many small jogs and turns with rough roads shooting off like branches on a pine tree, some going nowhere, some circling back. It was an easy place to get lost.

Zack walked back into the cabin and was delighted to find he had a cell signal. He called Eagle Feather and gave him the GPS coordinates for their new home. Right when he ended the call, his phone rang. It was Janice again.

"Zack, the new WIFI code is "Vanishedman" which is also the name of your operation. You'll find the fridge and bar well-stocked. We don't want you wasting your time shopping for groceries."

"Very considerate."

"There is a basement with a workshop and specialized tools should the need arise."

"Got it."

"One final thing, Zack. There is a garage in back. Use the vehicle that's in it and leave your Jeep there. Your red Jeep is too conspicuous."

"But Janice—"

Zack was reluctant to give up his Jeep, but Janice had already ended the call. He immediately went out and drove the Jeep around back. He found the same key that opened the cabin also worked on the garage door. There was a white Ford pickup truck inside. It looked like all the other white Ford pickup trucks he'd seen around the desert area. It had a logo on the door for a tree trimming service. After Zack exchanged the vehicles, he went back into the cabin, turned on his computer, and went back to his research on Dr. Scheidecker.

Zack spent an hour foraging into the man's background both officially and unofficially and found nothing that set off alarms. The man was a brilliant scientist without doubt, but did not appear to be in any way eccentric nor had he ever expressed any subversive or controversial viewpoints in public or private that Zack could discover. Turning to social media, he learned the man had a wife in Germany with whom he apparently maintained a happily separated existence most of the year due to his workload and travel, coming together generally only on holidays. The wife, named Sonja, appeared to be a content stay-at-home mom. They had one grown child, a woman in her twenties, married to a stockbroker in New York, and a baby grandson. His colleagues' tweets and Facebook comments painted a picture of a somewhat aloof but respected man, completely dedicated to his work, his social life limited to an occasional after-work beer and parties mandated by his job description. He was a true expert in his field, in great demand. EverSun had paid a huge consulting fee to coax him aboard the project.

Before suspecting Scheidecker of attempting murder, Zack needed to study the lab analysis data from the bomb removed from his Jeep. He wanted to decide for himself how the man's thumbprint had come to be on the steel cylinder. Zack knew Janice would forward the information as soon as it was available.

Now Zack turned to the EverSun Energy Company. Here he found a very solid and comprehensive energy company that backed its clean and renewable energy projects with substantial revenues from the solid consumer base and investor satisfaction of its two Florida electric utility companies. He could find no weaknesses in their portfolio or their operations. A large part of the company's security came in the form of Power Purchase Agreements from large utilities over long term contracts. Here he found a single dark cloud on the horizon.

A California utility with which EverSun had substantial PPA contracts, San Francisco Power and Light, had chosen bankruptcy to try to deal with suits arising from wildfire disasters attributed to the company's infrastructure. Once in bankruptcy, the company hoped to renegotiate its contracts to a lower price. EverSun continued to exude confidence for its stockholders, but Zack realized if SFP&L succeeded in gaining a price reduction not only would those particular contracts be devalued but other utility companies with EverSun PPAs facing similar liabilities from wildfire and drought could follow suit resulting in a domino effect and a fallout of huge proportions. EverSun was top of the Wall Street ladder now, but what about the future?

Could such a setback affect the energy company's plans for the hydroelectric project in the Eagle Mountains? Possibly. Could the bankruptcy situation and the missing scientist be related? Zack couldn't imagine any possible connection other than the fact that if the project failed to move forward, Scheidecker's contract would potentially be foreshortened, but he could find no cause and effect in this equation.

Zack turned his attention back to the EverSun Eagle Mountain project. Although the company owned the land, it was a risk to break ground until they were assured of the passage of SB 775 and the consequent guarantee the State of California would purchase their stored energy.

Regardless, they had hired a design and construction company, Santini & Marsh Design & Construction, to get started. They, in turn, had hired the now missing Dr. Scheidecker. The company was to inspect the designated pits for their suitability for water containment and conveyance, including inspection of the substrata for porosity and stability. Had that brought Dr. Scheidecker to the remote location of the lost oasis? Was it work-related, or something else entirely?

Zack decided the only way to learn the answer to that question was to talk to the rest of the team at the facility. Zack knew they would all have been interviewed by the Sheriff's Department and by the FBI. He had access to those notes. But at the time they might not have known the right questions to ask.

Zack looked up the name of the project foreman, found a number for him and phoned him.

An administrative secretary took his call.

"Santini & Marsh Design & Construction, Mr. Selder's office. Lucy speaking."

"May I speak with Mr. Selder?"

"He is out in the field right now. Would you care to leave a message?"

"I am FBI Agent Zack Tolliver. I wish to speak to him about Dr. Scheidecker."

There was a pause. "He has already spoken with the Sheriff's Deputies and the FBI. I believe they have all his information."

"I have been newly assigned to this case and will need to speak with all of Dr. Scheidecker's colleagues. I have new information and will be asking different questions, so you may be assured it will not be a waste of time."

"Very well. I'll set up an appointment for you with Mr. Selder. I can give you an hour at two pm next Thursday."

"I will need to speak to him first thing tomorrow morning," Zack said, his voice firm.

"Well, I don't—"

"And I can bring a warrant."

"Oh, that won't be necessary. I'll pencil you in for eight am tomorrow morning."

"Thank you, Lucy."

Zack ended the call thinking there did not seem to be a lot of concern for the missing scientist at the supervisor's office. It appeared to be business as usual.

As soon as he set down his phone, it sounded with Eagle Feather's signal.

"Hello, Eagle Feather."

"White Man, I will meet you at La Casita Restaurant at five pm."

"Any news?"

"I will tell you then."

"Where is this restaurant?"

"Just off Old Woman Springs Road near the intersection with Twentynine Palms Highway."

Zack set out to meet Eagle Feather at ten minutes to five. Even with his GPS, the restaurant was hard to find. He turned into a drive to what looked like a small home with a large parking lot. It seemed almost like a private club. There was no sign of Eagle Feather's truck. Inside, a tall, attractive girl in a colorful Mexican dress waited at a small counter. She looked up from her reservation book and asked his name. After she heard it, she smiled. Zack noticed her eyes were dark and curiously alert.

"You are expected. Right this way, please."

As she came around the counter, Zack saw the girl was even taller than he first thought. He admired the girl's graceful, athletic tread as she led him to a very small room, about the size of a living room in a small home. There were just five or six tables. Eagle Feather sat at one of them.

"You need to try the tortilla chips and sauce, White Man. They are special."

The girl waited for Zack to sit down.

"I am Maria," the girl said. "I will take care of you. Would you like to order a drink?"

Zack ordered the house margarita and reached for a chip.

After she had left, Zack glanced at Eagle Feather. "I didn't see your truck outside."

Eagle Feather shook his head. "Someone knows I am here. I left my truck with a friend. I will be staying with him. I need to remain unnoticed." He nodded toward a black helmet on the floor next to him.

Zack did remember seeing a motorcycle in the lot. He smiled. "Good idea. Your truck is...uh, distinctive."

"I will take that as a compliment."

Zack told Eagle Feather what he had learned about the missing scientist, the energy company, and the construction crew. "I am meeting with the project director and his crew, including several consultants, tomorrow morning. I too am driving a different vehicle, the white pickup with the tree trimming service logo out there, at Janice's insistence. The subterfuge won't last forever, but it might give me space for a day or two."

Eagle Feather nodded. "I have learned something about that odd pillar stone. It is a spiritual place, as we suspected, valued by the ancient ones. I have learned Dr. Scheidecker also asked about the place. He knew about it before he went out there."

"What was his interest?"

Eagle Feather shrugged. "I do not know. Maybe he just wanted to see a place of geological interest."

"Do people still visit the site?" Zack asked.

"Only shamans or the old people who still believe. They do not go often, I think."

Zack turned to another thought. "I tried to learn through Janice who might have known we were coming, but the possibilities are too numerous to quantify. I hope my interviews tomorrow narrow the pool."

Eagle Feather nodded. "Someone has had eyes on us from the time we arrived. They have followed you closely. I don't believe anyone followed me, but they know I am here."

"Yes." Zack sighed, sipped his margarita. "It was a full-time job to follow me that closely. Either someone took the day off work today, or they hired a professional. I will find out tomorrow if any of the construction crew or consultants took time off."

"White Man, how long does your phone remain on before it locks down?"

"The security delay was set for two minutes."

"That is not much time for someone to break into your room, find your phone, and use it. Perhaps this person is a professional."

"There are other possibilities."

"Not many."

They ate in silence. As they waited for the special flan dessert to arrive, Zack asked, "What do you plan next?"

"Tomorrow I will visit a shaman."

Zack smiled. "Are you feeling ill?"

Eagle Feather regarded him. "A shaman can cure more than just physical illness. The one I seek uses the spirit of the sun to heal."

CHAPTER FIVE

Zack left the cabin early. Although his destination, the
construction supervisor's office, was only some fifty miles
as the crow, or perhaps, the vulture flies, the distance by
road was closer to a hundred miles, and some of the
roadways were limited to forty-five miles per hour. The
eastern sky was pink, and the peculiar bright sun of desert
dawn cascaded over him as he walked to the pickup. The
truck was a late model Ranger with a powerful engine and
four-wheel drive. It was equipped with a satellite phone,
GPS, and encrypted links for searching remote FBI files,
all built into the central computer. The full leather seats
were deep and comfortable.

Two hours later, Zack reached the Kaiser Mining
Company town of Eagle Mountain, a ghost town that once
housed over two thousand people. Modern-looking
houses, stores, even a shopping center waited in ghostly
stillness behind a perimeter fence for a population that
would never return. A road followed the fence to the north
end of the town and branched off at a sign indicating the
EverSun Hydro Energy Project. This was a narrow but
well-traveled dirt road up a canyon to a ridge where
abandoned infrastructure from the old Kaiser iron mining
operation mingled with several new trailers. He parked in a
large lot full of dusty vehicles.

After climbing out of the truck, he stood for a moment
taking in the view. Beyond a rusted tower was an almost

apocalyptic scene, a massive pit carved deep into the earth ringed by access roads every hundred feet all the way to the bottom for the huge trucks used in quarry mining. After taking in the spectacle, Zack followed a dirt path edged by stones to a trailer bearing a sign that said Project Office. He pulled open the screen door which squealed to announce his presence. A woman behind the counter looked up.

"Agent Tolliver?" she asked.

"Lucy, I assume?"

"Mr. Selder is out walking the site. He'll be back at any moment. Please have a seat." She flashed a professional smile.

Lucy was a petite woman, narrow-faced with fine features. She wore a business suit and styled her hair in a tight bun. She looked quite professional for the middle of the desert, in Zack's mind.

Zack thanked her and sat in one of the plastic molded chairs along the wall. He glanced at the titles of a handful of dog-eared magazines in a rack near him: Architecture Today, Modern Archaeology, and National Geographic, and decided against all of them, instead contented himself by watching the top of Lucy's bun bob up and down behind her computer screen.

Five minutes later, the screen door screeched and a man entered the trailer. He wore a yellow insulated vest over a freshly ironed blue flannel shirt. His well-worn jeans had come that way from the rack, Zack decided. A thick leather belt with a monogram designed buckle held them up. Fine honey-brown hair floated across a sunburnt balding scalp. Care lines deepened when he looked at his visitor. He pointed a bony finger at Zack.

"You cost me a FaceTime meeting with my boss this morning."

Zack was startled but managed a smile. "Sometimes that's a good thing."

Selder walked over and slapped him on his shoulder. "In this case it certainly is. Come on in and get some coffee." He led the way around the counter into the back area.

The trailer was set up like a typical construction office with a wide window overlooking the mining pit, file cabinets along the wall beyond. A desk overflowed with sheets of paper, some weighed down with large bolts acting as paperweights, an in-and-out tray stack held manila files, and a laptop sat in the only possible space in the middle of it all.

Selder waved Zack into a chair and walked to a bookshelf filled with ring binders and poured a cup full of coffee from the machine. "Cream, sugar?"

Zack nodded. "Both, please."

Selden dumped in a spoon of sugar in the cup, added milk from a small pitcher, stirred, and handed it to Zack. He poured himself a coffee in a large mug decorated with a Ram's football logo, took it behind the desk, dropped into his chair, and spun to face Zack.

"Now, what do you need to ask me that none of the legions of cops and feds haven't already asked that's so all-fired important? And when are you going to find my missing scientist for me?"

"After I answer your first question, I imagine," Zack said, answering the second.

"Shoot."

"What was Dr. Scheidecker doing ten miles away in Great Wash?"

Selden shook his head. "That's the nub of it, isn't it? What the hell was he doing over there? That area has nothing to do with this project."

"What did you hire him for, precisely?"

"He's an expert in fluids, rates of flow in constricted conveyances, effects of evaporative loss on flow rate formulas, energy gains per rate of free flow descent, formulas for energy loss from mass and inertia of fluid versus crank weight, yada, yada, yada, all of which he should have been doing right here." Selden leaned forward and banged a long bony forefinger down on his desk. "He's got all the freedom he could want to do things in his own way, just give us the numbers, the possibles, the impossibles. What we didn't need was for him to wander off and get lost."

Selden jumped to his feet. He waved Zack over to stand with him next to the window. "Look out there. See that great big pit in front of you? We want to fill that with water. That's all. Then we want to pump it up a pipe to that ridge over there." He pointed. "There's another big mother of a pit up there. We want to fill it with the water from down here. Once it's all there, we want to open another pipe so it can flow right back down into this same pit. Then we wanna do it all over again. That's it!"

Selden waved Zack back to his chair and sat down himself. "We pump the water uphill with energy from wind and sun and capture that energy from the downhill flow of the water turning a turbine, just like all the damn dams do."

"I get how it works."

"Right," Selden said. "Okay, then, why was our expensive expert way the hell over on the other side of the mountains nowhere near the project we hired him for?" Selden shook his head. "I can only imagine he was on some sort of busman's holiday for his own interests."

"Such as?"

"Hunting for some kind of treasure, maybe, gold or silver, that's all I can think of. The man was an expert in everything including minerals, geology, seismic activity, volcanism, you name it. Maybe while looking at maps and charts he saw something that made him curious." Selden shrugged. "How the hell do I know?"

Zack stared at him. "You just used the past tense when you said he was an expert. Why?"

"Do you see him standing here? He's been gone a week, disappeared, vamoosed. That seems past tensely to me!"

"Fair enough. Tell me, what do you know about the area where he disappeared?"

Selden grew quiet for a moment. "I have heard it is a place with some kind of special meaning to the Indians. There's some sort of strange rock there, you know. Some topographical anomaly." He glanced at Zack. "I knew nothing about that location before Scheidecker chose it for his disappearing act. I still know very little about it, just what the cops and my men are telling me."

Zack raised an eyebrow. "Your men?"

"Yeah, my crew and the other consultants. There's been talk among them about the place, so I'm told."

"Before the disappearance?"

"I don't know that."

"Have any of your crew suggested any reason Scheidecker might have gone there?"

Selden leaned back in his chair. "There's the usual scuttlebutt, you know. Scheidecker was real smart. Everyone knew it and when he got a splinter up his ass about something, they all listened. So, yeah, there are some wild rumors about why he went there. Gold, for one."

"Anything else?"

"Indian artifacts was another theory."

"You think that might be it?"

Selden shook his head. "That's maybe the one area he didn't have a Ph.D. in—archaeology, paleontology, anything having to do with people, ancient or modern. You can add Sociology to that list as well."

"He didn't get along with people?"

"It wasn't that he didn't try to get along, he just didn't know anything about people. Didn't have a clue. Like he was raised on Mars or something."

"Did he antagonize people here? Anybody have a problem with him?"

Selden laughed. "Do you have a problem with your laptop? That's how people thought about him. He was a fact machine, a calculator. People went to him like you go to the internet. Nobody interacted with him. He didn't know how. He was, well, neutral."

"So he didn't socialize at all? Have any kind of buddy? Ever go out for a beer?"

"Never."

"What did he do at night?"

"How the hell do I know? Far as I can tell, he worked, ate, and slept."

Zack stared at Selden. "Okay. I'm gonna need to talk to your people. Can you arrange it?"

Selden didn't look happy. "Yeah, I can do that. Again. Do me a favor? Let me have Lucy arrange a schedule for you so my guys don't miss too much work. Again."

Zack was fine with that. "Starting today."

"Yeah, yeah, starting today. Starting now."

Selden went out of the office, returned shortly followed by Lucy.

She smiled at Zack. "If you'll follow me, please?"

Zack thanked Selden and followed Lucy. She led him to another section of the trailer and a different room. This was obviously a conference room, dominated by a long table with a WIFI router setup in the center. Unlike Selder's office, the chairs surrounding the table were cushioned.

Lucy led Zack to the far end of the table and invited him to sit. She set a stack of files on the table in front of him. "These are the people you'll see today," she said. "In order of appearance. Shall I go get Mr. Schäuble?"

Zack glanced at the top folder. The name on it was Blair Schäuble, Assistant Supervisor. "Absolutely."

After Lucy left, Zack flipped open the folder. This man, like everyone else he'd met so far on the project, was eminently qualified, with particular strengths in administration.

The man who knocked and then entered the room was wide at the belt with a large chest and spindly legs. He was fiftyish, bald, with very alert brown eyes. Zack had him sit, introduced himself and his mission, and asked him to verify a few things in his file. The formalities over, Zack held his eyes.

"Why do you think Dr. Scheidecker went up to Great Wash?"

Schäuble answered immediately. "I have no idea. Our concern is the area with the old Kaiser Mining iron ore pit mines, not anything way over there. He had no authorization to be there."

"Who could give him that authorization?"

Schäuble looked puzzled. "Well, any project administrator. But these aren't school children. We expect them to do what needs to be done to fulfill the terms of their contracts. These are professional consultants. Dr. Scheidecker was tasked with understanding the geology and mineralogy in this specific area relevant to the forces and flow qualities of water that we need to ascertain for the project. In other words, how successfully can we store large quantities of water at each end of an incline and how efficiently can we move it back and forth? There's a myriad of finite factors involved and Dr. Scheidecker was tasked with learning them. None of that has anything to do with where he was when he disappeared."

Zack thought about it. "You're saying there is nothing in that region that could in any way concern your project. Nothing to do with water flow from, say, flash floods, or maybe something he could learn from exposed minerals that might explain formations over here. Nothing like that?"

Schäuble coughed. "Don't get me wrong, Scheidecker was a brilliant man. But I have worked in this industry a long time and I can think of no reason for him to have been there that relates to our project."

"Your guess is it was something personal, then?"

"Has to be."

"Why did you use the past tense in referring to Dr. Scheidecker?"

Schäuble looked startled. "Did I? Well, I guess since it's been a week since he went missing we all kind of assumed the worst. I didn't mean to be callous."

"I'm sure you don't, Mr. Schäuble. Thank you for your time."

After Schäuble had left, Zack pondered how everyone at EverSun seemed to consider Scheidecker a person from the past and moved forward without a backward look. Sure, any business, particularly a huge corporation like EverSun and its contract companies, had to do so, but wouldn't you expect individual workers to show more feeling than this?

The next file had the name Arlene Pettigrew. Her job seemed also to be largely administrative, despite the usual lengthy list of academic titles. According to the file, her main responsibility was to manage the consultants on the project.

Arlene burst into the room without knocking, her inertia banging the door back against its rubber stopper. She came to an abrupt halt at the foot of the table, looked at her watch, and then fixed Zack with an intense gaze.

"I can give you exactly five minutes," she said. "You have my file. You know who I am and what I do here. Let's skip all that crap and get to what you want to know."

Arlene was a big woman. She had light brown hair cut short, thick eyebrows over ice blue eyes, and a square chin that gave her a bulldog appearance. If anyone could herd cats, Zack thought, it was this woman. He did not invite her to sit, somehow knowing she wouldn't.

"Very well. I need to know why Dr. Scheidecker was ten miles away from his job when he disappeared."

"And I want to know why it takes an entire sheriff's office and a flock of FBI agents to find a man playing hooky, but I know I won't get an answer to that one either."

Zack was taken aback. "You don't think something happened to him?"

"Yes, I think something happened to him. I think a need for a change in scenery happened to him."

"What do you mean?"

"I think he took a hike."

"Evidently he did, quite literally. But what do *you* mean by 'took a hike'?"

She shrugged. "He left. Got tired of the daily grind and left. Wouldn't be the first time."

"There have been other times?"

Arlene rested her palms on the table and leaned toward him. "Look, I've got nine other prima donnas to watch over and try to keep on task. It's like having a room full of ADD monkeys. Scheidecker is the worst of the lot. He gets some idea in his head and jumps in a car and takes off without a word to anyone. They're all like that to some extent. Last time he was gone for eight hours."

Zack stared at her. "Have you told this to anyone else?"

She gave a dramatic sigh. "Look, my job is to keep the brain trust on task. They all have their own contracts with individual expectations and parameters. Each is a highly respected leader in his or her field and used to working his or her own way. They do not play well together. The administrative supervisors on this project do not understand this mentality which is why they hired me. I'm not about to tell the bosses each time one of these people goes off on a tangent. They wanted the best minds in the business on this project, they got them, and hired me to make it work."

Zack raised an eyebrow. "How do you explain his footprints ending so abruptly that even my tracker, the best tracker in the business, can't tell me where he went?"

She gave her first smile of the interview, more of a grimace. "Your best tracker in the business is up against the best brain in the business."

CHAPTER SIX

The best tracker in the business was on a motorcycle
roaring along U.S. 10 toward the turnoff for Twentynine
Palms Highway. His destination was the Oasis of Mara in
Twentynine Palms. He had just left the Morongo Casino
where his friend Dan Singletree owned a suite of rooms.
Dan's tribal membership descended from one of the last
Chemehuevi Indian families to move to the Morongo
Reservation from the Oasis of Mara, and his rooms came
from both his tribal affiliation and his status among the
Chemehuevi. Eagle Feather's truck now resided in the
private underground garage where it could not be seen.
Chief Dan, in absentia, had authorized a key to be made
for Eagle Feather. The accommodations were very
comfortable, to say the least.

The morning was cool and the ride comfortable, the
smell of sage wafted under his helmet. The scenery on the
ride up through the Morongo Valley was beautiful and
Eagle Feather felt a sense of freedom on the Yamaha he
never quite felt in his truck. He thought of Zack in the
shack in the desert, probably thinking Eagle Feather was in
a homemade wickiup in the woods and grunted to himself
in amusement. Eagle Feather had no intention of telling
him the truth.

His ride warmed as the sun rose, and by the time he
turned onto Utah Trail in Twentynine Palms, he was hot
despite the breeze from the bike. He stopped first at the

historic oasis, intending to pay homage to the place his fellow Native Americans lived for centuries. He learned from the signs that Mara meant "the place of little springs and much grass", but found it a place of tall palm trees and much sand. When a shaman first led the Serrano people to the Oasis of Mara, he prophesied they would find gentle living conditions and give birth to baby boys. They were instructed to plant a palm tree for each baby boy born that first year. The tribe planted twenty-nine palms, a success story on both counts.

After a short visit at the oasis, Eagle Feather followed the directions given him to Old Dale Road and found the modest home of the shaman. The sign outside the residence listed the hours of dentistry for Dr. Silvia Mike, but in smaller font read "Puhwaganti by Appointment Only". Puhwaganti, Eagle Feather knew, was the Chemehuevi word for a shaman or healer. Fortunately, his friend Chief Dan had obtained an appointment for him and glancing at his watch, saw he was right on time. He parked his bike and knocked at the door.

The woman who opened the door was dark-skinned, tall and slender, with black hair and large brown eyes. She smiled was reserved yet friendly. Prominent cheekbones gave her face an impression of strength.

"Let me guess. You must be Eagle Feather."

"Yes."

"By the surprised look on your face, I'd say you were expecting a man."

She was right, but Eagle Feather didn't want to insult her by admitting it. Instead, he said nothing.

"Never mind," she said. "Come on in."

They entered a long corridor. To the right, a closed door with a mottled glass window had a sign that read, "Silvia Mike, D.M.D". A door to the left was open to a waiting room. They walked past both doors to the end of the corridor and a less official door and entered a living room. It was a large open space, quite different from the office atmosphere of the corridor. Various tribal talismans decorated the far wall above two sturdy wood-backed benches with seats of embroidered cushions of colorful design. Tall clay pots lined a second wall. A pair of comfortable leather chairs were arranged in the middle of the space. Dr. Mike waved Eagle Feather toward one of them.

"Water, coffee, juice?"

Eagle Feather thought about it and decided his early cup of coffee was inadequate. "Coffee, black if you don't mind."

"I'll be right back." She stepped through a curtain of hanging strung beads and into an alcove and disappeared.

Eagle Feather sat down in the large leather chair she'd indicated and looked around the room. He noticed a group of diplomas on the wall nearest him. He couldn't read them from where he sat but deduced one was an undergraduate degree, two others were masters degrees, and the last a doctor of dentistry diploma. A tall stick with a crook leaned against the wall beneath them.

Silvia came back with a steaming mug and handed it to Eagle Feather, then sat in the adjacent chair.

"Are you a hiker?" Eagle Feather asked.

She looked at him in surprise and followed his eyes to the stick. "Oh, that. Well, I am a hiker and a runner but the crook has another purpose. It is a Poros."

"I do not know what that is."

"I am a healer, a Puhwaganti, as you know. You are Navajo. You have healers."

"Yes, we have singers. But they do not use a staff."

She smiled and nodded. "All Chemehuevi people are singers. Each of us has a proprietary song about the land we own. These songs are passed down in our families from our ancestors."

"The Navajo do not own land. The earth is for everyone."

"Except the land the white people own," she said, with a mischievous look.

"Times have changed," Eagle Feather said.

Silvia smiled. "We still have our songs to identify our traditional places. In our dreams, we still own our land."

Eagle Feather chuckled. "In our dreams, the Navajo still hunt and fight our enemies."

Her smile was conciliatory. "What I meant was, for my people dreams are part of our songs. Our songs keep the world in motion, they address our landscapes, animals, people, and plants. We have sacred songs, hunting songs, and traveling songs as well. When we travel our trails we do so physically but also in dreams. This spiritual element is just as real as the physical, if not more so."

Eagle Feather cocked an eyebrow. "Do you mind if I ask? You are a healer, what many call a sachem, yet you are a woman."

"I'm flattered you noticed." Silvia looked amused. "In our culture, both men and women may be healers. Women practitioners are called *mamau puhwaganti*. The skill of healing is learned and practiced but is also part of our genes, passed down from parent to child, as are our songs. My mother was a healer as was her father before her. Our songs and skills are passed from generation to generation."

"Your particular skill involves the sun?"

"I heal with power from the sun. This power comes to me through my familiar."

"Your familiar?"

"All healers have familiars. It may be an animal, bird, reptile, or even insects. Healers do not talk about their familiars and no one else can see them when they come to us. When we heal, we call to them and wherever they are in the world they hear us. If they come to us, we know our patient will be healed."

"If not...?"

She shook her head. "The healing can not happen."

Eagle Feather shifted in his chair. "I have come to ask you about a place called"—he hesitated, then stumbled with the pronunciation—"*Ta'va Ma'ma'u*".

"Ah, you have done your homework. What do you wish to know?"

"You may have heard that a leading scientist went missing near that specific spot, a Dr. Carl Scheidecker."

"Yes."

"I followed his footprints in an attempt to locate him. They led to this place and then disappeared entirely."

"*Ta'va Ma'ma'u* is a sacred place, dedicated to the sun." Silvia looked thoughtfully at Eagle Feather for a few moments before going on. "I would not attempt to offer my thoughts to anyone who is not Native American. As a Navajo, you may be able to assimilate what I am about to say." She paused again to gather her thoughts. "The songs of the *Nūwū* people, the Southern Paiute, are important for more than sacred reasons, as I have said. But there is another tradition that is part of the identity of our people. We are great runners. Before the Europeans, before contact, as ethnographers call it, our young men ran great distances as a matter of course. The *Nūwū* bands were widely scattered and runners were our only means of communication. Our trails extended from east of the Colorado River all the way west to the Pacific Ocean. We have a song cycle describing these trails called the Salt Songs. These songs describe every twist and turn of the trail network including physical landmarks and tributary trails and all the emotions and thoughts as one travels the trail." Silvia paused, glancing at Eagle Feather. "Are you with me so far?"

He nodded.

"Good. Here's where it begins to get difficult. When we sing the Salt Song we travel the trail spiritually. Our souls, if you will, soar along them seeing every feature as if we were traveling it physically. In old times each Chemehuevi community had a small number of select runners, couriers, who knew the land intimately, knew all the shortest routes. All they needed for nourishment were small amounts of Chia and a little water. The runner went alone, and used his secret method to cover vast distances in remarkably short times."

"What do you mean by secret methods?"

Silvia gave a faint smile. "These select runners are able to merge the physical and the spiritual elements of the Salt Song as they run."

"I don't understand."

She paused. "Okay, let me tell you a story my grandfather told me when I was a little girl, something he witnessed. He spoke of a select runner who lived in his camp when he was a child. This runner was a particularly handsome man of extraordinary athletic build. He ran regularly as a courier for the community. My grandfather described how would he leave camp and run up the sand slope with long relaxed strides and disappear over the other side. One day, after the runner departed, my grandfather and some other children decided to follow the runner. They followed his tracks up the sand slope and over the top. On the far side, when they were out of sight of the camp, the tracks began to look different. Here they became staggered, farther apart. The interval between each track became longer and the impressions lighter and lighter until they disappeared altogether."

61

"What are you saying, that he flew or somehow transported himself?"

Her eyes went to his face. "I am telling you what my grandfather told me he had witnessed."

"Was this runner ever seen again?"

"My grandfather learned he had arrived at his destination that very same day—two hundred miles away."

Eagle Feather sat in silence for a moment. "When you first spoke of these runners, you used the present tense."

"Yes."

Eagle Feather let it sink in. He said, "My people also have legends and myths, some of which I believe to be true, but this is a lot to swallow. If you are telling this to me to explain the disappearing footprints, remember he is not Native American. He is a German scientist."

Silvia leaned forward. "What did his foot impressions look like just before they disappeared?"

"It was too difficult to tell. The ground was hard and many other people had stepped on his tracks. I could follow him only by a slight impression here and there."

"You should go back and view those impressions with a different outlook. Were the footprints obscured by others or did they grow farther apart and become less distinct on their own?"

Eagle Feather chuckled. "My white FBI agent friend will never consider the idea that the missing scientist flew away."

"Would you?"

He shrugged. "I do not dismiss such things without thought."

Her smile was gentle. "You asked me. I have told you what I know." She waved a hand toward the hall. "When I practice dentistry, I am a pragmatist." Then she waved toward the Poros. "When I heal souls, I am a spiritualist. I do not believe one supersedes the other."

"I, too, do not. Most other Native Americans do not. A white man like this scientist does."

Silvia looked toward the wall of diplomas, her expression thoughtful. "Each journey begins with the first step," she said at last. "Once you have taken that first step, the next step will reveal itself. Go back to *Ta'va Ma'ma'u.* Look again for the footprints of the scientist. Look at them with your heart, not your mind. That is your first step."

The interview was over. Eagle Feather thanked Silvia. She followed him to the door and watched him mount his motorcycle and roar off.

Eagle Feather rode over to the Tortoise Rock Casino for lunch. He was biting into a carne asada burrito at the Oasis Grill when George Madrigal found him.

"Mind if I sit?"

"It's your casino."

Madrigal grinned as he sat. "It's the tribe's casino."

Eagle Feather glanced at him. "You look like a man with a question."

"I guess maybe I do have one." He leaned back toward his right and waved an arm toward the waitress, calling to her. "Please bring iced tea for me and my guest, Susan." He looked back at Eagle Feather. "I am curious to know if you spoke with a Sun Doctor."

Eagle Feather nodded. "Yes, I just met with Dr. Silvia Mike. She is an extraordinary woman."

"She descends from the original leaders of our people and maintains the old ways."

"As well as the modern, more painful ones," Eagle Feather said.

"True," Madrigal said, with a rueful smile. "She is able to walk two roads."

"I confess I find the belief that a Chemehuevi runner can fly hard to accept. I can not accept that a German scientist can fly."

"She told you that?"

"Not in so many words, but she did tell me of the powers of Chemehuevi select runners."

"You do not believe it?"

"I do not disbelieve it. The practitioners of traditional medicine among my people claim powers that are difficult to understand. I have come to believe much from the evidence of my senses. Perhaps I will come to understand your runners the same way."

Madrigal paused as the waitress arrived with two glasses of iced tea. As she set them down he thanked her. After she left, he said, "Let me tell you what my teacher said about the reality of such difficult to believe abilities. He told me if you wake from a dream to find a monster crouched at the foot of your bed, you have two choices: you can accept that it is there and prepare to defend yourself, or you can decide it is not real and go back to sleep. If you fight the monster and it is not real, you will feel foolish. If you ignore it and it is real, you will be dead."

"Some will never accept that the monster exists."

"That is true. But you are not among those, I think."

"No, but most of the people I work with find such things difficult, and the monster Dr. Mike describes is quite large."

Madrigal laughed. "Yes, I suppose the belief that a man can fly is a leap in faith. But before the Wright Brothers came along, most people felt that way."

CHAPTER SEVEN

Arlene Pettigrew was not surprised to receive a phone call summoning her to Jason Selder's office shortly after she met with the FBI agent. Back when that old kook Scheidecker first turned up missing, Selder had gathered them all in his office. His worry had nothing to do with the welfare of an internationally known scientist, it had more to do with keeping the man's disappearance under wraps until they could locate the guy. Only when it became apparent they could do neither did he allow security to call in the law.

"Security!" she said to herself in disgust as she chugged across the dusty lot between trailers. She thought the company security department was a joke, a bunch of old fart wannabes strutting around with pistols on their hips and playing video games on their computers. Local law enforcement had been no more effective, she had to admit, and given their lack of progress and Scheidecker's reputation as an important foreign national, they had panicked and called in the FBI. That was days ago. A couple of agents came around, asked the same questions everyone else asked, then disappeared. No one knew what the hell was going on now.

Selder had sure been okay with that, Arlene thought, with a snort. For him, it was the FBI's problem, and he could get on with his work. That is until today. Now here comes another FBI agent, everyone gets questioned all over again, work is interrupted, and her gaggle of scientists is all in a dither. She figured her boss had to be pissed.

Lucy sent her straight through to Selder's office. He glared up at her from his desk when she entered. "What-a-cock-up! Why the hell couldn't you keep track of your consultants? That's what you were hired to do."

Arlene sat down without invitation. "Jason, we've been through all this. I was hired to synthesize data and chair meetings for these specialists, not babysit them. If you want to blame someone, blame whoever hired this Scheidecker guy. He's been a disruptive force ever since he arrived."

"Yes, yes, I know. He keeps finding problems where there aren't any. I'd be just as happy that he's gone if it wasn't for the uproar he's stirred up. It just won't die down." Selder leaned forward, palms on his desk. "What did the FBI guy ask you?"

"He wanted to know about Scheidecker, what he was like. I told him the man was a loose screw, wandering off places without telling anyone."

Selder nodded. "Did the agent tell you his specialty?"

Arlene looked at him in surprise. "He has a specialty?"

"Yeah, he does. I checked with a friend of mine who knows these things. Tolliver is called in when things get weird."

"Weird?"

"Yeah, weird, like mumbo-jumbo weird."

"No shit! The FBI has people like that?"

Selder nodded. "Apparently. More to the point, he works with a Navajo tracker, this character who can track a gnat across a gravel pit."

Arlene was delighted. "This is like a fucking movie!"

"Don't be so damn cheerful. If this Navajo is as good as they say, he might discover stuff we don't want discovered." Selder shuffled through an open file on his desk, found a memo, and slid it across toward Arlene.

She reached out for it and glanced at the title. She knew it right away. "What, this anomaly? We dismissed that a long time ago. There was a consensus that the disturbance was a fluke, insignificant. Scheidecker was the only holdout, and not because he knew anything different, only because that's what he does...did. He disagrees. It's his thing."

Selder made a teepee with his fingers. "I'm not concerned with your team's recommendation. I agree with the analysis. The harm can come just from people talking about it. Scheidecker could not have found a better way to underscore his disagreement with our findings than by disappearing where he did. If this comes to light during the FBI investigation and the media gets hold of it, the entire project could stall, regardless of right or wrong."

Arlene flipped the paper back to him. "Yeah, I see your point. But remember, it took a world-renown scientist to discover it and draw implications. No Indian scout is going to find out about it, no matter how many gnat's footprints he can follow. It was a fluke, for God's sake. It won't happen again."

Selder stared back at her, thinking about it. He stuffed the paper back into the file. "Okay, you're probably right. I've steered Tolliver away from your consultant group, told him you would be speaking for them. Our position is to be as helpful as we can with as little interruption to our work schedule as possible. Fact is, I'd kind of like to know what happened to the old goat myself. But keep a tight reign on your consultants. Make sure they know you are their spokesperson. They are not to talk about their work to anyone. Understood?"

Arlene stood and nodded. "Got it, boss."

CHAPTER EIGHT

Eagle Feather stood next to his bike in the casino parking lot, undecided. He glanced at his watch. The sun burned on his shoulders and shimmered on the blacktop. He knew it was going to be a hot day and the last thing he felt like doing was retracing his steps up that desolate wash to take another look at the scientist's footprints. He'd never had to review his tracking before, and didn't want to start now. But he was conflicted. Admittedly, the possibility that the scientist had flown away never occurred to him. Why would it? The man's tracks had been almost completely obliterated by eager but incompetent investigators and were incomplete even when they were visible, but nothing about them suggested an unusual pace. But flying?

There was nothing to debate, Eagle Feather realized. His tracking skills had been challenged. Now he would have to return to Great Wash for another look. He pulled on his helmet. The sooner he got this done, the better.

The ride south on Park Boulevard and along Pinto Basin Road was smooth and enjoyable. The many spectacular views and physical peculiarities for which Joshua Tree National Park is known were on full display. Even the unpaved surface of Black Eagle Mine Road was comparatively smooth for the Yamaha, equally capable on-road or dirt. He turned up the dry bed of Great Wash and followed the Jeep tracks, flying along faster than Zack had driven. Where the Jeep had stopped, he rode on.

LOST OASIS

Eagle Feather had a photographic memory for topography, an ability that served him well as a guide and tracker. He remembered where he had first found untrampled tracks of the scientist. He stopped there and left the bike and helmet, replacing the latter with his hat from the saddlebag. Once again he crouched and crawled along the hard pebbled surface looking for any slight indication on the ground. Sweat came quickly in the desert heat, trickled down his spine, oozed through the sweatband of his hat.

The first clear impression of Scheidecker's foot he found was a forefoot strike. The ground here was iron hard. It was impossible to determine if any extra force had been applied, as when running or leaping. Eagle Feather studied the impression for several minutes but could conclude nothing. He moved ahead looking for the next print. There was nothing but a confusion of disturbed ground within the distance of a normal stride or even a long stride. The next clear and identifiable print made by the scientist came many strides later. Eagle Feather mentally chalked up a point for the *mamau puhwaganti*. The print was impressed into the concrete-like surface, somewhat more so than the last. It could have been a harder strike, as when landing or as when leaping. It could also simply have been a stumble.

Eagle Feather's well-honed instinct gave warning even with his eyes glued to the ground. His peripheral vision caught a flicker of reflected light and he immediately dropped to the hard surface of the mesa. He heard a whistle as the bullet passed above him, and the report of a rifle.

Without a second's hesitation, Eagle Feather leaped to his feet, ran back the way he had come, weaving, changing speed. He could be in a worse place to be ambushed, he knew. Nothing but plate-like flatness surrounded him. His memory imaged the terrain he had just traversed, including a slight depression about fifty back. He ran toward it, running for his life.

He heard no more rifle shots, wondered what that meant. He reached the small depression and immediately dismissed it as too small. He had to keep running. He came to a tiny growth of ocotillo. He passed behind it, felt safe momentarily, but knew it would no stop a high powered rifle bullet. He kept running. All the while he wondered, would the gunman pursue him?

Who could have known where he planned to go once he left the casino parking lot? Even knowing his plan, no one could reach this area before him and set up an ambush. Maybe the rifleman was not targeting him specifically but was guarding something. But would the rifleman follow him? Was he even now on a parallel course, running along the edge of the widening wash, looking for his shot? The sniper couldn't know if Eagle Feather was armed. He would not dare venture out onto the wash and become a target. As the wash grew wider, the rifle shot from beyond its bank became less certain. All this went through the Navajo's mind as he ran.

His next thought was that the shooter may have left a vehicle somewhere nearby. His answer came immediately with the undulating chainsaw-like whine of a single stroke engine in the far distance. The shooter did indeed have a vehicle, and it sounded like a motorcycle. Now Eagle Feather stopped weaving and ran fast.

He sprinted the last fifty yards to his motorcycle. He flipped his hat into the bike's saddlebag, slipped on his helmet, turned the ignition and kicked the bike on, turned the throttle full. He erupted through the soft gravel in a cloud of dust. Once the ground beneath the bike tires became firm enough, he risked a glance to the east and saw a small wisp of rising dust. The race was on.

There was nowhere to go but south toward the Black Eagle Mine Road. Eagle Feather figured he had a slight advantage once he reached the road and turned right, knowing his pursuer must make up the width of the wash at that point almost half a mile. But all other factors were unknown. How well did the sniper know the lay of the land? How powerful was his motorcycle? How good a rider was he? The answer to those questions would play out soon enough.

The Navajo pushed his speed as much as he dared. He could not risk a fall. Any stop for any reason now would place him in extreme danger. The sight of the mine road was a relief. As he turned on to it, he glanced back and saw nothing. The dirt surface was firm and he gunned the Yamaha. A minute later he saw the dust of another vehicle in his jiggling rearview mirror. His pursuer had made up the difference very quickly and was gaining.

Eagle Feather knew if he could make it to the paved Pinto Basin Road, he would be safe. There would be a much greater likelihood of meeting travelers, his pursuer would probably not follow him beyond the road junction. But could he get there? He was going as fast as he dared on this road surface, but the rider behind was still gaining.

He flashed by the open gate into the park proper. That told him there were eight miles more to go to the intersection. He knew now he would not make it in time. His eye traveled constantly from the road to his rearview mirror. Suddenly it shattered. He first thought was the excessive vibration had broken the mirror until he realized it had been shattered by a bullet. The man who was trying to kill him was not only an excellent rider but also an amazing shot with a handgun. All of this was bad news.

He tried weaving his bike but this slowed him too much. As he crested the next rise he took advantage of the hill to straighten and accelerate down the other side. At the bottom of the downslope, he steered into soft dirt along the shoulder, a dangerous maneuver, but it created a momentary screen of dust to conceal him. But not for long. He heard a ping as a bullet dinked his handlebar. How the hell could the man ride like this and still shoot so well?

Eagle Feather was desperate. He needed a saving move. He saw his chance ahead where desert sand had drifted deep into the roadway, a dangerous spot for a motorcycle.

LOST OASIS

He slowed just in front of it and once in the sand braked the front wheel while accelerating, spinning the rear wheel in the drift to raise a storm of dust. But he was out of time. The pursuing bike was on top of him. He jerked the handlebar to one side and accelerated to avoid being hit. For one precarious moment, he lost control, then somehow managed to straighten the bike. The pursuing motorcycle slid by him on its side. Eagle Feather caught a glimpse of a red helmet with black visor, a red riding suit, one gloved hand gripping the handlebar, the other ungloved and waving in the air as rider and bike scraped along the rough dirt roadway.

Eagle Feather accelerated up the next rise. He did not know if the rider behind him was hurt. He did know the man would not have time to remount and catch him. He also knew his pursuer no longer had the pistol. He was safe, so long as he didn't spill. He felt a wave of suppressed adrenalin surged through him as he slowed to a safer speed. Dust coated his visor and nearly blinded him but he resisted the temptation to remove a hand from the handlebar to wipe a sleeve across it. He could see well enough to manage until he reached the pavement.

At Pinto Basin Road, Eagle Feather turned north and traveled on until he came to the first occupied turnout. Tourists were standing next to their car reading an informative sign. He parked his bike, climbed off, and cleaned the helmet visor, watching back along the road. There was no sign of anyone. He didn't expect to see any. When he put his helmet back his hands were shaking. The

Navajo looked at them with interest. The shaking was caused by adrenalin and was an indicator of what a very near thing it had been.

As he traveled back toward Twentynine Palms, Eagle Feather considered the situation. Someone was very interested in preventing anyone from taking a close look at the scene of Scheidecker's disappearance. Would the shooter be so dedicated as to stand guard in the broiling sun twenty-four seven? That seemed unlikely. But if not, the shooter had to have anticipated Eagle Feather's arrival, almost as if he'd listened in on his conversations of that day. The time required for the shooter to get into position appeared to eliminate Madrigal from suspicion, but not Dr. Silvia Mike.

Eagle Feather could not believe she would intentionally set him up that way. But after all, she was the reason he had returned to the wash. It was her challenging words that ultimately spurred him to re-examine the scientist's footprints. Could someone have been listening in on their conversation, or might she have mentioned it to a third party?

The Navajo was letting his prejudice in favor of the Chemehuevi shaman color his judgment. What did he know about Silvia Mike, anyway? She was a unique individual, living in the modern world and in the ancient past at the same time. Such an extraordinary person should not be underestimated. Nor could his liking for her, which he now admitted, be allowed to dissuade his rational line of thought. As a *tava-vuaganti,* a Sun Doctor, she had a real interest in protecting that sacred site. Was that what this was all about? Or, was the rifleman's presence at the time of his arrival pure coincidence?

When he reached Twentynine Palms, Eagle Feather rode directly to the pancake house. He went into the men's room, cleaned up as best he could. After claiming a table, he called Zack.

"White Man, we need to meet."

"Okay. I'm just finishing an interview at the project site. Where are you?"

"I am in Twentynine Palms. We could meet at La Casita restaurant, say in two hours?"

"I'll see you there."

Eagle Feather ordered a large milkshake and sipped it slowly. He went over in his mind everything he had learned from Dr. Silvia Mike about the sacred site *"Ta'va Ma'ma'u"* and Silvia's background as a Sun Doctor. Through everything she had said, one thing always dominated: she was a healer. Would a healer have a part in trying to kill a man, even to save her sacred site? He just didn't know.

With time on his hands, Eagle Feather went back to the Oasis of Mara. He left his bike and walked out among the palms. Many appeared dead or dying. In some places, he saw young palms protected by chicken wire. It seemed the park service was attempting to replace the original palms as they died, but they could not conceal the atmosphere of decay. How did the Chemehuevi feel about this, he wondered? Did they feel desperation at the prospect of their sacred sites fading away? Was it enough to drive them to protect them by force of arms?

As Eagle Feather walked back to the Yamaha, he had more questions than answers.

The parking lot of the little Mexican restaurant was crowded when Eagle Feather arrived. There were several white trucks, any one of which could be the one Zack was driving. Once inside, Eagle Feather went to the counter where a man in a flowery shirt reminiscent of Hawaii rather than Mexico asked him if he had a reservation.

"My friend Zack Tolliver made the reservation," Eagle Feather said.

The man ran his finger down a list, looking doubtful. Before he could respond, Maria emerged from another room.

"Never mind that, Raymond," she said. "I took Mr. Tolliver's reservation. I will seat this gentleman."

She led Eagle Feather to a table and took his drink order. The margarita he sipped as he waited for Zack remedied to some degree his stressful day.

Zack arrived ten minutes later, ushered to the table by the cordial Maria. He, too, ordered the margarita, after casting an envious eye at the one the Navajo was enjoying.

"Sorry I'm late," he said, as Maria went off to get his drink. "My last interview went long."

"I have enjoyed the quiet moment," Eagle Feather said"

"Well! While I've spent my day in a small stuffy room interviewing less than pleasant company employees, no doubt you've enjoyed riding about on your motorcycle."

"Yes, White Man. That is exactly what I have been doing."

Zack charged ahead with his news. "I have the lab results from the bomb. First, the forensic fingerprint expert confirms that the thumbprint on the bomb belongs to Scheidecker but suspects it was deliberately placed there, that belief based upon the fact the print is so perfect. He thinks Scheidecker's thumb was borrowed to make it, with or without him. He can't say which. He can say it wasn't put there using a casting. The bomb itself is simple but ingenious and effective. Had I not stopped to look, I would be dead now. The materials used to make it are common and almost impossible to trace since all are readily available and can serve many functions."

"Such as in construction?"

Zack gave a grim smile. "Yes, certainly in construction." He sipped his drink, then said, "I will say I did not detect a great deal of concern on the part of anyone at Santini & Marsh Design & Construction over their missing consultant. In fact, I thought I detected a sense of relief. I gather he was a bit difficult to work with."

"You said *was*. Do you believe Scheidecker is dead?"

"It seems most likely, given the forensic expert's conclusions, particularly. Still, they could be wrong."

Maria returned for their food order. She was cordial and charming. After she walked away with their menus, Eagle Feather said, "I think that girl believes you are special."

Zack raised his eyebrows but did not respond.

Eagle Feather asked, "Have you learned why an important scientist went on a hike to visit an Indian sacred site lost in the middle of the desert?"

"No," Zack said. "However, I did learn Scheidecker had a habit of disappearing from time to time. He wasn't very good at following company protocols." He eyed Eagle Feather. "You called it a sacred site. What have you learned about it?"

Eagle Feather described his meeting with Dr. Silvia Mike.

"The place is important to her as a Sun Doctor because it is the source of her healing power."

"She is a shaman."

"She is an unusual woman. She is able to blend ancient traditions and modern medicine."

"I sense unusual admiration on your part," Zack said, grinning. "Don't you already have a Southern Paiute girlfriend?"

"Can I not admire a woman without feeling a romantic attachment?"

Zack grinned. "I give up. Can you?"

CHAPTER NINE

After digging into steaming heaped plates of tangy soul-satisfying Mexican food, the friends leaned back in their chairs to contemplate the possibility of dessert. Zack sipped the dregs of his margarita and eyed his friend.

"What else did you learn today? I've heard nothing to suggest a reason for the urgent tone in your message requesting we meet."

"Two things," Eagle Feather said. "Chemehuevi runners can fly, and someone is anxious enough to protect the *Ta'va Ma'ma'u* sacred site to kill me."

Zack stared. "You saved those tidbits for dessert just to startle me?"

"I have no designs on your emotional state," Eagle Feather said. "I did not mention it before because we were discussing something else."

"Okay, then." Zack took a deep breath. "I think we should begin with whoever tried to kill you."

Eagle Feather took Zack through the events in Great Wash. In the end, he offered his conclusions. "It appears most likely to me either Dr. Mike told someone about our conversation or we were overheard in some way."

Zack sighed. "Well, first of all, that was a very near thing and I am extremely happy to see you here. I won't continue this line of thought because I know it makes you feel uncomfortable. Just saying. As to how this assassin knew to find you there…well, that is a puzzle."

"I need now to tell you about flying runners," Eagle Feather said. "Certain Chemehuevi runners were thought to have that ability. It appears to be a spiritual, dreamlike state to the Chemehuevi yet almost inseparable from reality. Before you comment, think about this: can a Skinwalker change into an animal? We have both dealt with that before. Is that concept very different?"

Zack shook a head heavy with doubt. "Both are an extreme challenge to my traditional belief system."

"Yet many of you white people believe a man can walk on water, raise people from the dead, and return after death."

"Okay, okay, we don't need to revisit this debate. But you felt Dr. Mike challenged your tracking skills?"

"No, not directly. Her belief in a runner's ability to fly offered another interpretation to the appearance of the scientist's tracks, one I had not considered."

"With good reason."

Eagle Feather shrugged. "You say you do not wish to return to the debate."

"No, no. Go on."

"Her interpretation was my reason to go back. I did feel challenged."

Zack was lost in thought for a moment. "You know I am not a believer in coincidence. But isn't it possible someone else was concerned enough to prevent the discovery of something out there that they or their agents make intermittent trips to the area and just happened to see you?"

"It is possible, but you do not believe that."

"No, I guess I don't," Zack said. He grinned at his friend. "Well, what do you think? You went back and looked at the prints. Did the scientist fly?"

"I did not have time to study more than two prints. I could not eliminate the possibility."

Maria returned.

Zack smiled at her. "I will have the flan," he said.

She smiled as if he had done her a personal favor and looked at Eagle Feather, who shook his head.

"I have eaten too much already."

Eagle Feather continued his thought. "I think someone was in a nearby room, listening."

"Was there another car out front? Did you hear noises? Do you remember anything to support that?"

"Nothing. But I can think of no other explanation."

"Someone planted a bug in her house, maybe?"

"Why? Who knew I would go there?"

"Maybe it wasn't just about you. Maybe someone wanted to know everything about Dr. Mike's connection to the site."

"Who? Why?"

Zack paused when Maria returned with the flan. She watched him take a bite.

He looked up at Maria. "This flan is unbelievable." He glanced at Eagle Feather. "You made a mistake not ordering it."

Maria walked away, looking very pleased.

Zack took several more bites before speaking. "What if there is a connection between the energy project and this remote oasis? That would explain why Scheidecker went out there in the first place. If someone wanted to know more about the site, wouldn't this Dr. Mike be a good source? But what if she didn't want to talk to a company exploiting the region, in her view? It certainly would not be beyond the capability of a huge corporation like EverSun Energy Company to bug her home."

Eagle Feather gave a slow nod. "That is a good theory, White Man. Can we prove it?"

"Maybe you could ask Dr. Mike to allow the FBI to search her home for a bug?"

"I do not think she would permit it. Remember, she has no more reason to trust the FBI than to trust EverSun."

"Even if you ask her?"

Eagle Feather shook his head. "As soon as I ask on behalf of the FBI, she will see me as one of you."

Zack nodded. "Okay, let's save that as a possible later option. Do you need to go back and make a more thorough examination of those footprints?"

"I do not think I would find anything different from what I already know. I would not be able to eliminate flying as a possibility. I also can not eliminate alien abduction as a possibility."

Zack grinned. "We can agree on that one." He stood. "I'm for a good night's sleep. Tomorrow I will find a geologist and ask him for his thoughts on that lost oasis site to see if we can connect it to the energy storage project."

He left a large cash tip on the table.

The two men walked out into the pre-twilight glow. The Little San Bernardino Mountains loomed in stark relief. They stood side by side at the doorway enjoying the evening warmth.

Zack glanced at Eagle Feather. "What are your plans for tomorrow?"

Eagle Feather stared off into the distance. "I did not enjoy running for my life. I will go back and find this man who ambushed me."

"Whoa, there. Not by yourself."

"If I need help, I know where to find it."

The sun was behind the mountains by the time Zack steered the pickup north on Old Woman Springs Road. The sandy turnoff was not well marked and hard to spot in the dusk and the complicated intertwining of dirt roads even more so. Zack was relieved when at last his headlights illuminated the small cabin. He drove behind it and parked in front of the garage. Once the pickup lights were off, it was very dark. He removed his handgun from the glove compartment, locked the truck, and waited for his eyes to adjust. Stars were beginning to prick the sky above and the air smelled of dry dust and sage. The moon had not yet risen but light still lay faintly over the Joshua trees and yucca plants on the rise beyond.

Zack's mind was full of his conversation with Eagle Feather. He worried about the Navajo and his determination to track down his assailant. It was clear someone was desperate to keep them from learning their secret, whatever it might be. He glanced at the cabin. The safe house was as much protection as Zack could expect under the circumstances, but it was apparent that the person or persons who had made two concentrated efforts to kill each of them had access to technology and inside information. If that information came from inside the FBI somehow, this place might not be as safe as he thought. No one had followed him here, but now in his heightened awareness, it seemed possible someone could be waiting inside.

A bit unnerved by that thought, Zack cocked his Sig Saur P226 before approaching the cabin. He knew the doors were alarmed and any interruption to the alarm system would send an alert to the local FBI office, but anyone connected to the FBI would be aware of it and could find a way to defeat it. Zack approached the rear door on silent feet, inserted his key which automatically silenced the alarm and pushed the door open a few inches. He listened. He reached in and flipped the light switch, listened again. Leading with his pistol, he entered the cabin. It was empty.

Once the shades were drawn, Zack felt relief. He might be overreacting to the danger, but better safe than sorry. He found a beer in the fridge and settled in an armchair to peruse his notes. His feeling from his interviews today

boiled down to one thing, he decided. Nobody at Santini &
Marsh was spending a lot of time worrying about the
whereabouts of Dr. Scheidecker. He sensed an
undercurrent of relief that the man was gone. Should Zack
put that relief down to the simple fact an eccentric, brilliant
man who was a major pain in the ass was no longer
rubbing everyone the wrong way? Or was it something
deeper, more sinister, such as the fact someone close to
discovering a naughty company secret was now out of the
way?

He had more interviews lined up for tomorrow. Zack
wanted to hear some real examples of the arbitrariness of
Dr. Scheidecker to learn more about the man and the
situation before his disappearance. So far he'd met only
with supervisors. He wanted to meet with a few of the
other consultants, the ones who actually worked and
debated with Scheidecker, but Zack felt there was a subtle
resistance to allowing that. Well, tomorrow would tell. He
planned to force the issue.

His thoughts turned to Eagle Feather. His friend had
been extremely lucky today. Although the Navajo's recital
of the facts had been basic and unemotional, it was clear to
Zack only the man's uncanny instincts had saved him.
Their foe seemed to be a determined professional. He'd
used a simple but terrifyingly effective bomb on Zack's
Jeep, perhaps hoping to leave the impression of an
amateur. But the long-range rifle shot and the motorcycle
skills pointed to more than that. Was he a professional
hired by Santini & Marsh or EverSun? If so, he was meant

to protect something at the old oasis site at all costs. Both Zack and Eagle Feather had their lives threatened after approaching the place. It wasn't a stretch to think Scheidecker hadn't been so lucky.

Now Eagle Feather planned to walk into the lion's den. Zack had every confidence in the Navajo's abilities. A tracker and guide, the wilderness was his playground and no one could match his skills. But the killer they faced was displaying exceptional skills of his own. One mistake, and...

Zack picked up his phone, texted a message. *Take a rifle.*

He went back to his thoughts. A moment later a ding sounded. *Why?*

Because I am your boss.

I do not have one.

Come by here early. House is an armory.

There was no response, from which Zack presumed consent.

It was predawn when the roar of the Yamaha neared and a knock sounded at the door. Zack was already up, the coffee was on. He let Eagle Feather in. The Navajo nodded his greeting.

"Cups are in the second cabinet right of the stove," Zack said.

Eagle Feather found one and poured himself some coffee.

Zack walked to a cabinet on the inside wall of the living area. He unlocked it and slid open the door. A wide array of weapons were hung on hooks and ammo boxes stacked on shelves. Several rifles stood upright. Zack took one down. He flipped the bolt and inspected the chamber, then closed it. He found a box of 308 Winchester shells and loaded a five-round magazine. He handed the box of shells to Eagle Feather and clicked the magazine into the rifle, then held up the gun.

"This is the FBI issue HRT rifle. It weighs eleven and a half pounds with the scope, more than that old lever-action Winchester you are used to, but has a lot more range and utility with these shells. I think you'll be up against a professional with sniper capability and I don't want you outgunned. Ever use one?"

Eagle Feather put down his cup and took the weapon. "I have used a similar weapon." He threw the bolt, checked the load. He removed the tripod attachment and handed it to Zack. "That will just get in the way," he said, setting down the rifle.

Zack watched his friend drink his coffee. "I'm a bit concerned..."

Eagle Feather waved him off. "Do not be. No unnecessary chances. Scouts honor," he said and raised two adjacent fingers. He gulped the remaining coffee, set down the cup, picked up the rifle and box of shells, and walked to the door. "I'll check in tonight," he said and slid out.

Zack had just settled down with his coffee and some fresh donuts provided by a thoughtful FBI shopper when his phone rang. It was Janice Hooper. She was abrupt. "Zack, you need to suspend operations. We've been called off."

"What do you mean, called off?"

"Someone way above my pay grade canceled this mission. That's all I know. We have to pull out right now."

"Janice, we can't. Eagle Feather has just gone out to the desert to track the guy trying to kill us."

"Call him back."

Zack struggled for words. "Janice, you know I can't do that. This is Eagle Feather. There is no way I can contact him until tonight."

There was a moment of silence. "Well, he is the Indian who doesn't exist, as we agreed. He's not FBI. But you are. You need to pull out now."

"I won't leave Eagle Feather unsupported."

"Officially, yes, you will." Janice hung up.

CHAPTER TEN

Arlene Pettigrew chewed on the temple tip of her glasses. Many impressions in the soft plastic indicated this was not an infrequent habit. She was studying a memo that had just popped up on her computer from her boss.

"The FBI is no longer investigating the disappearance of Dr. Carl Scheidecker. At this point in time, no official law enforcement agency is actively engaged in the case. Therefore no interviews will be granted from this point forward on the subject."

Arlene was not unhappy to be allowed to continue her work uninterrupted. Nor was she unduly sorry she wouldn't be chasing Scheidecker all over the countryside as usual. But during her meeting with Agent Tolliver, she had not gotten the sense he was ready to let it go. On the contrary, he seemed to be just getting started.

Her phone rang. It was Lucy, summoning her to a meeting with Selder. She slid out from behind her desk, put on her sweater against the cold of the air conditioning the old coot liked to keep on low and walked across the lot to his trailer. When she arrived, Lucy smiled and nodded her head toward the inner office.

"You got my memo?" Selder said without preamble while he shuffled through a stack of files, found one, and pulled it out.

"I get all your memos," Arlene said.

Selder ignored that. "We have fallen behind our schedule because of all the interviewing and re-interviewing and now we can finally get on with our work. Nicolás Constantine at EverSun wants us to hire another pumped storage expert to replace Scheidecker. He sent three names as possibilities." Selder pulled a sheet of paper from the file and handed it to Arlene. There were three names listed and numbered with contact information under each. "They are in order of preference. I want you to begin interviews immediately. We want the best fit for this project."

He closed the file, lay his forearms across it, and leaned toward Arlene. "This guy Tolliver seemed very gung-ho. The FBI search for Scheidecker is over, but Tolliver might pretend he didn't get the memo and show up. You are not—I repeat, not to give him the time of day, you understand? Just send him to me or, better yet, tell him to get the hell off the property."

"Jason, how—?"

"That is all." Selder turned back to his work.

Arlene walked out, gave an eye-roll to Lucy as she passed. Outside the trailer, the day was heating up. Men in hard hats were scurrying about the huge equipment garage, trucks were starting up, the smell of diesel fuel was in the air. She glanced at her watch. Time for the meeting with her herd of consultants. After that, she'd start researching the names on this paper.

But her mind was on Scheidecker. She couldn't believe they were just writing the guy off. EverSun must have tremendous pull to get the FBI to drop the case, more than she would have guessed. But despite his orneriness, his narcissism, his provocative manner, Carl Scheidecker was a human being, and you don't just let a human being disappear while on the job and do nothing about it.

By the time she returned to her trailer, four of the five remaining consultants were milling around the coffee machine and nibbling at the pastries.

"Where's Thomason?" she asked.

Faced with blank cow-like expressions, she shrugged. "Okay, let's get started. Have a seat."

They worked toward the meeting table, bits of conversation trailing off, and took their seats. All faces turned toward Arlene.

"Okay, folks, what have we got going today?"

A mid-thirties woman, her dark hair streaked with gray, spoke up. "Turner and I think a liner may be required for the upper reservoir for two reasons: first, the relative instability of the footing material could cause eventual cracks in the concrete and second, to help limit infiltration loss."

Arlene groaned. Costs were mounting daily. "What kind of liner?"

Turner Booker responded first. "We do not entirely agree on that. Sheryl thinks PVC is sufficient, but given the proven porosity of the base material and its conduciveness to seismic vibration, I'd say we should consider a ten to twelve-inch polymer which is more flexible yet—"

"Whoa, TMI. You two sort that out today. This time tomorrow I want your report giving me your five best reasons for and against a liner for the upper reservoir.

Then we can dig into what material to use." She looked at the other two. "What's going on over there with you two?" The two men attracting her eye were holding a whispered conversation of their own at the end of the table.

They looked up. The man who responded first was bald with thick-lensed glasses on a round face and a mat of black hair curling up from under the unfastened top button of his shirt. "We continue to hold out for site three for the upper reservoir," he said. "While we grant it may cost us more to construct than sites one or two, and hold less water when complete, in the long run, we think it will operate more efficiently and generate more power using a lesser volume of water." He glanced at Turner. "Apropos the conversation regarding the need for a liner, site three would require a smaller liner, less concrete, and a less powerful pump which should translate into immediate savings. We can demonstrate how—"

" Tim, Tim, we've been through all that. We made our decision a week ago for site two. We can't keep going back and rethinking."

"But now is the time to get it right," Tim said. "We need to think a decade down the line when water is an even scarcer commodity and efficiency is a mandate. If we don't plan for the long run—"

Arlene banged a palm down on the table. "Tim, that's it! The decision was made. Work on a design for site two has already begun. Move on!" She glared around the table. "What else?"

Sheryl put up a timid hand. "When will Carl rejoin us? We need his input for all this. He's the one who first suggested a liner." She glanced around the table. "I know he can be annoying, but he really knows his stuff."

Arlene's response was short. "He's not. I am tasked with deciding his replacement. He has wandered off on his own little field trips one time too many. I'll be meeting with each of you individually to get your input." She stood and clapped her hands like a teacher with a kindergarten class. "Okay, off to work!"

The group straggled out of the conference room amidst animated conversation.

A head peeked in the door. "So sorry to be late. Did I miss anything important?" The man grinned and stepped inside. He wore a neatly trimmed squared-off beard, his red hair was slicked down, and his blue eyes seemed to reflect a constant sense of wonder at the world around him. He was a big man, six feet tall, and broad-shouldered.

"Everything we talk about in our morning meetings is important, Ned. That's why I ask you to attend."

Ned stepped into the room. "I am sorry. I had car trouble."

Arlene relented. Of all the kooks she cradled here, she liked Ned Thomason, the geology expert, best. "You know, you really ought to replace that car. I could have used your help when Tim tried to revisit site three for the upper reservoir, but we got through it." She glanced at her notebook. "What have you got on for today?"

Ned slid into a chair. "I'm supposed to talk to the FBI Agent this morning about Scheidecker."

"Well, that's off now. The FBI has ended the investigation."

"Ended it?"

"Yes, rather mysteriously, I must say. I don't know why. Regardless, you can now attend to other work this morning."

Ned was silent. His eyes grew large. "I'm surprised they are not more concerned. I think I could have helped the agent."

Arlene looked sharply at him. "How so?"

Ned's face twitched. He shifted in his seat. "I did promise Carl I wouldn't repeat this, but I feel the time for confidentiality is passed. He did a seismic study of this entire area, much wider afield than prior studies, including the U.S. Army Corps of Engineers. He expressed some concern about what he found."

"Go on."

"As you know, Joshua Tree National Park is known particularly as a place of transition from the Colorado Desert, also known as the Sonoran Desert, to the higher Mojave Desert."

"Can we get past the tourist pamphlet?"

"Yes, yes, sorry. Well, Scheidecker mapped the transition belt, or zone, between the two deserts to their full extent against a seismic map and found an interesting thing: seismic activity stops abruptly at those zone boundaries along the entire Pinto Basin. Nowhere do faults continue east into the Colorado Desert.

"Okay, that's interesting but hardly breathtaking."

"Well, he had previously learned about an extinct oasis east of here about ten miles."

"The place he disappeared?"

"Yes, exactly. All the oases in this region were caused by seismic activity resulting in cracks in the earth allowing water from the aquifers to seep upward, and vegetation to flourish. But he realized that extinct oasis could not have been formed the same way. He believed the only other explanation was volcanism."

Arlene stared. "So he thought there might be a volcanic intrusion, a weak area in the earth's crust, underneath our project? Is that what you are saying?"

Ned looked upset. "He came to me to test his theory, to see if I thought it could be possible. He planned to visit the area, to study it. He wanted me to come along, but that day I had something else I was working on and didn't want to take the time. So he went alone."

Arlene was staring. "And never returned."

Ned shook his head, his eyes downcast.

"Wow!" Arlene shook her head. She sat in silence for a moment. She looked up. "Okay, not a word of this to anybody. I mean anybody! Understand?"

Ned nodded.

"I'll take it from here. If I need your help, I'll call on you. Meanwhile, put it out of your mind and get back to your work. Got it?"

Ned nodded, his face pale, and backed out of the room.

CHAPTER ELEVEN

Zack was stunned. He stared at his phone on the table where he had dropped it. Never in his entire career as an FBI agent had any of his investigations been closed down so summarily. Never, ever had he left a man in the field. His anger grew.

If Janice knew anything about him, she knew he would not leave a comrade dangling in harm's way. Especially not Eagle Feather. How could this happen? How could Janice allow it?

But even amidst his anger, Zack saw the answer to the question. She wouldn't, not if she could help it. He thought back to their conversation. It was peremptory, curt, short. Janice was the very model of efficiency, but she was diplomatic and thoughtful, especially with Zack. That brief, dictatorial conversation was completely out of character.

She had mentioned someone above her pay grade. Janice never followed orders blindly and very few people were so far above her pay grade that she would. This must have come from the director himself. Zack had little direct contact with the director but knew him for a measured, fair-minded man, not a man to suspend an operation so abruptly. Unless ordered. And there was only one man who could order him to do so: the president.

Who would, who *could* influence the POTUS to force the suspension of an FBI operation? It had to be someone or some group with vast political power. There were plenty who fit that description, but which of them cared enough about this investigation to expend that amount of political capital? EverSun Energy Company came to mind immediately. His previous research had revealed the extensive contributions EverSun and their affiliated companies made to various political campaigns. It was not a stretch to imagine POTUS had benefitted from EverSun along the way and that they were now cashing in their chips.

But why? What did they fear from this investigation? A scientist went missing in the middle of the desert while on some undetermined, unauthorized side trip. His employers at Santini & Marsh could not be held responsible for the man's disappearance, they had not authorized his excursion. It was clear to Zack from his interviews that the man was a loose cannon and went off on his own frequently. So what could benefit EverSun from shutting down an investigation into the man's disappearance?

Zack shook his head. He was stumped.

One thing was sure. He was not about to leave Eagle Feather out there on his own. Nor did he believe Janice expected him to do so. Her last emphatic statement came to mind. How did she phrase it? *Officially, yes, you will.* She had used the word *officially*. To Zack, that made all the difference in the context of her order. She was saying she did not expect him to leave Eagle Feather unsupported.

Zack realized her careful choice of words throughout the conversation came from knowing it was likely being recorded, a fact further suggesting the order came from the director. He was mulling all this over when his phone buzzed.

He glanced at it. It was not Eagle Feather and it was not FBI. It was a private number, one he did not recognize. He did not wish to talk to anybody else in his current state of mind, but he answered anyway.

"Hello."

"Is this Agent Tolliver?" The voice was low, almost a whisper.

"Yes, it is. To whom am I speaking?"

"Oh, I'm so sorry to bother you. This is Arlene Pettigrew at Santini & Marsh Construction. I have become aware of something I think you should know."

"Ms. Pettigrew, I'm afraid our investigation has concluded. I can not—"

"I am aware of that, Agent Tolliver. And I think I know why."

"I see. Ms. Pettigrew, you are an intelligent person and as such, I expect you realize I am not at liberty to talk to you about this. On another subject entirely, as we concluded our interview yesterday I recall you recommended a restaurant in Blythe. What was the name again? I thought I'd try it for dinner on my way home." Zack held his breath, hoping the woman would grasp his meaning.

There was silence for several seconds. "Oh, you mean Garcia's Restaurant on Hobsonway. Affordable and fun. They have a great Happy Hour from four-thirty to six."

"Yes, that's the one. Thank you. I'm sorry I can't be of help to you. Goodbye."

Of course, Arlene had never recommended the restaurant to Zack. He had taken a risk, hoping she was clever enough to get his meaning. It seems she was. He would drive to Blythe and go to Garcia's Restaurant at four-thirty and hope she would turn up.

It was easy to clear out his few things from the safe house. Used to traveling, Zack never took much with him and at arrival didn't tend to spread out much. Anything he took away from the safe house, such as weaponry, he would simply enter in the data file and turn it in elsewhere.

He would, however, borrow the white truck for a while longer. He would drop it off and reclaim his Jeep once Eagle Feather was safe. Until then, he preferred no one know his whereabouts.

Zack locked everything up, closed the blinds, and departed out the back door. He was careful to use cover to avoid sniper fire, just in case, but he doubted the location of the safe house had been exposed. No FBI agent, no matter what the reason, would ever do that. Besides, with the investigation ended, the reason to kill him should have ended as well. But on the other hand, Zack didn't want that thought carved on his tombstone.

He turned his mind to finding Eagle Feather. He was fairly certain the Navajo intended to return to the place in the desert where he had been ambushed. But Zack doubted he would approach Great Wash from the road, rather from somewhere else where he could cut the assassin's trail and backtrack him. Wherever that turned out to be, it was likely a place with a view of the lost oasis.

One question loomed large in his mind. With the FBI investigation terminated, had the assassin been withdrawn? Zack thought it unlikely. If the man was a hired professional, as Zack suspected, his communication with his employers would be infrequent. He might well remain out of contact until the job was done. So he was probably still out there.

Zack climbed into the pickup and started it up. He had his plan, and it was simple. He would drive out to Great Wash and take the truck as far up as it could take him and continue on foot to the oasis. He knew he would be a potential target the entire way. If Eagle Feather was in position, perhaps Zack's presence would serve to distract the assassin and thus give the Navajo an advantage.

Zack had taken an HRT rifle from the arsenal at the safe house. He would carry it with him and if needed use it to protect himself, but he knew he'd be lucky to get the chance, even if he was fired upon. After he reached the pavement at Old Woman Springs Road, he took the most direct route across Twentynine Palms Highway to Pinto Basin Road and turned south. He turned onto Black Eagle Mine Road, the scene of Eagle Feather's narrow escape. Once he reached Great Wash, he stopped, put the truck in low four-wheel drive, and began the tortuous crawl up the sandy bed.

Before he'd gone half a mile the hair on the back of Zack's neck began to prickle. He knew he wasn't safe in the cab of the truck. A good sniper could easily anticipate the truck's forward movement and put a well-placed bullet through the windshield. The feeling became so overwhelming he stopped the truck, turned off the engine, and climbed out. He sniffed the air, felt the heat rising. It was just midmorning, but sweat came quickly to his brow. He listened. There was no sound, no birds, no insects. Every living thing was already sheltered from the heat. He cast his eyes over the ridges to the west and then the east, searching for any sign but with little hope.

Ultimately there was nothing to do but drive on and become a target. Every instinct in Zack's body mutinied against it, but there was no other way. The distance was just too great to cover on foot and he needed to be in place should Eagle Feather and the assassin discover each other. The sun glared through the passenger window and on the windshield and effectively obscured that entire side of the wash from his view. He was driving blind. His entire body tensed in expectation of a sudden bullet impact.

He came to the gully where he had left the Jeep that very first day, now eons ago in his mind. He stopped the truck and climbed out again. This time he searched for a place to cross. He found it a few hundred yards to the west. Here the gully widened slightly and its sides, while still extremely steep, seemed passable. He slid down into it and after a quick inspection, decided to give it a try.

The gully offered the advantage of excellent cover and he used it to return to the truck. Zack knew the longer the truck sat in one place, the more likely it was to be spotted.

The sniper may even now have zeroed in on it, waiting for the driver to return. With that in mind, he stayed low, crawling out of the gully and over to the truck. He climbed in and drove west to his chosen crossing point. Once there, he didn't hesitate but took the truck right over the gully lip. The vehicle slid and crawled to the gully bottom. The job was half done.

The opposite wall of the gully was steep and the dirt was soft, but there was a band of red sandstone part way up. Zack thought if he could reach that band with his front wheels, he had a chance, although the truck would be nearly on end at that point. Well, it would be interesting.

He remembered seeing several large stones along the gulley bottom. He found them and carried them over and pushed them into the soft dirt wall to construct a path for his wheels up to the sandstone patch. He glanced at his watch. This effort had cost him ten minutes. He hoped it was worth it. He felt as if every second now was critical.

He climbed back into the truck, reversed as far as he could up the slope behind him lining up with his new stone road, then accelerated toward the steep wall as fast as the low four-wheel drive would allow. He felt the tires grip and spin on the stones, advancing sporadically in a fury of flying sand and dust. At one point the front tires dug deep into the sand, the forward progress stalled, then one of the rear tires touched a stone surface, gripped, and pushed the truck just far enough for the front tires to find the band of sandstone. Now the truck thrust upward, caught the gully lip, and stood almost on end. For a long moment, the truck hung that way, then the rear tires gripped stone, and in a furious blast of sand and dust the truck shot up and over the rim. At that moment the windshield shattered.

CHAPTER TWELVE

At this moment of extreme danger, time seemed to stop for Zack, stilled by an intense concentration upon each minute detail and his overpowering realization of the enormity of the consequences of an incorrect assessment. As the safety glass of the windshield crumpled back and chunks of laminated glass piled onto the passenger seat next to him, he knew instantly a professional with a high-powered rifle had shot at him, that the shot had come not from the east side of the wash as he expected but from the west side, that the shot had been meant to enter his window and then his skull but had missed forward by a matter of inches, that the next shot would be accurate and would be coming immediately.

In the next second, Zack threw himself over the front seat onto the bench seat behind. As he did, the driver's side window burst, and glass blew everywhere as a bullet plowed through the passenger seat upholstery. Without pause, Zack reached around the back of the passenger seat for the door latch, pushed it open, and rolled out onto the desert sand. He rolled and rolled until his body found a hollow and covering himself with sand, lay still. He heard the truck chug forward, cough several times, shudder, and stall.

Everything now depended upon the rifleman. Had he seen Zack exit the vehicle or would he believe he had accomplished his goal? Zack wondered if the truck had died between him and the rifleman to offer cover but dared not move to look. He must be still, wait, and listen.

The first seconds were vibrant with apprehension and dread. Those seconds became minutes, and those minutes dragged into more minutes. The sun grew hotter. Zack felt sweat break out all over his body. He dared not move. His mind began to wander and he remembered how certain Indian tribes would torture their captives by staking them out on the sand in the hot sun. Then they died. He tried to think of other things. He knew his thirst would increase until it finally drove him to move. His water bottle was in the truck, he could hear it calling to him. Would the assassin come to check his victim? Or had he already left?

Zack tried to refocus his mind. He went over his options, which were pitifully few. His rifle was in the truck and could do him no good. He did have the Sig Sauer at his belt. But it was useful only at a short range. He needed the killer to approach the truck, to make a noise to reveal his presence, and then be courteous enough to wait while Zack burst from the sand, pulled the Sig Sauer from his belt, cocked it, let his eyes adjust to the brightness and shoot. The prospect was impossible, ridiculous, but if the man approached, it was his only option. Meanwhile, until then, he dared not move a muscle for fear of giving away his position.

More time went by. He tried to calculate how long it would take a cautious professional to decide to cross the open wash bed and approach the truck. He couldn't hold the thought, though, for the heat was growing too unbearable. Sweat dripped into Zack's eyes and stung them, his entire body swam in moisture. He might not even be able to grip his gun in his sweaty, sand-covered hand, he realized. If he waited much longer, he might not be able to function at all.

That was it. His plan changed. He would burst from the sand and run toward the truck and just see what happened. As Zack tensed to make his move, he heard the crunch of a foot on the sand next to his ear. It was too late. He'd waited too long. He tried to explode upward but his cramped muscles would not respond, his hand could not find his gun, the sun blinded him.

"Whoa, White Man, take it easy. The shooter is gone."

Zack stared. It took several moments for the dark, sun-haloed figure holding a rifle to become Eagle Feather.

"Where did you come from?" Zack asked.

"I was on the east bank. I watched your truck approach. I saw you exit the truck. A wise move, although I do not understand why you did not leave it sooner. The loud sound of the motor and the dust rising in that gully warned every creature in the desert of your approach."

Zack walked to the truck and leaned in the door for his water bottle. He drank and then began the arduous job of removing sweaty sand from his clothing and body.

"So we've lost him."

Eagle Feather was watching Zack's efforts to clean off the sand with amusement. "Maybe not. He is on foot."

"How do you know this?"

"He saw me coming this morning, even though I took precautions." Eagle Feather kneeled by the truck. "I came down the wash from the north. I left my bike more than a mile above the old oasis and came on foot. I hoped to cross his trail and backtrack him from there. I almost succeeded. I came across his bike near the old oasis. He was cut off from his ride, that was good. But he had seen me somehow."

"What happened?"

Eagle Feather took the water bottle from Zack, sipped, and handed it back. "There were many fresh footprints where his motorcycle was hidden. He has used that place for many days. There was a small rise nearby with a long view. Footprints led south along the edge of the wash. I followed them. I did not think he would cross the open wash bed, but he did. He knew I was tracking him and crossed when he knew I couldn't see him."

"You didn't know he was over there?"

Eagle Feather shook his head. "No. When I saw you coming, I thought maybe he would show himself, and then I could distract him. He did, but he was not where I thought he would be. I could do nothing to stop him."

Zack glanced over at the opposite side of the wash. "So we've lost him," he said again.

Eagle Feather stood. "Not yet. Maybe we can run him to ground. I disabled his motorcycle."

"So even if he doubles back it will do him no good." Zack peered over the truck, keeping his head low. "How do you know he isn't still there?

"He would have shot me."

"Well, he's had a good head start. We'd better get to it," Zack said, putting away his water bottle.

Eagle Feather didn't seem to be in a hurry. "Why are you not interviewing more people today?"

Zack grimaced. "I forgot to tell you. Janice called and told me in no uncertain terms I was to drop the case and leave immediately. The investigation is ended. We are no longer official."

"But here you are."

"Yes. I couldn't leave you out here all alone, now could I?"

Eagle Feather raised an eyebrow. "You planned to drive up this wash, make much noise, draw the killer's fire, and save me."

Zack felt sheepish. "Well, it sort of ended up that way."

Eagle Feather looked at the truck, then back to the gully. "Can you get this truck back to the road?"

"Uh, yeah, I guess so."

Eagle Feather knelt and used a finger to sketch in the sand. "Here is where we are. Here is Great Wash running down to the Black Eagle Mine Road. Here is where the killer was when he shot at you. He will cross here to this arroyo. It is deep and will offer him cover. He will try to turn north to get back to his bike, or he may know I have disabled his bike and go to the mine road. The arroyo comes to the road here. You will drive there, hide the truck, find a place to shoot. When he comes out of the arroyo, you will shoot him. That is all." He stood.

"And you?"

Eagle Feather pointed the rifle barrel down at the map. "I will go up here, north of his position, and turn him and drive him toward you."

Zack went around the truck and peered in. He removed the glass that remained in the window and scraped more off the seat. To his relief, the truck started up right away. He turned the AC on full, still feeling the effects of his overheating. By the time he turned the truck around, Eagle Feather was nowhere in sight. He drove down into the gulch with some anxiety but thankfully, the far side was less steep and he was able to negotiate it without much difficulty.

He drove as fast as he reasonably could but it was a full half-hour before he came to the road. He turned west and drove with frequent glances through the passenger window, looking for the arroyo Eagle Feather had described. There was a sameness to the land here, wide-open desert and stone and brush-covered hills. When the arroyo came into view, there was no doubt.

He pulled over and stepped out to study the terrain. There was no place to hide the truck. As soon as the fugitive came to the arroyo mouth, he would see it. Zack would have to use the truck as a visual decoy and position himself somewhere away from it. The narrow opening of the arroyo was three to four hundred yards away, well within the capability of the HRT, but Zack hoped for a closer shot. He wanted to wound the sniper, not kill him. He wanted him to talk.

LOST OASIS

Debris from flash floods was piled near the arroyo entrance, a good place for cover, a place the fugitive would likely go once he saw the truck. Zack grabbed his rifle and water bottle and jogged to a position overlooking the pile. He set up the tripod, squirmed into a reclined position, and focused the scope on the debris. He took a long drink of water and settled in.

Once again the sun burned down on him but he did not sweat as much, and that was troubling. He knew he was dehydrated, his head ached, and his vision swam. He moved his eye from the scope from time to time to rest and refocus it. Every muscle in his body complained.

Zack looked away. When he looked back, a figure had appeared at the debris pile as if by magic. The man was crouched in the shadow of the tangled rocks and trees just at the periphery of the scope's bullseye. Zack held steady and waited for the target to move fully into the crosshairs. He could not see a face under the man's hood. The man's rifle was arcing around from the Jeep, searching for Zack.

Zack's emotions tried to hijack the discipline of his mind, crying out for him to shoot. But Zack wanted to wound, not kill. He waited. When the man's shoulder was squarely in the crosshairs, he pulled the trigger.

The bullet took just long enough crossing the interval for a sudden movement of the victim's head to spoil the shot. Something had alarmed him, the hooded head moved fully into the crosshairs, into the path of the bullet, and blood spurted out the back of it. The figure disappeared.

"Shit!"

Zack kept the scope on the debris pile, but the figure did not reappear. He knew he had killed the man. He shifted the scope, searching for whatever had alarmed him. Eagle Feather walked out of the arroyo.

Zack reassembled his gear, took a sip of water, and walked down to the debris stack, reluctant. He watched while Eagle Feather kneeled, checked the victim's pulse, and studied the wound.

"Nice shot," he said. "Your bullet went right through her temple."

"Her?" Zack was stunned. "He's a her?"

Eagle Feather nodded solemnly. "She was a she," he said.

CHAPTER THIRTEEN

Eagle Feather rolled the body over and pulled back the hood enough to expose the victim's facial features. The bullet had passed through the side of the head, leaving the face untouched. It was the face of a woman in her mid-thirties. Sightless brown eyes stared skyward, the mouth was slightly open exposing a gold tooth, her skin was olive, her hair black.

"A real professional," Eagle Feather said.

Zack felt no compassion, just regret. "She could be from anywhere in the world," he said. "We'll probably never know, now." He looked closely at the rifle, half pinned beneath her. "This is an M24 army issue. A good choice. It wouldn't draw unnecessary attention like these would," he said, indicating the HRT rifles the two men carried. "Yet it's practical and extremely accurate."

"Do you think she is American?"

Zack shook his head. "Can't tell. Look at her dress. Every item is dedicated to some practical purpose. Those sunglasses, for instance, are coated to prevent reflective flash, and probably have some sort of imaging capability software. The cargo pants look like French Foreign Legion issue, but that synthetic hooded shell probably goes for a thousand dollars at some specialized outdoor store in Switzerland. No, my guess is this lady was an international assassin and did not come cheap to whoever it was hired her."

"What do you want to do with her?" Eagle Feather asked.

Zack shrugged. "We have to leave her. There's no point in searching her. We won't find anything helpful."

"We will leave her here?"

"Yes." Zack gazed out toward the road, then back at Eagle Feather. "I was ordered off the case. As far as anyone knows, I left the area. Someone will find this body eventually. When they do, maybe it will reopen the investigation. If that happens, no one can stop it this time. The right questions will be asked." He gazed around. "Do you think there's any chance we can find the bullet?"

Eagle Feather eyed the loose sand and gravel that constituted the desert floor along the trajectory of the shot. "Not a chance."

Zack sighed. "I didn't think so. So be it."

"Our footprints are here."

"I'm not worried about that right now," Zack said. "Too many things can happen between now and when the body is discovered." He cocked an eyebrow at Eagle Feather. "Do you think she had a partner?"

"A good question, White Man. Her footprints are the only ones I have seen out here in the desert. But it is possible someone else attached the bomb to your Jeep and invaded your motel room. The person who called me on your phone sounded like a male."

"The voice could have been disguised." Zack laid a hand on his friend's shoulder. "We still need to watch each other's backs, as you watched mine today. Thank you."

"Someone has to hold your hand, White Man."

Zack grinned. "Now you need to go back and collect your motorcycle," he said. "I am moving my base of operations. I have a meeting in Blythe tonight, so I will find a place to stay there. Once I'm established, I'll call you."

"You will continue the investigation," Eagle Feather said.

"Yes. I hope to find another way to approach this. We are no closer to whoever is pulling the strings, and we still have no idea what happened to Dr. Scheidecker."

Eagle Feather turned and trotted back up the arroyo.

Zack stared at the body a while longer before walking back to the truck. But for a chance movement by the victim, he would now be interrogating a wounded witness. He found that hard to let go.

When he reached the truck, he took a good look at it. It would not do to be stopped by a ranger or a policeman. He cleaned up a bit more using a rag to brush glass from the seats and pulled away glass fragments that still adhered to the windshield. With all traces of the windshield gone, it might take longer to notice it. Zack hoped so, anyway.

He drove back the way he'd come, but turned south on the park road to the intersection with Interstate 10 and headed east. He intended to find a motel in Blythe, look up an auto glass repair shop, leave the truck, and rest in the motel until his meeting with Arlene Pettigrew. He did not believe he was in further danger so long as it was believed the FBI had dropped the case but would take no chances.

He had no idea what Arlene intended to tell him but hoped her information would open a new line of investigation.

Blythe was located thirty-five miles further east on the Colorado River. The town grew out of an area of pasturage made fertile by conveying water from the great river through a series of conduits, the brainstorm of a passing engineer who convinced financier Colonel Thomas Blythe of San Francisco to invest in the project. Due to the engineer's efforts, the land blossomed and later became the town of Blythe. The engineer's name is lost to most, but the town ended up named for the Colonel who visited the area but once in his lifetime.

It was two-thirty pm and one hundred eight degrees when Zack drove into Blythe. He followed signs to the Best Western on West Hobsonway. He had no difficulty booking a room for the next few nights, using the Jeep description and license plate to register. He knew no one would care enough to check. The hostelry had WIFI and a continental breakfast, all that he needed.

Zack relaxed in the air conditioning while searching online for auto glass replacement facilities. He found what he needed and went there. He was glad to see they did their more serious work in a garage, where the truck would be hidden away. He got a ride back to the motel from the manager, sent a brief text to Janice saying "Navajo safe!" and then dozed in the AC until it was time to walk the four or five blocks to the restaurant. He planned to arrive shortly after Happy Hour.

LOST OASIS

Zack entered Garcia's Restaurant at four forty-five. The small stucco building with its extended eave shelter for outdoor seating delivered what he'd hoped for, plain, practical table seating in a small but pleasant room. He found Arlene seated at a table near the wall and sat in the chair opposite her.

"Thank you for meeting me, Agent Tolliver," she said extending a beefy hand.

Zack shook it. "Please call me Zack." He hung his hat on the back of his chair. "So how can I help you?"

"Well..." As she began to speak the waiter approached. "I've already ordered. You go ahead."

"What's good?"

"Everything, really," Arlene said. "But the chimichanga is real good."

Zack put in his order and asked for a Corona.

When the waiter walked away, Arlene said, "Here's how my day began. I got this notice from Jason Selder that the FBI has discontinued the case and I am not to take any more interviews. Then he called me into his office just to make sure I understood his memo and that I will make sure the consultants understand." She paused to sip her water. "Like they give a shit. Anyway, one of my guys, Ned Thomason, whose specialty is geology, came late, missed the meeting. I gave him the company line and just before he left he tells me of this conversation he had with Carl Scheidecker just before his disappearance. I was surprised that Scheidecker had talked to anybody. But what he told Ned was even more surprising."

Zack's Corona arrived. He looked at Arlene. "No drink?"

Arlene held up her water glass. "Already got one. Got to keep my trim figure, you know."

Zack grinned and watched as the waiter left. "What did he tell Ned, then?" he asked.

"I'll try to keep this simple. Scheidecker told him he'd mapped the transition zone between the Mojave Desert and the Colorado Desert in that area and found all recorded seismic activity stopped at that zone. Meaning there are no faults whatsoever in that section of the Colorado desert. So, okay, so what? So it turns out Scheidecker, the famous snoop, discovered remnants of an oasis about ten miles east of our project, near where he disappeared, in fact. So how could that be, considering all the oases in the area were formed by seismic activity causing cracks in the aquifers? Scheidecker concluded there was only one possibility." Arlene looked at Zack as if expecting a response.

Zack put up his hands. "If you are expecting me to fill in the blanks, I'm gonna need help."

She grinned. "Sorry. Dramatic effect, I guess. Anyway, it can only mean volcanic intrusion, an upheaval of magma through a weakness in the earth's crust directly beneath the area, up through the aquifer. In geological terms, it was recent. Over the eons, it cooled, solidified, and eventually healed to the point the water no longer seeped upward, and the oasis died."

Zack thought about it. "Okay, I think I can connect the dots, but can you spell it out for me?"

"Oh, yeah. The reason for Scheidecker's little side trip that day was to confirm his suspicions. Now if he was correct, and if any investors happened to learn about it, they would immediately withdraw their support…"

"—because the whole area under your project was weak and subject to potentially subject to volcanic activity…"

"—yes, and even the slightest bit of activity could crack or even destroy the reservoirs we are building at great expense to hold water for our hydroelectric storage battery."

Zack stared at Arlene. "So the whole project goes up in smoke."

She nodded. "Yup."

Zack sipped his Corona. "It's worth killing people not to let that secret get out. But who might be that worried?"

She laughed. "You name it! You can start with Santini & Marsh and move to EverSun and from there to certain powerful lobbies in Congress. Or you can look at the people who stand to make fortunes out of this."

Zack shook his head. "Lots of powerful people."

"Very powerful. Now you see how the FBI can get called off a murder case." Arlene pushed her face closer to Zack. "But what the hell can you do about it?" Her eyes narrowed. "Let's not forget, I just put my big ass in your tender palm just now. If word gets out I spilled the beans to you, I won't just lose my job, I'll lose my ass."

121

Zack's eyes held hers. "You said this other geologist, Ned something, learned all this from Scheidecker. Who has he told?"

She shrugged. "He swears he only told me. After Scheidecker disappeared he started putting two and two together, realized how dangerous that information might be. But"—she shrugged—"he was supposed to go with him that day but something came up at the last minute. He could have mentioned it to anybody."

"Where do these consultants stay?"

"Wherever they want. A couple of them have families, they brought them with them. One or two are right here in Blythe. You know, I think Ned stays here in Blythe, come to think of it."

Two heaping plates arrived. The conversation was suspended until the waiter was gone. Zack's appetite was sketchy now and from the look on Arlene's face, as she stared at her meal, she was in the same condition.

Zack spelled it out. "I would consider Ned to be in extreme danger. Someone obviously learned Scheidecker's intent. He may have told someone besides Ned, but from what you've said about him he was a loner. So Ned strikes me as the most likely one to have let it slip." Zack had picked up his fork, now he put it down again. "These people don't mess around. There have been two attempts on my life since I got here, both of which came very close to succeeding."

Arlene's normally ruddy complexion turned pale.

"Where are you staying?" Zack asked.

"Uh, here in Blythe at the Palm Drive Apartments, 200 North palm Drive."

"Parking garage?"

"No, outdoor canopy at my unit."

Zack leaned back, sighed. "Okay. Now that I'm off the case, I no longer have the resources to protect you, or Ned, for that matter. You need to protect yourself. First, appearances. You can't change anything you do or how you do it. Stay calm. If anything, go slower than usual like you've got all the time in the world. Second, buddy up all the time. Wherever you go, be near people. Do not eat or drink anything you haven't seen prepared, don't accept food or drink that anyone hands you."

Arlene stared at him. "Jesus Christ!"

"Places to watch." Zack put up fingers, ignoring her outburst. "Your office. Keep the door open, blinds down on all windows, move around a lot, be on the telephone a lot. The bathroom. Go to ones used frequently, wait for someone you know to go in first, then go. Elevators. Never ride one by yourself or with a single stranger. Wait for a crowd. Driving. If you can share the commute with a colleague, do it. In any case, change up your habitual commute times, at least by ten minutes or so. Do nothing at your regular, habitual times." Zack saw he was losing her. "You get the picture."

"Jesus Christ," she said again, only softer.

Zack felt compassion, knowing what she was going through as she gradually comprehended the full extent of the situation. But he had to say a lot in a short time. "I'm most worried about Ned. I'm amazed he's still alive. You said he missed your meeting. Why?"

"He said he had car trouble."

"Anything specific?"

"No, and I didn't ask."

"He might have already dodged a bullet," Zack said. "I need to know where he is staying ASAP. Same goes for all your consultants. Ned might have said something to one of them as well. As I said, I no longer have the FBI's resources, but I do have help. We need to try to safeguard anybody who might now be vulnerable. When you have the information, put it in an envelope, write "tax info" on it, and leave it on the back seat of your car. I'll get it."

Zack wrote on a card, handed it to her. "That is my private phone number. Call me only in an emergency. That second name and number is another agent I trust. Call her only if you can't reach me. When you do, tell her you tried my number. She knows I always answer, and she'll know what it means if I don't."

CHAPTER FOURTEEN

When Arlene Pettigrew left Garcia's Restaurant her heart
was pounding like a pile driver. Never a timid woman,
always one to assert herself and let the chips fall where
they may, she was unused to the abject fear she felt now.
The fifteen steps it took to reach her car in the parking lot
seemed like ten miles. Every other car in the lot looked
sinister, with threatening opaque windows conveying to
her an image of dark unseen strangers within, watching
her.

She reached her yellow Volkswagen Bug with its flower
on the antennae and wished for the very first time she
hadn't purchased a car so blatantly obvious, so
recognizable. Why hadn't she selected a white pickup truck
or a black sedan that blended into the background,
chameleon-like? Her shaking hand dropped the ignition
key twice before she successfully inserted it. And just as
she was about to turn it, the thought of a bomb flashed
into her mind and she froze, terrified.

Arlene sat there, her hand on the key, frozen by fear
into immobility. Her brain refused to function normally.
One fearful thought after another raced through her mind,
each feeding upon the next, growing larger with each
scenario.

"Jesus Christ!" The apex of her fears erupted into anger
and that shouted, furious outburst brought a reality check
to her panic. "What the hell is wrong with me?" This new

emotion brought determination and she started her little car with a roar that rattled the tailpipe. "Enough!" she told herself. "Get hold of yourself."

She gained a new calm with the philosophical reiteration that what will be, will be. There was no going back. She had brought herself to this point trying to do the right thing, a heretofore unsuspected but apparently very much alive part of her personality, and having started down this road there was no option but to continue. So, screw it, she would make the bastards pay.

She remembered Zack's caution to continue her activities in a normal fashion, and with that in mind drove back to her apartment and parked in her canopied spot. She glanced surreptitiously at the street but saw nothing to suggest she had been followed. Once inside her apartment, Arlene took her water bottle from the refrigerator and walked into her tiny office. A file cabinet stood next to her desk. Here she hoped to locate the file with the current addresses of her team. She had paid this information scant attention in the past, not caring a fig about how the consultants lived their lives outside the workplace, but the information had suddenly become vitally important to her. It was a great relief when she found it.

Arlene had remembered correctly—Ned had submitted an address in Blythe, an apartment complex not far from her own. She took an envelope from a drawer and wrote Tax Information on it. Then on a sheet of paper, she wrote down the addresses of each of the consultants beginning with Ned and put the sheet in the envelope.

As she was about to step out the door, it occurred to her that carrying a single envelope to her car might look a bit strange if anyone was watching. She went back to the office, grabbed a random pile of files, and carried those out to the Volkswagen as well. She put the whole pile in the back seat with the envelope on top.

Back in her apartment, Arlene felt a surge of restless energy. She was used to meeting problems head-on, bulldogging them into a solution immediately. She had followed her instructions from Tolliver and now there was nothing else to do. Her mind raced on regardless. Was there some way to pinpoint the people responsible, those so desperate to prevent anyone learning about the potential seismic danger to the project that they hired a killer, people with enough influence or political capital to force the FBI to shut down the case?

Arlene went over in her mind the conversation she'd had with Jason Selder—was it just this morning? It seemed like days ago now. He had mentioned a name, hadn't he? Now she remembered. It was Nicolás Constantine, a big wig at EverSun. Selder had said he was the one who contacted him, which made sense because he was the man running the project and the man who had hired Santini & Marsh. There was no reason to believe this man was any more involved in murder than the next person, but he was the only person she knew from EverSun directly connected to the project. And he fits all the criteria—he was vested in building the energy storage facility, he was a spearpoint of EverSun's political influence, which was massive, and he had a hand in their treasury.

A quick Google revealed he had earned a bachelor's degree in economics from the University of Massachusetts, a master's law degree in corporate finance, and a Juris Doctor from Suffolk University Law School. He'd been with the company eight years, served in many departments having begun his career as an equity derivatives sales trader and was on a fast track for promotion. His company portrait showed a ruddy-cheeked, pleasant-faced man with a serious combover.

Arlene followed link after link but could find little to raise her suspicions. EverSun already had two similar hydropower storage facilities up and running in the southeast, she noted, but this desert project was the first of its kind in such an environment and the first such facility in the West. This meant the project hung on the energy subscriptions of several western energy utilities, new clients/partners for EverSun. Arlene imagined such clients must have been thoroughly vetted by the huge corporation. Still, new partnerships on such a scale were dicey. And since Constantine was where the buck stopped on this project, he would certainly want to keep it on track. Still, she saw nothing about the man to raise concerns— happily married with two kids, no whiff of shady dealings, no workplace transgressions, nothing.

Arlene sat back in her desk chair, frustrated. She knew large corporations such as EverSun carefully controlled their optics. Any news releases involving company personnel would be carefully handled by their publicity department. And using political clout to halt an FBI investigation or smother a Grand Jury finding was not unheard of with such huge companies. EverSun might have done so in this instance simply to prevent bad publicity, not to hide nefarious activities. Regardless, the shield they constructed around the inner workings of the company would be impenetrable to outsiders.

And what about Santini & Marsh Design & Construction, the company that hired her? A minuscule company compared to EverSun, the company still had its reputation to maintain and was heavily invested in this contract. Her thoughts turned to her boss, Jason Selder. He was arrogant, pushy, and demanding, for sure. They'd locked horns many times. Still, it was hard for her to imagine him hiring an assassin to kill someone for any reason, even if he could afford it. His way was to point the finger of blame and shout.

Still, she could be wrong. Arlene decided to try an experiment with Selder, try to draw him out. She needed to think of something to say or do that would force his hand but only if he was the guilty party. But what?

When it came to her, Arlene felt her entire being relax. Her hard-charging personality could never be at ease without a plan of action—and now she had one.

After leaving Zack with the body, Eagle Feather retraced his footsteps up the arroyo and headed east into the Great Wash. He walked north along the west bank. The sun was high, a bit past noon, and the bank above him provided little shade. He'd left his motorcycle a mile or so beyond where the wash narrowed and jogged to the east.

When he reached the bend he decided to cross to the far side. When he was partway there, something caught his eye, a quick flash of reflected light from the brush somewhere on the far bank. He stopped. The flash of light meant he was not alone. Someone was there, concealed among the rocks and chaparral, likely wearing a watch or piece of jewelry that had just signaled his presence.

The thought of a second assassin came to Eagle Feather's mind in an instant. It made sense, one killer backing the other, ready now to exact revenge. The crosshairs of a rifle might even now be on his face. He quelled the instinct to dive for cover. If he was not yet seen, a sudden motion might catch the eye. He kept his movement slow and smooth, one leg at a time, his upper torso and arms still. He reached the cover of the far bank and exhaled in relief.

No one had shot at him. That was good news. Perhaps he had not yet been seen. Of course, there was always the possibility it was merely an off-course hiker, but as far as they were from anywhere made that seem unlikely.

He needed to resolve the question and began his stalk. Staying low, he moved along the wash bank until he reached the mouth of a narrow gulley. He followed it to the shade of smoke trees along its upper edge and used them as cover to climb out. The terrain before him was mottled with large boulders, sagebrush and yucca, and occasional scrub oak. He assessed his direction, determined where he'd seen the flash, and moved ahead. He followed animal paths where they suited him around boulders and brush and in and out of small ravines.

He came to an area of sand and there he found a boot print, then another. He knelt to study them. They were Vibram soles, size nine or ten, with the look of a standard hiking boot. The prints led south along an animal trail. Eagle Feather kept on, his eyes searching. Ahead, the ground sloped downward and the trail wound around a boulder. He could not see beyond it. Eagle Feather approached, waited, and listened. His patience was rewarded with the sound of a soft cough and the scrunch of shifting feet.

He edged around the rock and caught a glimpse of blue. It was the back of someone's T-shirt. The person was kneeling, arms up and elbows out as if holding field glasses. Eagle Feather stepped close, brought up his rifle, and cocked it.

The figure before him froze at the sound.

"Drop the glasses and raise your hands."

Rubber coated field glassed dropped into the sand. Beefy arms went up.

"Turn toward me keeping your hands up."

The figure turned, knees shuffling to change position in the soft sand. It was a large man with blue eyes and a neatly trimmed red beard. He wore a floppy canvas hat. He looked terrified.

"Where is your weapon?" Eagle Feather asked.

The man stammered in his fear. "I…I don't have any weapons," he said.

Eagle Feather observed the large watch on the man's wrist, the obvious source of the flash that had given him away. He nudged the field glasses with his foot. "What were you watching?"

The man's face was red and coated with sweat. Fear almost prevented him from speaking. "I…I was watching a bird."

"A bird that has not moved for half an hour?"

The man hung his head, had no answer.

Eagle Feather studied him. This man was certainly not a killer. He had no weapon. He had no clue. But he was not here to watch birds.

"We both know you are not here bird watching. You waited for me to return to my motorcycle. Why are you spying on me?"

The man didn't reply, he simply hung his head.

"Okay, sit down, relax. I will not hurt you if you will not lie to me." Eagle Feather waited while the man settled his large frame into a sitting position, obviously relieved to bring down his aching arms.

"I have an idea. You will tell me if I am correct," Eagle Feather said. He eyed the man, then went ahead. "You are a friend or colleague of Dr. Scheidecker. You are here to try to understand his disappearance. Am I correct?"

The man nodded his head, a hopeful look entered his eyes.

"My partner and I are here with the same question," Eagle Feather said. "Someone does not want us to learn the answer. I think we are on the same side. Who are you?"

Relief showed on the man's face. "I work…worked with Carl Scheidecker," he said. "My name is Ned Thomason. I am a geologist. Carl had suspicions about this area."

"You mean about the possible volcanic activity here?"

"Yes," Ned said. "I came to try to read the geology for myself. I wanted to be certain before I expressed my concern.

"To whom?"

"I intended to take my concerns to the FBI. I think someone did something to Dr. Scheidecker to prevent him from revealing the nature of the underlying geology here and its danger to the energy storage facility we are constructing."

"You should not do that," Eagle Feather said.

"Why not?"

"Someone has stopped the FBI investigation, someone very powerful." Eagle Feather waved an arm toward the south. "A killer was here today. Did you hear shots?"

Now Thomason showed fear all over again. "I thought I did."

"Those shots nearly killed my partner."

"What happened?" Thomason's voice was breathless.

"Let's just say the killer did not succeed." Eagle Feather looked intently at Thomason. "Who else have you told about Scheidecker's suspicions?"

"No one. Well, wait, I did mention it to Arlene Pettigrew. She is my immediate superior. She told me not to tell anyone."

"That is good advice. Your life may be in danger. You likely have increased that danger a great deal by coming here."

CHAPTER FIFTEEN

Zack opened his door enough to allow Eagle Feather to slide in. The Navajo glanced around the motel room, looked at the king bed, the wall AC unit grinding and pulsating, the narrow door to the cubicle bathroom, and his face showed amusement.

"Nice digs, White Man."

"It'll do for now," Zack said with an answering smile. He waved an arm as if to encompass the Taj Mahal. "Find a chair, any chair, make yourself comfortable."

"I will take the chair, you can have the bed."

Zack grinned. "Let me mix you a drink," he said. He reached into the mini-fridge and tossed Eagle Feather a can of beer, took one for himself. "What have you been up to?"

"I just captured a geologist in the desert."

"Never a dull moment."

Eagle Feather told his story. Zack imagined the time, effort, and discomfort the Navajo went through just to find a confused and unarmed scientist at the end of his stalk. He shook his head, smiling.

"It is funny to you, White Man."

"Such things do not happen to you often, my friend. I laugh when I can."

Eagle Feather's expression did not change. "I think this man is in danger."

"I think so, too," Zack said, the thought sobering. "Where is he now?"

"I carried him out of the wash on my motorcycle," Eagle Feather said. "He had left his truck on the Black Eagle Mine Road, in plain sight. He told me he had quarters in Blythe and was going there. I waited and followed him at a distance to see if anyone followed him. I left him at his home just now, safe for the moment."

"No sign of a tail."

Eagle Feather shook his head.

Zack then told the Navajo about his conversation with Arlene Pettigrew.

"I think your lady friend is in danger also," Eagle Feather said.

"There is no doubt of it in my mind. My first instinct is to remove both of them from the situation, just put them in a safe house somewhere and go on from there. But we need the information they can provide. They are our only link to the inner workings of this project. If we remove them, the people who hired the assassin will know we are on to them and cover their tracks, maybe even do away with Dr. Scheidecker, if he is still alive, and then we are left with nothing."

"I think they would always be in danger for what they know," Eagle Feather said.

Zack sighed. "Even down the road, if the plant is built and volcanic activity causes any problems, Arlene and Ned would be seen as dangerous witnesses to the fact that the builders were aware." Zack shook his head. "No, I think the best safeguard is to find the guilty parties now and to do that, we need those two in place."

"What is next, White Man?"

"I need you to break into a car," Zack said. He explained his arrangement with Arlene. "When you get back, we will need to talk to Ned."

Eagle Feather went off to run his errand. He returned a half-hour later with the envelope labeled "Tax Information" and a Subway sandwich that he ate while Zack looked over Arlene's information.

"The consultants' living quarters stretch out over a large area, from Palm Springs to Indio to Blythe," Zack said, studying the list. "For now, we have to assume only Ned and Arlene are in on Scheidecker's secret. Let's see what we can learn from Ned. If he has spoken to anyone else about it, no matter how briefly, we need to know."

It was a pleasant, if still hot, evening as the men climbed aboard Eagle Feather's motorcycle. They rode down E Hobsonway to the units at 2450 and parked outside Ned's living quarters. Eagle Feather knocked on the door. Several minutes later the door opened to the chain.

"It is okay, Ned. My friend is an FBI agent."

The door swung wide enough to allow the two men to enter. They were in a foyer with a coatrack and narrow, mirrored table. Ned Thomason looked at them with red-ringed eyes and unkempt hair. He was a man on the verge of panic.

Zack extended his hand, introduced himself.
Thomason's grip was firm despite his anxiety. He was a
large, robust man, probably not accustomed to feeling fear
in his protected life.

"Let's all sit down," Zack suggested.

Thomason led the way to a living room. Zack sat on the
couch. Eagle Feather and their host each took a facing
chair.

"What has happened? What's going on?" Thomason
asked.

Eagle Feather answered. "Nothing new has happened.
My friend needs to ask some questions."

"Uh, okay," Thomason said and waited.

Zack wondered where to begin. "Ned, you may know
the FBI has been called off the Scheidecker case. Someone
with great power has wielded their influence. As far as
anyone beyond you, Arlene Pettigrew, and Eagle Feather
know, I have dropped the case and have gone home.
However, I met with Arlene today and she told me of the
conversation the two of you had this morning. I am aware
of Scheidecker's discovery at the lost oasis. That
knowledge is the likely reason he was abducted, for I now
have no doubt that is what happened. Although I'm off
the case, I have no intention of deserting you and will
continue to investigate. But for now, my investigation must
be unofficial and discreet. No one can know of my
continued presence here." Zack looked hard at Ned.

"What should I do?" he asked.

"Absolutely nothing. It is essential both you and Arlene carry on as you normally would. Forget about anything but your work during the workday. We will reach out to you when we need you. Are you willing to do this? Our only other option is to remove you from the situation altogether and try to find a safe place for you. However, that would be difficult as I would be acting unofficially, your absence would raise suspicions, and I still would not be able to entirely guarantee your safety." Zack watched Thomason's face as he spoke.

Ned hesitated. "What did Arlene say?"

"She prefers to tackle this head-on. She will continue to work with us."

"Then I will do the same."

"That's fine. I know this isn't easy, but you will need to look relaxed. You don't look relaxed right now. Pay attention to your appearance, keep shaved, keep your hair combed, keep your clothes neat. Think of this as a theatrical performance, including maybe even a little makeup." Zack put a finger to his eye to indicate Ned's eye redness.

Thomason nodded. "I understand." He looked from Zack to Eagle Feather and back again. "How long will this go on?"

Zack lifted empty palms. "That will be hard to say until we know more. Somebody hired a professional assassin, probably to protect the secret of the lost oasis area by any means. We have eliminated that particular threat. However, we think it possible they may have engaged other

139

professionals, and if so the remaining killer or killers continue to be a danger. To find them and to remove that threat, we must identify the heads of the conspiracy and expose them. That's where we will need your help."

"How?"

"We don't want you to be proactive in any way. Just maintain your role. Never, never talk to Arlene about this. There are likely to be bugs all over your work area. But keep your ears open. We'll know the questions to ask you. The other thing is, be cautious. Stay around people whenever possible. Drive directly to work and directly home again. Leave when everyone else does, try to arrive when you know they will mostly all be there. No eating out. Cook at home. If you must order in, find a way to confirm the delivery person's identity. In other words, if there is an assassin still out there, don't present him with a golden opportunity." Zack tried to reassure him with a smile. "If you follow these steps, you should be fine."

The anxiety had returned to Thomason's face in spades.

"Here is a number to reach me if you must. Give me your phone." Zack took the smartphone Thomason handed him and entered a number. "Only use this number in an emergency. You'll know when that is, I think. Meanwhile, we'll be keeping an eye on you." Zack handed back the phone. "Now I have just a couple of questions, but you must answer them as truthfully as you can. First, have you told anyone other than Arlene about your conversation with Dr. Scheidecker? Even the slightest hint? Think carefully."

Thomason shook his head. "I've gone over that in my mind since this morning. After Carl told me of his suspicions, I had it in mind to consult with the team, to ask some "what if" scenario questions like what might be the impact of a temblor or similar occurrence on the reservoirs and how could we protect them. But I never did, thinking Carl would probably do that himself. Then when he didn't return that day, I grew worried and suspicious and decided not to say anything."

"Nothing to anybody?"

"No."

"Okay, second question. Did Carl mention saying anything to anyone else?"

"No, he didn't say anything about that. But I had the impression he came to me first because he wanted my opinion as a fellow geologist. Frankly, he was a bit of loner and didn't seem to value the opinions of others all that much."

After leaving a shaken Thomason behind, Zack asked Eagle Feather what he thought. "Did Ned really keep that conversation to himself, do you think?"

"I do not think the man capable of deceit," Eagle Feather said. "But he might have let something slip without knowing it."

Zack nodded. "My thoughts as well. But so far as we know now, the discovery remains a secret, the only assassin we know about is now dead, and whoever hired her probably doesn't know that yet. If we are lucky enough for all those things to be true, we might be able to accomplish something before the status quo changes."

Zack had Eagle Feather drop him a few blocks from his hotel, just to be on the safe side. "The perps know about me," Zack said to his friend, "but they may not know about you."

"Someone does," Eagle Feather said. He reminded Zack of the threatening call from his own phone.

"With luck, only the deceased assassin had that information. These professional killers do tend to work alone."

Eagle Feather gave his head a slow shake. "I think we ran out of luck."

"Why?"

"The voice of the one who called me from your phone was a man," the Navajo said.

Arlene Pettigrew woke early. As her consciousness crept in, she felt a sudden surge of excitement remembering her plan. As much as she had feared an assassin's bullet when she first learned the danger from the FBI agent, she now anticipated the challenge of her planned course of action. Arlene was motivated by action, stubborn in the face of resistance, the very qualities which had made her the perfect choice for herding cats—or scientists. These qualities also helped her replace the fear in her gut with a plan in her brain.

LOST OASIS

The day, as always in Blythe during the summer, was clear and hot. A mantle of blue sky swept to the far mountain horizon and the early sun was a spotlight in her rearview mirror. Few cars traveled the freeway this early. Arlene accelerated to eighty miles per hour. Speed exhilarated her. She enjoyed the surge of power at her command and the sense of flying along with dotted white lines racing toward her attempting to become one.

The construction sign requiring her to slow to forty-five mph came as a surprise. It was not been there yesterday, of that she was sure. Another sign informed her the right lane was closed and an arrow directed her to move over. Then came angled cones and a "slow" sign. She slowly crested the rise and saw a construction worker in a reflective vest and hooded sweatshirt holding a stop sign. She slowed, came to a stop, apparently the first in line. Beyond the worker was a blue pickup truck with a construction logo on the door blocking the lane. The man ambled to her car, she rolled down her window.

His face was partially obscured by the hood of his sweatshirt. "Good morning, miss. I'm afraid we have to send you on a very short detour around our drainage work here. Please follow that truck." He pointed to the blue pickup.

"How long will I have to wait?"

"No wait, miss. There is very little traffic this morning. I'll take you around myself."

The man put the handle of the stop sign into the top of the cone, walked to the pickup truck and climbed in.

Arlene lined up behind the pilot truck as it drove off. They left the pavement and went onto a dirt road leading away from the interstate. Dust billowed behind the pickup and Arlene held her vehicle back a bit. The dirt road crested a rise and then dropped steeply down the far side. Ahead, the dust had stopped and Arlene had to brake hard not to hit the truck. The man climbed out and walked back to her. She rolled down her window.

"What's the matter?" she asked.

The man's hood had fallen. He had black hair, an olive complexion, and a sweet face with a friendly expression. He rested both hands on the window sill, peering in at her.

"I'm afraid your detour may take longer than expected," he said.

Arlene had the sudden premonition of danger. Instinctively, her hand went to the automatic window button and pressed it to raise it. At the same time, she threw the car into gear.

The man's face changed instantly to a hard mask. His hands tried to come in the window but he was too late and the window almost caught them. He pulled away with a curse as the VW moved away from him. But the truck was there and Arlene braked and went into reverse and gunned the little car. She saw a flurry of movement as the man leaped out of the way and grabbed for her door. He seemed incredibly agile. Then it was all dust in front of her. Driving with the rearview mirror she flew up and over the crest of the rise backward. The VW's rear tires lifted into the air momentarily and it was enough to skew her steering so that the vehicle slid backward off the hard-pack into the sand. The wheels spun.

Arlene shifted into drive and hit the gas. The wheels kept spinning. She felt panic begin to surge in her chest. She forced herself to breathe calmly, then shifted to another gear and lightly touched the accelerator. The tires seemed to catch momentarily, then spun again.

Movement caught her eye. Looking up, she saw the man coming over the crest, running hard. He had a gun in his hand.

CHAPTER SIXTEEN

Arlene's knuckles were white on the steering wheel, but anger overtook panic and she focused her mind on extricating the VW from the sand. Her strength was disciplined thought, both as a scientist and a manager of scientists. She recalled the VW bug had its engine in the rear thus most of its weight was over the rear wheels. In her present situation, with the car angled uphill, she needed her most direct gear to wheel ratio with slow acceleration to best utilize the engine's power and ease out of the sand without spinning the drive wheels. She shifted up to high gear, held her breath, let in the clutch slowly, praying the engine would not stall, for that would mean her death. As the clutch engaged, the car shuddered, the engine coughed. Arlene gave it incrementally more gas, felt the little car inch forward, while in her peripheral vision the man's shape grew closer. Panic had started to reassert its grip in her just as the bug's tires caught on firmer ground. She gave it more gas. The man had stopped running, was aiming his gun, but by now she had the little car in a tight turn on the dirt road, accelerator to the floor, while dirt and sand spit from the tires creating a storm of dust that obscured his view. She roared back along the dirt road toward the interstate. The shot never came.

When Arlene reached the freeway she had no choice but to continue in her original direction on the westbound lane, scattering cones freely as she went. But should she go on to her office, now that it was clear someone wanted her dead? It seemed a little late in the day to go about her life as usual as Agent Tolliver wanted. Whoever that man was, he knew her routine inside and out, right down to the exact time she drove to work each day. If he could engineer the complex subterfuge he'd just managed, coming within an inch of success, it seemed to Arlene he could take her life almost at will. She couldn't count on having people around her enough of the time to stay safe. Her smartphone might even be bugged. What now?

When she arrived at the exit for Desert Center, she turned down the ramp as usual but drove directly to the post office, the only business now active in the virtually extinct town. She walked in. The window was closed, it was too early, but she could access the payphone. She found Zack's card in her purse and called the number. Her hands still shook, she had difficulty pushing the buttons accurately.

Zack answered at the first ring. "Hello?"

"Your plan is for shit! I almost got killed."

"Whoa, hold on. Is this Arlene? What happened? Where are you?"

Arlene gave a hurried synopsis of what had just occurred. "Where can I go now? I can't go to work, they'll see I'm still alive and correct their mistake."

His voice sounded calm through the phone's earpiece. "On the contrary, that is the one place you will be safe. If someone with Santini & Marsh hired this killer, the responsible party will not want your assassination to occur

147

on his doorstep. Even if it is someone with EverSun or any other involved company, the same must apply. No, you are safest there, at least until quitting time. By then I will have a safe place arranged for you to stay. We will have a reason for an extended absence worked out for you by then as well. But you need to get back in your car right now and go. You are vulnerable until you reach the office. I promise you this case will blow wide open before long, and your life will go back to what it used to be. But right now you need to go on to the office as if nothing happened."

Arlene clanked down the earpiece and walked quickly out of the post office. She scanned the small street for a blue pickup truck but didn't see one. Once in her VW, she drove past the deserted town buildings and headed up the road toward the old Kaiser company town filled with dread.

Zack put his phone down on the dresser. The question that had been in all their minds was now answered, he thought. There was another assassin and he was very inventive, an obvious pro. All of their lives were in danger until he could be stopped. He thought for a minute, then picked up the phone again.

Eagle Feather answered after several rings. "Yes, White Man?"

"We almost lost Arlene Pettigrew this morning," Zack said. He related the story of Arlene's narrow escape. "She had enough presence of mind not to use her cell phone to call me. Got to give her credit."

Eagle Feather sounded unusually terse. "My fault, White Man," he said. "I had planned to watch her, but I thought she was safe once the assassin died and the FBI was off the case. Either this killer does not know that, or he does not care."

"Probably the latter. He still wants his paycheck."

"What now?"

" I will arrange for her to go to the safe house after work today. But I will need to bring Janice Hooper into this."

Zack heard a chuckle on the line. Eagle Feather enjoyed working with Janice. He thought of her as feisty, worthy of the Navajo's respect, Zack figured. "She can help us create a bonafide reason for Arlene to be absent until this mess is cleared up," Zack said. "However, there is another concern. We also need to protect Ned Thomason. The assassin may have that name on his list as well."

"Where is Thomason now?"

"I don't know, but he should be at the job." Zack glanced at his watch. "I'll go check his place to see if his car is gone. If it is, I'll leave him to you."

Zack called a cab, then choked down the toast he'd brought back from the meager continental breakfast. He was watching out the window when the cab arrived. Grabbing a banana and the remains of his coffee, he climbed into the cab. On the way to the glass repair shop, Zack had the cabbie detour to Thomason's home. They cruised by. Ned's vehicle, an ancient blue Toyota Tacoma, was gone. He went on to the glass shop and messaged Eagle Feather—*he's yours*.

Zack paid the cabbie. The repair shop was not yet open, it would not be until eight am, another ten minutes. He sat on the curb to wait. The manager arrived five minutes later. He saw Zack and smiled. "You're all ready to go. Come on into the office and sign off."

Zack did so. He charged the bill to the FBI but had the manager put a three-day hold on it. He didn't want anyone knowing he was still around, even the agency. The manager agreed without question. He'd probably noticed the bullet hole in the upholstery.

In a truck more or less like new again, Zack drove back to the motel room. This next part would be tricky. After his cryptic conversation with Janice ending the official investigation, he no longer trusted that their conversations were private. He needed to involve Janice without tipping off anyone who might be listening in.

He called. She answered immediately.

"Janice Hooper, Supervisory Agent FBI, speaking."

She'd responded formally. A good start, he thought. "Supervisory Agent Hooper, I am calling regarding my letter to you asking for your endorsement of my application to the academy," Zack said, pitching his voice higher and, he hoped, younger.

Janice responded without pause. "Yes, of course. You must be Mr. Richardson."

"Yes, ma'am."

"Mr. Richardson, before agreeing to this, despite your excellent credentials, I would need to meet with you in person. I have some time around ten this morning. Let's say my office at nine forty-five. I can give you until ten sixteen. Will that do?"

"Yes ma'am, thank you."

After Zack ended the call, he pondered Janice's reply. He knew she had just told him a means to communicate, but he had to puzzle it out. On a Best Western pad, he jotted down every word she had said, looking for code words or numbers. He came up with Richardson, credentials, ten, nine forty-five, ten sixteen. It wasn't until he'd written out numerically the times she specified that it came to him: 9:45, 10:16. A telephone number, 945-1016, probably for a throwaway phone. With the 435 area code for her St. George office, he had the entire number.

Zack resisted the temptation to call right away. Her office itself might be bugged if she were being monitored. She had said she'd be free around ten, perhaps she meant the time specifically. He'd call the number then.

With about two hours to kill, Zack decided to drive the route Arlene had taken this morning when she was ambushed. He got on the interstate and headed west toward Desert Center. Within five miles something orange caught his eye. He pulled over for a closer look and saw it was a highway cone half-hidden in a bunch of coyote brush just off the shoulder. Zack got out and inspected it closely. It seemed quite new but showed signs of impact, undoubtedly from Arlene's VW as she made her escape. He turned and walked back along the highway until he found the dirt road she had described.

Zack went back to the truck and backed it along the shoulder, then turned into the dirt road. He drove down it. Within a quarter mile he came to a short rise followed by a steep downslope, fitting her description. It was a perfect spot for the ambush, invisible from the highway. He stopped and got out, looking for tire marks. He saw Arlene's story written clear as crystal on the dirt surface, the sudden stop, the spin marks from suddenly accelerating tires, the reversal back up the rise. Zack walked along, found the place she'd gone off the road, and a channel in the sand her spinning tires had dug before her escape with the tight fast U-turn.

He returned to the rise, inspecting the ground. He found several toe impressions where the killer had run after Arlene, then nothing more. He saw no returning prints and was confused, then realized the man had walked into the vegetation along the road to hide them. Very careful, this man. He must have been furious at Arlene's escape after planning so well.

Zack took pictures of the prints with his phone, then walked down to where the man's truck had stopped. When he found a clear tire impression, he took another picture. He searched the area thorughly but found nothing else of use.

LOST OASIS

He drove back to the freeway, thinking how well the man had chosen the spot and how lucky Arlene had been to escape. Now he could only hope Ned had an equally lucky morning.

Zack took the off-ramp at Desert Center, passed several big rigs dozing in the wide parking areas on either side of the road, and entered the ghost town. The post office was marked by a flag pole. It was in a long narrow building with a porched walkway. Other storefronts in the building seemed to be used for storage. He drove slowly. Two large buildings that had once been cafes came in view on his right, another with a faded sign announcing itself as a market. They all seemed to be completely deserted.

Zack had an eerie feeling about this place. He had heard Desert Center had a population of about four hundred people, but none lived or worked in the town itself. It was a ghost town. Just beyond the market, he came to a State of California maintenance service area, beyond it a private, fenced-in home. Zack turned around and drove into an empty lot between the two deserted cafés. There was another home there, a cabin-like construction. Another set of buildings appeared to be a deserted motel. That was it. There appeared to be nothing else here.

This place would be a perfect hideout for someone who did not want to be noticed, Zack thought. He could park his vehicle behind any one of these empty buildings, arriving after dark to sleep, leaving quietly before dawn. Zack doubted the people living behind their fences would notice another vehicle over the sound of trucks roaring in

153

and out of the parking lots, or care, for that matter. It would be useless to search now, though. But maybe he could wait here at dusk, wait to see what happened. At least it was something.

Glancing at his watch, Zack saw it was time to try the number Janice sent him. He called it. Janice answered at the first ring.

"Hello, Zack. You can call this number for the next twenty-four hours. After that, I'll get a new number for you. You've apparently pissed off some powerful people."

"Yes, people who aren't afraid to spend money on professionals," Zack said and gave Janice a quick synopsis of events. "It's now all about trying to keep two potential witnesses alive."

"What do you need from me?"

"I need a safe house in Blythe, but one known only to us. How high do you think this thing goes?"

Janice didn't hesitate. "Right to the top. But I have an agent I trust completely. I'm sending her to you. We can't use any existing safe houses, she'll have keys to a new one we've set up. You should use it yourself since you are no longer expected to be in the area. How is the Indian who doesn't exist?"

"He's taking care of himself," Zack said.

"Does the other team know about him yet?"

"We think yes, but he's not high on their priority list."

"What else do you require?"

"I'm sending a couple of photos now. Any info you can get from the tire tread will be helpful. Oh, and I'm keeping the truck. If you can keep teams away from the Yucca Valley safe house where my Jeep is stored for the next few days, that would be great."

"Done. You need to conduct this investigation as if you do not exist. Not just to stay alive, although that may be important to you, but for my sake, which I hope is more important to you."

"Of course it is, Janice."

"Okay. Final thought. I expect updates every six hours. I will have an answering device on this phone. Got it?"

"Got it." Zack grinned to himself. He could always count on Janice to be a step ahead. He noticed he had a call. It was a voice message from Eagle Feather confirming Ned Thomason's truck was parked at the job site. He had not seen Ned but assumed all was well.

Zack called him back. "Eagle Feather, where are you now?"

"I am on a slag heap overlooking the office trailers."

"Can you see Arlene's yellow VW in the lot there?"

"You can't miss it."

"Excellent. Our babies are safe for now. Next will be to safeguard their return trip at the end of the day."

"I will watch to see if our subjects leave here before then."

Zack paused, thought about it. "Okay, do that. If I need you elsewhere, I'll call. I'm considering a proactive strike tonight, but we'll need to get our sheep safely home first."

After ending the call, Zack drove back to Blythe. He needed time on the internet.

CHAPTER SEVENTEEN

Arlene was in bad shape. The drive from Desert Center to the workplace had been horrible, every vehicle she passed a potential danger in her mind. On her walk from the parking lot to her trailer, she inwardly cringed, her back tensed against the impact of an imagined bullet. In her office, she threw away what was probably perfectly good coffee, made by Lucy every morning, and made a fresh batch of her own.

"This is ridiculous!" she said to herself as the coffee maker groaned and burbled. How could she go for an entire day like this? But she must. Agent Tolliver said the end of the day would bring safety for her. But first, she must get through these hours in good form and not behave suspiciously.

The first item on her agenda this morning was the meeting of the consultants. Ned Thomason arrived first. Always pale of face, he now looked blanched. His red beard stood out like a distress signal. They were alone for a moment. When he opened his mouth to speak, she silenced him with a motion of her head.

If I'm having trouble with this, she was thinking, *how the hell will this guy ever make it?* She was bothered that he was first to the meeting since he was usually last. At a time when it was essential to keep his normal routine, he'd already made a muck of it.

LOST OASIS

The others drifted in, not a care in the world. Arlene was envious. These academics were clueless, she thought, never knowing the undercurrents passing around them, never suspecting the dangers that lurked near them in dark places. Someone would always protect them. They lived on their own academic island and never saw the sharks in the water.

Finally, everyone was present. Booker and Buker argued over materials for the reservoir lining, Sheryl Hunter was lost in space, Thomason was ominously quiet. Arlene prayed no one would notice him. The big surprise came when Blair Schäuble, the project's assistant supervisor, walked in. Although he had a perfect right to attend, and probably should, he had never done so before. He nodded, harrumphed, and sat down in an empty chair, his beady eyes going around the table. If anything, Thomason managed to look whiter. Arlene was sure he would give the game away.

She called the meeting to order, then called on the consultants to report. There was nothing new, the big item being the liner for the reservoir. Each turned in their homework, the five reasons for and against the liner. The top item in the 'against' column was cost, the top item in the 'for' column was the possibility of cracks caused by seismic activity. Turner Booker continued the argument for the liner, maintaining that any earth movement from any cause could cause cracks which could lead to water loss on an ongoing basis which would be unsustainable. Arlene was surprised when Ned interrupted to state unequivocally that there would be no seismic activity in the area.

"Although there are many faults at lower elevations of the Sonoran in this area, none have been found this side of the transition belt between the Mojave and the Sonoran deserts," he said. He shrugged. "There just aren't any." He seemed calm.

Arlene wondered if by engaging his mind in his area of expertise he was able to forget, at least momentarily, the danger he was in. She noticed Schäuble's brown eyes were glued to Thomason as the scientist spoke. There was something about Schäuble that repulsed her.

The meeting ended, the group still split on the issue of the liner. When the last consultant had filed out, Schäuble remained.

"Where are you on the liner subject?" he asked, fixing her with his bug-pinning gaze.

"Ultimately, I am prepared to recommend it," she said. "Yes, it is costly, but it is a safeguard against possible future problems leading to even greater expenditures. Besides, similar existing projects use them."

"Those projects reside in different geologies with different temblor potentials."

"Geological faults can be hidden," she pointed out.

He stared at her. "What position did Scheidecker take on the matter?"

The mention of Scheidecker almost undid her. Had the man brought him up on purpose to watch her reaction? She couldn't tell from his fat, blank face. She didn't let her fear show. "He never said specifically. He disappeared before we touched on the subject of a liner."

"But he must have engaged in discussions about potential seismic or other activities affecting the reservoirs."

She shook her head. "Again, nothing specific to my knowledge."

He rose from his seat, walked toward the door. He turned, his hand on the doorknob. "You are doing fine work for us, Arlene. I just wanted you to know how much we appreciate you." He turned and left, shutting the door quietly behind him.

What the hell was that all about? she wondered. But when she thought about it, the truth was she didn't know the guy and had no way of knowing if his appearance this morning was significant or just coincidence. She'd be sure to mention it to Tolliver, though.

Arlene remembered the test she had decided to try on her boss, Jason Selder. Shaken as she was by the morning's events, she was determined to try to learn if Selder was involved. He looked up when she appeared at his door, his normal abrupt self.

"What is it?"

"I've heard rumors and I want to check them out with you."

"Rumors?"

"Rumors about why Scheidecker was out in Great Wash."

Selder closed the file he was studying and looked at her. "What rumors?"

"Rumors that the company did something to Dr. Scheidecker to keep him from reporting a seismic anomaly that could sidetrack our project."

"What seismic anomaly?" Selder stared hard at Arlene.

She threw up her hands. "I don't know, maybe the same report from the California Institute of Technology Earthquake Data Center that we thought we'd put to rest a while ago."

Selder looked frustrated. "We went through all that. Your own team pointed out that underground tremors can have numerous causes. Your own team put it to rest. It's not like the earth is just one big concrete ball, for Christ's sake." Selden was getting worked up now. He glared at Arlene. "Somebody thinks this company would harm a world renown-scientist for something as trivial as that? Harm him? None of this is so important anyone should be harmed over it. That is ridiculous! You scotch those rumors, Arlene. And give me the names of anyone spreading them. I won't have that kind of loose talk going on around here." Selder waved her away and reopened his file.

As Arlene returned to her office, she was pretty sure she had her answer about Selder.

LOST OASIS

Eagle Feather lay in a small depression atop the slag heap, his elbows deep in dirt to steady his hands holding the field glasses. He wasn't worried about the lenses giving him away, they were coated and he'd long ago tested them for telltale flashes. They worked as advertised. His bike was concealed at the bottom of the rubble heap. He was surveying the entire project site, viewing it with the glasses in an oval pattern, right to left across the old towers and slag heaps and back across parking lots, trailers, and the fenced machine yard and barn. He'd been at it about an hour, with time out to talk to Zack. It was warming up considerably, but Eagle Feather was prepared and did not notice.

Now he swept the glasses along the hangar doors, pausing to look for movement inside the shadowy openness but saw none. At this hour of the morning, all the workmen were down in the pit and office personnel were inside the air-conditioned trailers. Eagle Feather did not expect much activity until nearer lunchtime. He moved the glasses along the barn and began the return survey over rooftops and the old girder tower. At the end of his sweep, there was another rubble pile nearly as tall as his own. He scanned it, the large rocks springing into focus as he moved the glasses. Something new came into view, half-obscured by the rock he was viewing. He adjusted his focus. The object leaped out, a rifle and scope pointed directly at him, so clear now he thought he could see an eye in the scope. He instantly rolled to one side, falling backward on the rubble. He heard a ping on a stone where

161

he had just vacated. He did not hear the report of a rifle.
The killer was using a silencer, perhaps the reason Eagle
Feather was still alive, as they are notorious for inhibiting
accuracy.

Eagle Feather had left his old Winchester repeating rifle
mounted on his bike at the bottom of the slag heap. He
plunged, running, sliding down the loose slag. He was
protected on this side of the mound from the sniper but
knew the man would now be running down his own hill of
rubble to find another firing position as Eagle Feather tried
to escape. His bike and rifle were where he had left them.
He pulled the bike upright, jumped on, started it, and
accelerated across the open ground toward the dirt road.
He glanced at the slag heap where the sniper had been,
calculating how long it might take the man to descend. He
figured he had a few seconds to spare once he hit the dirt
road. He reached it, roared down it at full throttle. He
heard another ping, this one on his rear fender just as the
road took him behind a protecting ridge. It had been a
near thing.

Eagle Feather was not content to be chased away. Once
protected from view by the side of the mountain, he
turned off the road and into a small arroyo and motored
up it as far as he could. He dropped the bike, took his rifle,
and scrambled up the steep slope to a ridge where he could
look down upon the roadway. He lay the Winchester out in
front of him and waited. He'd found a good spot, the road
was within easy range of his rifle.

He heard the distant whine of a motorcycle. He steadied his rifle on a particular patch of road. The motorcyclist appeared more suddenly than he expected, moving fast. With little time to react, Eagle Feather pulled the trigger.

The rider's head turned, his helmet visor angled toward Eagle Feather's position even as he increased his speed. The road was visible for a long distance and the Navajo sent two more shots after the cyclist, knowing even as he did his target was out of range. He watched the figure gradually blend into the distant landscape.

Eagle Feather hated to quit, had a momentary thought of pursuing the killer further, but realized he'd never catch him. The killer would not return here today. The Navajo scrambled down to his motorcycle and rode back to the construction camp to resume his surveillance.

Zack's online search was interrupted by a knock on his motel door. He peered out the peephole and saw FBI credentials naming Agent Sarah Whithers. He opened the door, his eyes widening as he stared at the young woman who stood there.

"Janice?" He asked, yet he knew it could not be.

The woman gave a great smile, her green eyes sparkled and perfect white teeth glistened. "Agent Sarah Whithers," she said. "Janice sent me. May I come in?"

"Yes. Please come in." He marveled as she slipped through the entranceway. His boss Janice Hooper had the same facial features, perfect teeth, same green eyes and her smile, when she chose to use it, was brilliant, just like this woman. How could two different FBI women agents look so much alike?

"Please, sit," Zack said, waving toward the chair. Before he could help himself, he blurted, "You're not related to Janice Hooper by any chance, are you?"

She had started toward the chair, now turned and looked at him in surprise. "How on earth did you know? I've not met you before, have I?"

"Oh, no, no. It was just a guess," Zack said and perched on the end of the bed. "None of my business."

She settled into the chair. "It was a good guess. I am her niece."

"I see." It explained to Zack why Janice felt she could trust this particular agent.

Sarah smiled again. "I am here to help you move to the safe house." The smile brightened. "Now," she said.

The last word was soft but unmistakably firm, another Janice trait. Zack prevented a smile of his own, rose from the bed, and went to close his computer. "I'll pack right now."

Although claiming a population of a little over twenty-one thousand souls, the small city of Blythe did not lack for condo rentals and homes for sale, a fact Zack had appreciated when first Googling the condo units where Arlene lived. But Sarah Whither's little Ford hybrid led

Zack in his truck to the west of town and then north, away from the sprawl. Like many desert towns, Blythe had no suburbs but came to an abrupt end where the public water supply ended and fields or desert began. This was a preferred location for FBI safe houses as it offered a clear view to one side of the building at least, and a place for a helicopter to land if necessary. Zack was not surprised to pull up to a large one-story home with its entire east side facing a field of broccoli. They were on a cul de sac at the end of East California Ave. The large house with its low, wide porch faced inward toward a second, smaller home with which it shared the lot. Between the house was a wide parking area, beyond which an el construction on each home led to a shared patio.

"Who lives there?" Zack asked when he met Sarah in the parking lot.

She flashed a smile. "Me."

Zack nodded. Pretty neat. They had their own home, lots of openness around it, good visibility, and the nearest neighbor would be his support team. "What's to the north?" He couldn't see the area beyond the patio.

"It's an alleyway, another potential escape route. Beyond that is a large home, but they have a ten-foot wall all the way around and lots of yards. There is no visual into this place unless they employ a drone." She smiled again. "But even then, I have radar." She pointed to the adjoining home.

Zack felt a growing concern. This layout was almost too perfect. "Who else knows about this place?"

Sarah's face had the look of someone about to announce they'd just won the lottery. "No one. That's the beauty of it. Aunt Janice… I mean Agent Hooper had just purchased the place on her own but had not yet added it to the list of agency assets. Because these purchases are always made through a chain of buyers and real estate agents who can't be traced, no one knows of this property but her—and now you and me."

Zack shook his head in wonder. "I'd never say this to her face, but your aunt is an amazing woman."

Sarah laughed. "Yes, she is an amazing woman and, no, I would not say that to her face either."

Zack backed his truck to the garage of the large house. Sarah helped him move his few belongings into a small bedroom with a window facing the field. The move didn't take long.

"We need to pack up Arlene Pettigrew's things and move them here as covertly as possible," Zack said, stretching his back. "Can you help with that?"

"I am yours to command," Sarah said. "At least until Janice needs me, of course." She pulled out a shirt from the closet. "We anticipated that move. This maintenance worker's shirt is from the apartment units where Arlene lives. Throw that on. I'll have a clipboard and pen and with the truck, we'll look downright official."

"You plan to stand around and check things off while I work?"

She smiled. "Great plan, isn't it?"

166

CHAPTER EIGHTEEN

Zack was intrigued by the many subtle ways Sarah reminded him of her aunt Janice, a younger, more relaxed version for sure, but a tintype nonetheless. Like Janice, Sarah was unpredictable, full of startling ideas, totally outside the box in her thinking yet never off task, always responsible. And her will was unmitigated.

The removal of Arlene Pettigrew's personal items from her apartment went off without a hitch. Fortunately, as it was not a permanent residence for her, Arlene had relatively few possessions there and, best of all to Zack's mind, the furniture had come with the condo. If any neighbors noticed Zack and Sarah moving suitcases and boxes out of the apartment, they made no inquiries. The landlord never learned Arlene had moved out. Arlene would write a rent check at the end of the month, as usual. As far as anybody knew, she still lived there.

When Zack drove away with his loaded truck, Sarah took a position far enough behind to protect him from tails. They took an indirect route to the safe house. Sarah gave Zack the all-clear by phone and he went ahead into the cul de sac. Then it was simply a matter of moving boxes from the truck into the house.

Sarah observed where Zack was placing Arlene's things in the master suite, placed hands on slender hips.

"Not bad for a man," she said. She peeked in the bathroom, glanced at the makeup counter. "Oh, no, she'd never put this here," and moved lipsticks and an eyebrow pencil case to another location, with a little smile.

Zack shrugged. "I simply tried to remember where she'd had them."

Zack's phone rang, saving him from her reply.

"Hello, Eagle Feather."

"Hello, White Man. The second assassin is alive and well and tried to send me to my ancestors this morning."

It took Zack a moment to understand, then the implications flooded him. "How?"

"He ambushed me from another slag heap. I do not think he had expected me, just happened to see me. He took a shot at me, I returned the favor. He got away."

"Where are you now?"

"I am back on surveillance. I do not think he will return here."

Zack thought for a moment. "He knows most of our secrets. He certainly knows about you. He knows we will try to protect Arlene Pettigrew. I hope he doesn't know about Ned Thomason." Zack glanced at his watch. "We've another two hours before quitting time for Arlene. Keep an eye on her, follow her when she leaves. Okay, my friend?"

"As you wish, kemo sahbee."

Zack chuckled.

"Things are heating up," he told Sarah. "The most critical part of this operation will be to move Arlene here undetected."

LOST OASIS

Zack and Sarah sat together at the kitchen table working out their plan for the remainder of the day. Once every detail was considered, Sarah went to work on the chain of events that would support Arlene's temporary leave of absence.

Zack turned his thoughts toward the ambush he hoped to spring on the assassin. He believed there were two possible locations the killer would likely hide. First, and most likely, he could have a sanctuary in Eagle Mountain, the Kaiser company ghost town just a few miles from the Santini & Marsh construction site. It was a huge place full of empty buildings. He could easily find a break in the fence. Once inside, no one would ever find him. It was an empty city.

But the second possibility, the one that intrigued him, was the ghost town of Desert Center. To hide there, the assassin would not have to climb fences or break into houses, just slip into some abandoned broken-down building late at night, roll his motorcycle in with him, no one the wiser. That is where Zack hoped to find him.

He picked up his phone. There was one more thing to try.

"Hi, Janice. Please initiate an internet search for a pair of international assassins for hire, one male, the other female, probably work as a pair, maybe even a husband and wife duo." Zack went on to describe the female's physical appearance.

Janice had two tough questions. "What makes you think the two weren't contracted separately? And what makes you think there aren't more out there?"

"There is something about their modus operandi that feels similar, even beyond the motorcycles. Hiring two separate killers at the same time can cause conflict, something a client would want to avoid."

"Like they could shoot each other," Janice said.

"Like that."

"Once I find a pair matching your description you'd like me to try to find a money trail and follow it."

"You're the best," Zack said.

"I know."

"By the way, your niece…" Zack realized he was talking to himself.

Sarah came back.

"How's it going?" Zack asked.

Sarah grinned. "You were just speaking to my aunt, weren't you?"

"How did you know?"

"Conversations with her always end with the expression you just had on your face."

Zack grinned, abashed. "That obvious, eh?"

Sarah referred to her notes. "Anyway, we've set Arlene Pettigrew up with a close friend named Marty Swinger who slipped and broke his pelvis last night and needs care twenty-four-seven. She'll learn of this after leaving work today from a telephone call she'll receive when she arrives home. Assuming her phone is tapped, we'll use a tape and help her dub the call. She'll then call her workplace and leave a message with a request for immediate leave."

"That all sounds good." Zack glanced at his watch. "Now we've little more than an hour to plan to intercept her and get her here. We can't risk calling her. In fact, after we dub her fake call, we'll need to fix her phone so they cannot locate it. Here's the plan." Zack explained his idea to Sarah.

Usually imperturbable, Arlene was nervous as a cat when it came time to leave the office for the day. She had heard nothing further from Agent Tolliver and could only hope he had arranged a safety net as promised but had little faith. In her experience, men seldom followed through on their promises but were always quick to apologize. This time that behavior wouldn't cut it.

Ned Thomason passed her office on his way home and cast a bad dog glance her way. He didn't attempt to speak, but obviously wished he could. The man wore every emotion he felt on his face like semaphores. Arlene wondered if Mr. Brilliant FBI man realized how vulnerable they all were because of Thomason.

She picked up her purse and walked out into the sunshine. Other employees were headed to the parking lot, chatting away with friends or intent upon some plan for the evening. She was unpleasantly surprised when Blair Schäuble fell in with her.

"How was your day, Arlene?" he asked. With his eyes squinting against the sun, his pudgy face reminded her of Elmer Fudd. She was almost a foot taller than the man and his slicked black combover looked like a torn fishing net from this perspective. Still, there was something about him that frightened her.

"Just ducky," she said. "Can't wait to hit the highway."

He smiled up at her. "I have days like that."

What is the little creep up to, Arlene wondered, but responded, "I'm sure you do."

"Arlene, I hope you keep in mind our concern regarding seismic potentiality for the lower pit. I need to know any thoughts your specialists may have on the matter."

"Cross my heart," she said and turned away abruptly toward her yellow Bug. As she unlocked it and climbed in she found her heart beating a tattoo. She wasted no time starting the little car and drove out of the lot.

Arlene watched her rearview mirror the entire way along the dirt access road. She passed along the fence guarding the ghost town of Eagle Mountain and at the junction with Kaiser Road headed south toward Desert Center and Interstate 10. Billows of dust followed her, the other Santini & Marsh employees headed home. She passed the turnoff to Desert Center and drove under the interstate bridge. Where she waited to turn up the interstate ramp at the far side of the underpass, she saw a hitchhiker, a woman in jeans, an overlarge sweater and a great floppy hat holding a beaded bag. There were always young people hitching along the desert roads, a flower child carryover, she imagined. Poor kid. The temperature gauge mounted in the VW read one hundred four degrees. She was ready to drive on when the woman caught her eye and opened her sweater. A sign suspended across her chest said, "Arlene, pick me up. I am FBI."

Arlene's response was panic. She dropped in the clutch but did so too rapidly and the little engine sputtered and quit. "Shit!" She quickly moved the stick to neutral and started it again, but by then the passenger door had opened and the woman slid in.

"Keep driving," she said. "We don't have much time."

Arlene did as she was told. "Who the hell are you?"

"I am Agent Sarah Whithers, FBI." She flashed her identification. "I work with Agent Tolliver. We are taking you to a safe house now, but we will need to engage in a little subterfuge along the way. There is a rest area as we approach Blythe. Turn in there, and park near other cars."

Arlene did as she was told. The minute she parked, Agent Withers said, "I'm getting out now. You wait a minute, then go to the ladies' room. I'll meet you there."

Again, Arlene did as she was told. The heat was such that the tiled bathroom walls were sweating, but it was noticeably cooler. Agent Withers was waiting at the sink. Arlene went to the basin next to her.

Sarah spoke into the running faucet. "Slip your car keys into my purse right there." Arlene did. "When we walk out of here," Sarah went on, "put on my sweater and hat, there on the hook by the door. Walk across to the other side of the rest area. You will see a white pickup truck with a pink flamingo hanging from the antennae. Climb in the passenger side. Agent Tolliver will be in the driver's seat. He'll explain the rest."

Arlene walked to the door, took down the raincoat and put it on, then walked out into the blasting heat. She ignored her VW and walked across to the large vehicle parking area. There were two white pickups among the trucks and cars. One had a stuffed pink flamingo attached to the antennae. She walked to the passenger door and climbed in. Zack grinned at her.

"Welcome to my world," he said.

"Right now it's better than my world," she said.

"Before we leave, I'll need your phone. We need to make a little recording together."

After the phone message had been recorded, Zack backed the truck out and drove to the highway ramp. "We will drive west toward Desert Center until I can be certain we don't have a tail," he explained. "Then I'll turn around and we'll go to Blythe." He glanced at her. "But not to your old apartment. You'll be staying with me in brand new digs."

"What about my stuff?"

"It's already been moved."

Arlene was silent for a moment. "What then? For how long?"

Zack checked the rearview mirror, then glanced at her. "We are using the tape you just made to arrange a leave of absence for you. Your yellow VW is about to disappear. You will be safe with us until this matter is concluded."

Arlene had another thought. "What about Ned Thomason? He's barely holding himself together. Isn't he in danger too?"

"Frankly, we don't know," Zack said. "The killer showed his hand when he tried to catch you this morning. But there does not appear to have been a threat toward Thomason. They may not see him as a danger. He has a way to contact me if he needs to, but he hasn't. The problem is, if we pull Thomason out the same way, we lose our last eyes and ears inside the project." He looked at her. "I hated to pull you, for the same reason, but…" Zack shrugged.

"Well, I'm glad you did. I never again want to go through anything like happened this morning."

Zack found a place to turn and drove back to Blythe, confident they were not being followed. He drove to a section of the town Arlene had never visited, a neighborhood with large properties and big homes, many of them walled in with tall fences. They seemed to travel in circles, returning to the same place more than once, to be certain no one had followed them. At last, they turned into a short road that brought them to a complex of two houses at the edge of the fields. Zack parked the truck near the large house.

"Honey, we're home," he said.

CHAPTER NINETEEN

Agent Sarah Whithers strolled into the safe house an hour later, cool and calm. She smiled when she saw Zack and Arlene settled in the sunny parlor, each in an easy chair, each with a drink in hand, smiling and chatting like old friends. They looked up at her arrival.

"Did everything work out okay?" Zack asked.

Sarah smiled brightly. "Yes, just fine. Your Indian friend was right there when I needed him, and he gave me a ride to my car before disappearing like a ghost. I felt like saying, 'Who was that masked man?'"

Zack laughed. "You would have aged yourself considerably beyond your tender years if you had said that."

Arlene looked at Zack. "So might you, I expect." She turned to Sarah. "What did you do with my little yellow Bug?"

Sarah walked over and dropped a key in her hand. "It's safe in a storage unit right here in town. That's the key to the unit, but we won't tell you which one until it's time to retrieve the car when we're sure you are safe. That little car is cute, but it is somewhat noticeable." She turned to Zack. "I intend to put my feet up for a spell. Long day so far. When's dinner?"

"Whenever you fix it. Unfortunately, I will need to excuse myself from you two lovely ladies very shortly." He caught Sarah's eyes. "You're certain you weren't followed?"

"Absolutely. Your Indian on the motorcycle saw to that." She looked at Arlene. "Stay comfy. I'll be back in half an hour and we'll make some dinner. I live in the little house across the terrace if you need me. Just come on over. But let me show you something before I go." She beckoned Arlene to follow.

Arlene rose, drink in hand, and followed Sarah into the kitchen area. There was a telephone on the wall. "This line goes to my house, nowhere else. Just pick it up and it will ring me. But over here"—she took several steps toward the wall—"is the emergency button. Step on this tile next to the wall and a signal will come to my phone. I'll be over here in seconds."

Then Sarah shone her brilliant smile on everyone, waved, and left.

It was dusk when Zack pulled into the rest area on Interstate 10. He parked and waited. Five minutes later, a motorcycle arrived and parked next to him. Zack grabbed his rifle case from the passenger seat, climbed out and locked up the truck, took the helmet offered him, and climbed on the motorcycle. They roared off.

"You know where we're going?" Zack asked, shouting against the wind.

Eagle Feather's words floated back. "Yes, I know a place."

No more was said. Twenty minutes later they were riding down the off-ramp at Desert Center. Eagle Feather motored across the wide parking area among several slumbering semis. He turned onto a narrow track that wound into the desert. The sun's orb had just dropped completely behind the mountain range, and sagebrush along the narrow path, fading to ambiguity in the twilight, cast impenetrable shadows. The sky had become phosphorescent purple and dusk settled over everything. Eagle Feather turned off the bike's headlight and used a headlamp on his helmet to illuminate their way. The path dropped into hollows and climbed small ridges, and unexpected bumps threatened to unseat the riders from time to time. Far across the landscape lights from homes twinkled off and on as intervening brush interrupted the line of sight. Eagle Feather slowed the bike, his helmeted head swiveled side to side, then he stopped and turned it off.

"We get off here," he said.

Zack stepped off into soft sand, removed his helmet, and handed it to Eagle Feather. He stretched his cramped leg muscles and removed his rifle from its case. Eagle Feather had exchanged his helmet for his black reservation hat. Now he handed his Winchester to Zack to hold while he pushed the bike a short way off the track and deeper into the hollow.

When he returned, he whispered, "The abandoned motel and cottages are over there." He pointed. "I think it is the most likely place for the killer to hide out."

"Lay it out for me," Zack said.

The men knelt, Eagle Feather shone his headlamp on the sand and drew with his finger. "The cottages of the motel line up side by side like this," he said, drawing parallel slashes. "Most are full of junk, but these two toward the end are nearly empty. The motel office has large windows and is opposite those empty units."

"What if he stays elsewhere in the town?"

"All other buildings can be seen from people's homes and any light might be noticed. I do not think he would use them."

"That's it, then," Zack said. "We'll set up our surveillance in the motel office."

Eagle Feather led and they moved from shadow to shadow across the desert. Full darkness descended swiftly. A building appeared before them with magical suddenness. Eagle Feather touched Zack's arm. He followed the Navajo around it to a concrete step and a steel frame door. The door was ajar by several inches.

Eagle Feather gripped the door by its edge, lifting and pushing it inward. It squealed slightly as it opened. The Navajo slipped through, Zack followed.

The interior was black as a tomb. They were in a corridor with no windows. Zack kept close to Eagle Feather. He knew the Navajo was listening, getting a sense of the building. If anyone was inside, he would know it.

After a minute or two, the Navajo switched on his headlamp and began to work his way around the junk scattered on the floor. There were bits of rusted shielded cable, some old clothing, and piles of seeds and nutshells indicating a vibrant mammal population. They went down a long corridor leading toward the front of the building. Eagle Feather's headlamp shown on an open space with large glass windows. He crouched down and turned off the light.

They waited in silence for their eyes to adjust. Gradually a counter materialized out of the gloom and Zack began to discern some chairs in a small lobby area. The large pane window was beyond the counter. A door was directly in front of them, the main entrance to the office.

Zack followed Eagle Feather around the counter, crouching. They entered another space with a large corner window. Peering through, Zack could see the dark hulks of the small cabins, all in a row. He stood far enough from the window not to be seen from outside and studied the outlines of structures and trees to familiarize himself with the stage so that he would notice any new player who appeared, no matter how subtly.

He felt Eagle Feather close to him. For them, it was now a matter of waiting.

Eagle Feather sat, legs crossed, eyes fixed in front of him, and was still. Zack knew this posture. He'd seen it many times and knew it meant Eagle Feather was dismissing his eyes and placing his reliance on all his other senses. The Navajo seemed to have acquired the ability to completely isolate each of his senses, pouring all his powers into one or two while shutting off the others. When asked about it, he always claimed the skill came from his hunting experiences, but Zack suspected these were not talents just anyone could cultivate.

For his part, Zack found a comfortable ledge with a view out the window but far enough away from it not to be seen. His best sense was his vision and he counted on movement to help him.

The next hour unwound like a bandage from a burn, slow and uncomfortable. The moon would not rise for another hour yet and the darkness was complete. The cold of the desert night grew in the room and crowded away any memory of the daytime heat. Zack felt the urge to rub his hands together and move about for warmth, but he dared not.

His vigil was not uninterrupted. Once, a flicker of movement caused his eye to dart to the first cabin. He stared hard, his gaze just to one side, a technique he'd learned for better night vision. He watched, waited, and was rewarded with more movement at the far side of the cabin's dark outline as something eased out of the shadow. The size and sinewy smoothness of motion told him it was a cat, probably from one of the nearby privately owned homes. Zack wondered as he often did how an ordinary cat managed to survive at night among coyotes, wildcats, and owls. He could only conclude they must have even more senses than Eagle Feather if that were possible.

Thinking again about his friend, he turned to look at him seated in the darkness with no view to the outside. Without moving anything but his lips, Eagle Feather whispered, "Cat". Zack turned back to his surveillance, impressed yet again by the Navajo's powers.

At some indeterminate point in the long vigil, Zack felt a touch on his arm. The moon had not yet risen, the night's veil was undiminished. Eagle Feather stood close, his mouth at Zack's ear. "Listen," he whispered.

Zack listened. He heard nothing. Then he heard something. Before he could identify the sound, it stopped. He was unable to tell where it had come from, not near, but not very far. Now again, nothing. Yet he could tell from Eagle Feather's increased grip his friend was hearing something. They waited.

Then the grip pulled Zack down to the floor. Eagle Feather faced the rear of the building.

A small sound came to Zack, this time a familiar sound, a slight squeal. It was the door they had used to enter, the door to the very building they were in. Someone was coming into the building. Zack felt what the tiger hunter must feel, waiting high in his *manchan* over a goat, when he suddenly realizes the man-eater he hunts has begun to stalk the hunter.

Zack leaned his rifle against the wall and opening his jacket, inched the Sig Saur from its holster. He aimed it at the darkness above the counter beyond which was the corridor through which they had entered.

There was no sound now. Was the killer listening for them as they were for him? Zack remembered the dust on the concrete floor. They would have left footprints. The killer would not have missed them. He knew they were here. What would he do? Retreat? Or attack?

There was a slight creak from a footfall on wood. The killer was in the corridor. Zack's arm tensed. He dared not cock his weapon, the click would sound like castanets in the stillness. When he fired he would have to pull the trigger hard to override the cocking mechanism. It was something he practiced at the range, for just such situations.

The next sound he heard came as a surprise. A low voice spoke in an articulated sigh. "You bastards. You killed my partner. For that I will kill you."

Before the echo of the words had fully died away, the Navajo moved. His vague form hurled over the counter. There was a crash, a flare of brightness, the sound of a silenced pistol. Zack fired at the gun's flame. He heard running feet, the crashing scattering of junk, the squeal of the outer door now more of a howl, running steps, silence.

Zack was on his feet. There was a moan on the far side of the counter.

"Eagle Feather!" Zack banged his side on the corner of the counter as he fought his way around it. "Are you hit?" He saw a crumpled dark mass on the floor near the counter's base. Zack switched on his flashlight, directed it at the stoic face of his friend. He heard a motorcycle starting up outside somewhere, the engine whirring like a distant chainsaw.

Eagle Feather's gaze went to the side of the counter and Zack's light followed. There was a hole in the plywood just a foot above his friend's head where the bullet had gone.

The Navajo sat up, grimaced. "Do not worry. I am not hit. The floor is very hard and I am not so young as I like to think I am."

"Are you sure you are okay?" Zack hovered over his friend like a hen with a chick.

"I may have bruises on my arm and shoulder and there is a very large bruise to my ego. No more than that."

Zack shook his head in wonder. "What on earth were you thinking?"

Eagle Feather levered himself upright, testing his limbs as he did so. "He was right here, right where I landed, ready to shoot us over the counter. I thought he might be wearing night-vision goggles. He would have killed us. I believed our only chance was to try to disrupt his plan."

"It worked, but you were lucky not to be hurt."

"Yes, that is so. I believe he would have succeeded in killing us if his anger had not made him declare his intentions first. That speech gave me the seconds I needed." Eagle Feather raised his left arm, easing the ache. "White people tend to let their emotions get in their way."

CHAPTER TWENTY

Zack returned to the safe house well after ten to find Sarah and Arlene in the living room enjoying a nightcap. He helped himself to bourbon on ice at the bar. He saw with approval that the bar was well stocked. If things continued as they had gone tonight, he would need it.

"You certainly take after your aunt in terms of attention to detail," he said, grinning at Sarah. He dropped into an armchair.

"Actually, I'm not so sure Aunt Janice would approve of that particular detail," Sarah said, shaking her head. "She is a stickler for sobriety on the job."

Zack raised his glass. "Here's to being off duty, then," he said and sipped.

"Where did you go tonight?" Arlene asked.

This woman doesn't beat around the bush. Zack shrugged. "We thought we might have an idea where the killer was hiding out. We went to see if we were right."

"We?" Sarah asked.

"Yes, I went with 'the Indian who doesn't exist' as your aunt would say."

"Oh, the Navajo," Arlene said. "Were you right?"

Zack shook his head ruefully. "We were right, but that information will no longer help us. He got away, and will not return there any time soon." He shrugged again. "So back to square one."

"Are you any closer to knowing who hired the assassin?"

"Unfortunately, no. There are powerful people involved and we have any number of suspects. And now the assassin is even more alert and dangerous." He looked at Arlene. "So please stay within the confines of this safe house, out of sight."

"I get it. I just don't like it."

Zack stood, finished off his drink in a gulp, and set the empty glass down on the coffee table. "I'm to bed. Morning comes early and I have a breakfast meeting."

"Will you walk me to my house?" Sarah asked.

Zack raised his eyebrows in surprise. "Uh, sure."

Arlene said good night and retreated to her sleep area. Zack followed Sarah out the door to the terrace. It was a typical desert night, a chill on the breeze but warmth still radiating from the flagstones. The stars were almost touchable.

Sarah put a hand on Zack's arm. "I'm sorry to drag you out here. I know you must be tired. I heard from Janice tonight. The security people at Santini & Marsh have discovered the body of the first assassin. They brought in the local Sheriff's people who in turn informed the FBI, as a courtesy. Aunt Janice is pushing buttons to reopen the case, or failing that, open a new one on the grounds the killer was an unregistered alien."

"She was?" Zack asked. "We found nothing to identify her."

"That is precisely Janice's argument. We cannot prove the woman's nationality." Sarah grinned. "Either way, she feels confident you will be back in official standing on this case by tomorrow morning."

"Has she met resistance?"

Sarah shook her head. "She didn't say. But I'm guessing so." She turned to look up at Zack. In the soft glow of the muted terrace lights, Zack couldn't help notice she was extremely attractive. She shared many of Janice's features, her white teeth glimmered behind bright red lipstick, her soft green eyes given greater depth by the shadows. If he had met Janice as a twenty-year-old, she would not have looked much different, he thought. Sarah's next words brought him back to reality.

"Aunt Janice doesn't want anyone to know about this safe house, not even the FBI. She suspects a leak. She doesn't think she can safeguard our witness if anyone beyond the three of us knows this location."

"The four of us," Zack said.

Sarah smiled. "The Navajo? He doesn't exist, remember?"

At five-thirty a.m. a beam of sunlight spoiled Zack's comfortable world of darkness behind closed eyelids and he awoke, realizing he'd forgotten to close the window shades. He sat up, rubbing his eyes.

The house was still. Hopefully, it meant Arlene was getting some much-needed sleep. Zack padded across the thick carpet to the small bathroom and climbed into the shower where he let the hot water cascade over him as he pondered the news Sarah had given him. So Janice suspected a leak at the Bureau. Meaning, he guessed, an agent who was motivated more by hard cash than a sense of justice. It wouldn't be the first time, but it was rare among these dedicated people. The worst case was probably William Philip Hanssen who spied for the Russians against the United States from 1979 to 2001, was finally caught and brought to justice when exposed as an ex-KGB officer. He had been just the third spy in FBI history, at least as far as anyone knew, and that was the key, of course. It hadn't cost a lot to turn Hanssen at first, about thirty thousand dollars earned in his first three years. But he had gone on to earn well over a million before he eventually ended up in his final home, prison.

If an FBI leak was responsible for turning off Zack's investigation, a lot more money than that must have been waved around, probably with political benefits as well. All of it so far above Zack's pay grade it made him dizzy to contemplate. And motivation? Was the discovery of a volcanic intrusion indicating a possible weakness in the earth's crust a full ten miles away from the projected water reservoirs enough to begin such an expensive chain reaction with bribes and obfuscation, kidnapping, even murder? It just didn't seem to fit, in Zack's mind. There had to be something else.

The forecast called for another hot day. Zack threw on a T-shirt and a light windbreaker to hide the holstered Sig Saur and a pair of lightweight nylon pants. In the kitchen, the coffee had already gurgled into the pot started by the electric timer. He poured a cup into his travel mug and walked out to the truck.

He glanced at Sarah's little house as he passed through the terrace. He thought he saw a curtain flicker. He'd never been in the little house and wondered what it was like. He glanced around at the fields and open spaces before climbing into the truck. The nearest visible building was over a mile away across a field of peppers. Janice had chosen this location well.

Zack stopped at a donut shop, bought several jelly donuts of the kind Eagle Feather loved, and drove out to the interstate rest area. He parked and took the bag of donuts to a shaded picnic table and sat. Before long Eagle Feather ghosted over from wherever he'd been and sat down with him.

The Navajo peeked in the bag and eyed the jelly donuts. "A good friend brings donuts," he proclaimed and reached for one. After several bites, he glanced at Zack. "What news?"

Zack told him about the discovery of the assassin's body. "Much as we'd hoped, the case went to the local cops who informed the FBI. Janice is pushing her boss to get us back aboard."

"Do you think she can do this?"

"Probably, but there's a complication." Zack relayed Janice's suspicions regarding a leak at the Bureau. "There may be some very influential push-back against involving the FBI."

"They could not know the two cases are connected," Eagle Feather said.

"Exactly my thought. Janice will likely present it as an entirely new case. I'm sure she will succeed because if someone in the FBI objects on the grounds it is the same case, that person would have to know about the assassins. The only other possible grounds for comparison between the cases is geographic proximity, but that shouldn't be enough to forestall an investigation. There is too much room for coincidence."

"The leaker will dare not object."

"Probably not."

"This means you will now be able to pay me, White Man."

Zack grinned. "Yes." He set down his coffee mug. "There is one caution to pass along to you. We four, you, me, Janice, and Sarah, are the only ones who know the location of the safe house. It needs to stay that way."

"Does this Thomason man know about it?"

Zack scratched his chin. "Yes, he knows there is one, but he doesn't know where."

"What are we do about Thomason?"

"We wait. He has my number to call in an emergency. When did you last see him?"

"His truck left the company parking lot just before Arlene left yesterday."

"Good." Zack glanced at his phone. "Ned should just be leaving for work." Zack pushed some buttons. "Yep. He's motoring down Hobsonway as we speak." Zack grinned at Eagle Feather's questioning look. "When I put my number in his phone, I also added an app. He can't see it. It's a tracker."

Eagle Feather grunted. "Handy. Where does this leave us?"

"We will continue our surveillance on Thomason. We hope he learns something that can help us, but if anything suspicious happens around him, we will have to pull him out immediately. We are waiting to see if Interpol can help Janice identify our two assassins and then try to find a money trail back to whoever hired them."

"That seems sketchy."

Zack grimaced. "Yes, it is, but it's all we've got." He darted a glance at Eagle Feather. "It's too bad we were unable to trap the second assassin."

Eagle Feather's expression did not change. "He is a true professional. Even if we took him alive, a difficult thing, he would not talk."

Zack sighed. "No doubt you are right."

The two men sat in silence. A light breeze played in the branches above their heads and brought a wisp of sage. Zack glanced at his phone. Thomason's vehicle had now moved on to the interstate. He pressed the screen to refresh. Nothing changed.

"That's funny. I wonder if there is some interference. He hasn't moved in a while."

"Where is he?"

"He's on the interstate about five miles east of us." Zack frowned. "He still hasn't moved. These map locators take a while to reload sometimes."

Eagle Feather shot a glance at Zack. "You are thinking about what almost happened to Arlene."

Zack nodded, still staring at the app. The icon still hadn't moved. He stood. "Let's go. We'll have to take your bike. We need to go east, then find a way to cross over."

The men ran to the motorcycle. Eagle Feather unstrapped his extra helmet, threw it to Zack, and strapped on his own. Zack was barely on when the Navajo started it up and moved off. Seconds later, they were flying east on the interstate. Zack held Eagle Feather's shoulder with his left hand while he watched the phone display in his right palm.

"Watch now, we're getting close," he called after a few minutes. He glanced over at the opposite lane and there it was, the blue Toyota pickup, on the shoulder in front of a large black SUV.

"There he is," Zack yelled. "He's got company. We've got to get over there now."

But the median was too rough here. They sped on until an emergency vehicle crossover finally appeared.

"Hang on," the Navajo called. The bike decelerated almost to a stop, leaned hard, spun wheels, and quickly reaccelerated back on the pavement, now headed west.

Zack glanced at his phone. "He moved," he yelled.

A minute later, they flew past the place where they'd seen Ned's pickup. Both vehicles were gone.

"Slow down," Zack called. They slowed, studied the roadside, Zack looking for any dirt track off the highway the vehicles might have taken. They found none.

"They must be ahead," Zack yelled. "Let's try to catch them."

The bike immediately surged to a higher speed. The wind increased on Zack, tugging at the phone in his hand. The screen had changed. Ned had advanced west somewhere in front of them.

The motorcycle roared on. They flew past a truck and several cars.

"There!" Eagle Feather called over his shoulder.

They came up beside the truck and they glided along next to it. With their faces hidden behind the dark plastic guards of their helmets, they could be any two riders. Zack saw Ned Thomason glance at them, then back at the road, his expression tranquil. He was all alone in the truck.

CHAPTER TWENTY-ONE

Arlene had heard Zack move about the kitchen from the snugness of her bed. She saw by the digital clock on the bedside table it was almost six a.m., but the blinds and curtains were closed, the darkness in the room was complete. She almost always rose before six and liked to leave the windows uncovered to allow the sunlight to awaken her, but a note pinned to the curtains instructed her to leave them closed for safety reasons. She had obeyed.

Now she found herself enjoying the comfy warmth of the covers and the extra doze time, a rare treat. Her conscience nagged, finally she got up, but by that time Zack was gone. She heard bubbling and noticed he had restarted the coffeemaker for her. Nice guy, but married. All the frickin' nice guys were married. Not that many ever noticed her, anyway, though. She probably scared away more than a few guys because of her size and directness. Fuck 'em, she thought and yawned.

What to do today? Arlene never in her life, that she could remember, had so much empty time on her hands. The shock of her sudden departure from work, the abrupt mental switch from complete absorption in a difficult task to now nothing at all to occupy her mind, hadn't hit her until now. She envied Zack, rushing off to work, challenged by difficult problems. Shit, she thought, he probably wishes he was me right now.

LOST OASIS

She sipped her coffee, and her mind began to leap as it always did after that first cup of java. She was stuck here. Nothing to be done about that, but maybe she could help solve the mystery with her brain alone. If Scheidecker's disappearance was related to the discovery of a volcanic intrusion near enough to the worksite to endanger the project, it seemed to her that in her capacity as a synthesizer of the experts' findings and her direct liaison to upper management she was in the supreme position to uncover clues to the culprits, if indeed clues were to be found. She simply needed to recall meetings, conversations, attitudes, careless remarks—in short everything she could remember leading up to and shortly after Scheidecker's disappearance. Arlene did have a remarkable memory, in her opinion, it was one of the assets that made her good at her job.

She rummaged around, found some carbs in the form of a pumpkin muffin, refilled her coffee, found a notebook and pen among the materials in her briefcase, and sat down at the kitchen table to begin.

But begin where? When had Scheidecker first learned about the lost oasis? She remembered the general topics at her morning meetings and thought back to Scheidecker's remarks at those times. They had mostly discussed reservoir and conduit proportions, conduit grades and size, basic stuff like that to feed the engineers even as the construction boys were working on it. They were like navigators in a flight of B-52s over Germany, fine-tuning directions as the pilots flew the planes. Scheidecker was a smart ass at those meetings, saying little until someone proposed a specific measurement, then caustically corrected it by an inch. What an asshole, she thought.

As she raced down memory lane, more detail popped into her head. Now she recalled a morning when Scheidecker made a strange comment, something way off topic as if his brain had gone off in some quirky direction. He had said something about Indians, said it right in the middle of a discussion about the earth under the large reservoir. What was it again? Something about sun worshipping, or shamans conducting energy down from the sun, or some such nonsense. What a fruitcake! He had thrown that out just when the geologist was reporting on his analysis of the soil beneath the reservoir. Everybody at the table had turned to look at Scheidecker, their mouths agape. There had been this moment of complete silence as they stared at him. After an awkward moment, waiting for him to explain himself, which he didn't, they continued their discussion. By then they had grown used to strange utterances from the man. Arlene had been on the verge of recommending to Selden that they can the man on the grounds he was mentally unstable, but as usual, he'd come up with something brilliant right after that to solve a problem, and she had resigned herself to the fact they needed him.

Now she jotted down that discussion along with the date. What had happened the next morning? Nothing remarkable came to mind. But now she remembered why– –Scheidecker had been missing. He'd come in late that day, no explanation just shuffled by her door on his way to his office without even seeing her, as she recalled. She wrote that down, too.

Then she remembered something else. It had been the next morning, the one after he'd come in late when he suggested the reservoir liner. She'd forgotten that he was the one who started the whole bruhaha about the liner that morning with one of his arrogant remarks. That was, what, two days before he disappeared? Something like that.

Arlene outlined the chronology in her notebook day by day beginning with the meeting when he made his random Indian remark. Looking over her notes, she thought there might be a pattern to Scheidecker's thinking. There also seemed to be a pattern to his strange remarks and suggestions. They seemed to follow days he had been late or absent completely. She'd tried to get him to explain his absences but without success. Instead of answering her questions directly, he'd go off on some diatribe about soil layers and magnetic fields and stuff she couldn't connect to reality and she just gave up. Selden had told her not to obsess over it, to give the nutcase his space. She was only too happy to oblige.

When had the liner question emerged after that? She was pretty sure it was after Scheidecker had gone missing, but no doubt he had put it in a few people's heads before then.

Arlene threw down her pencil. She was getting nowhere. It seemed Scheidecker first became suspicious about the stability of the earth underlying their project during that first day he was absent. He'd learned something then. Had he spoken to someone about the site, about ancient Indian practices, about the geology there? In that case, more than one other person might know about Scheidecker's concerns, someone who could potentially have leaked this information to an individual or group who wanted it kept silent.

If Scheidecker had been to Great Wash the day he was absent, the day before Day One in Arlene's notes, and met someone there, that person would be a valuable source. If there was a way to know this, if there was a way to find that person, *if, if, if...*

Arlene's musings were interrupted by a knock on the patio door, two quick, a pause, and then a single knock. A simple recognition device, but effective. Sarah opened the door and came into the kitchen.

"You've got your coffee, I see."

"There's plenty," Arlene said. "Help yourself."

"I will, thank you." Sarah poured herself a cup and took a seat at the table. "What are you working on?"

Arlene explained her attempt to reconstruct the days leading to Scheidecker's disappearance, hoping for clues to the culprits.

Sarah listened to her findings. "I agree, his Indian remark is interesting. I'll pass that along to Agent Tolliver when he calls." She took a sip of coffee, then asked, "Do you have thoughts about who might be desperate enough to kill people to protect this secret?"

'I'd been thinking about that," Arlene said. "Anyone with a financial interest in the project would have a motivation, of course. But enough to kill? Every company, large or small, knows projects of this sort carry risk. People would be upset if their investment went out the window at this point, no doubt about it, but that is a part of being in business. You don't kill people every time you lose on an investment."

Sarah nodded. "How familiar are you with the investors?"

"Not very. Most are financially involved by way of futures."

"Futures?"

"They have Power Purchase Agreements with EverSun, contracts to purchase the power the generator will create and store. These PPAs are long term financial commitments. If the plant isn't built, they become null and void."

Sarah frowned. "But then they won't have lost anything financially, right?"

"Well, no, not really, although some utilities will pay forward on the contract to guarantee they are serviced first, but not very much, in the scheme of things." Arlene paused. "I suppose the greatest liability might come from betting everything on this future power. For instance, some utilities might turn around and contract with other companies to supply electricity they don't yet have and can't get except through this project."

"Kind of a long chain linked to a skyhook."

"Exactly. And for some, this gamble might be a desperate throw of the dice."

Sarah leaned forward. "Do you know any PPA investors who are in that situation?"

Arlene shook her head. "No, that would be a closely guarded secret, of course. Stock values would ride on that information. But there sometimes might be indicators. I'd look for sudden, severe rate hikes, personnel layoffs, and of course bankruptcies."

Sarah smiled. "That's a good line of inquiry. We'll pursue it." Her phone chirped and she walked a few steps away to answer it.

Curious, Arlene watched Sarah's face as she spoke on the phone. Her expression did not change from her last words with Arlene, whatever the news. Arlene wondered if they learned how to do that in FBI school. When Sarah ended the call, she was still smiling.

"I have to go back to my little house and do some work," she said. "The FBI investigation into the dead assassin has been approved. That will open some resources for us." She waved, her heels beat a cheerful tattoo on the terrace tiles as she walked away.

After passing Thomason's truck, Zack tapped Eagle Feather's shoulder and shouted, "See if you can catch the SUV." Eagle Feather nodded, the bike accelerated. The roadside brush became a blur. Vehicles appeared in front, grew large, and disappeared behind them, but no black SUV. Minutes passed—ten, fifteen, and then they came to the Desert Center turnoff.

"Which way?" Eagle Feather shouted.

Zack didn't know. He flipped a mental coin. "Keep going," he yelled.

The bike whined to a higher pitch. As they neared Indio, traffic grew denser. Eagle Feather pointed. A large black SUV was just ahead.

They caught up to it quickly. Zack read the license plate, tried to memorize it as they came up behind. The highway had broadened to three lanes westward at this point. The black SUV was in the center lane. Eagle Feather shouted again, pointing. In the far right lane beyond the black SUV was another black SUV, exactly like it. Both were Escalades. Then Zack saw yet another on the exit ramp.

He groaned inwardly. "Forget about it," he yelled. "Let's go back to Desert Center."

Eagle Feather took the offramp and then the bridge over the highway to reverse direction. Ten minutes later, they were back at the Desert Center exit. They decided to see if Thomason had made it to the office. They drove up the access road to the parking lot. Ned's blue truck was there, right where it should be. No doubt he was back to work, thinking no one the wiser about his mysterious meeting along the highway.

They stared at the truck but there was nothing to be done.

"I will drop you at the rest area and come back here to keep watch," Eagle Feather said.

Zack shook his head. "Don't bother. Let's go back to the safe house and have a meeting." He was feeling discouraged. To his mind, all their efforts so far were fruitless.

Eagle Feather dropped Zack off at the rest area. Walking to his truck, Zack tried to imagine what Thomason's meeting with the black SUV might mean. Who had he met? Who had set up the meeting? It was clear they had not wanted to be observed, and wouldn't have been if Zack had not placed the app on Thomason's phone and then glanced at it at just the right time. Thomason gave the appearance of an open, ingenuous type but the meeting along the freeway indicated anything but that, it was the result of skillful planning and good timing, a professional strategy. Was Zack reading Thomason completely wrong or was someone else controlling the scientist? Maybe it was a little of both.

Zack drove on toward Blythe, his mind racing. Janice was worried about a leak in the FBI. Was there also a leak among the consultants hired by Santini & Marsh, namely one Ned Thomason? And the black SUV? Was that the FBI leaker? Or was it someone from EverSun? Either way, Zack's ongoing role in the investigation was no longer secret.

Zack was so absorbed in his thoughts he never noticed the black SUV approaching to pass him suddenly swerve out of its lane and into his truck.

CHAPTER TWENTY-TWO

Zack had no chance. The large SUV struck his truck at the driver's door and now turned hard into him, forcing him toward the shoulder. Zack reflexively turned the wheel back hard to the left but even with a curb weight of forty-six hundred pounds, the Ranger was no match for the huge vehicle with all its momentum forcing him sideways. As he felt his truck lift onto two wheels, Zack immediately spun the steering wheel to the right to go with the direction of the force, but too late. By now he was on the shoulder, the passenger side wheels had caught in sand and the truck hurtled off the road and onto its side.

It was all in slow motion in Zack's mind, the impact as the truck landed, the glass cracking and tearing, the strain of his body against his harness as he was thrown forward and down toward the opposite side of the cab, the immediate inflation of the airbag pinning him and obscuring his view, the grinding of metal on dirt, the forward jerking slide and sudden stop that flung him forward again. His truck engine clucked, sputtered, and died. Then there was silence.

Zack was alive but did not know how badly he was injured. He dangled in his synthetic web in the cab, the two deflated airbags limp around him. His ears rang. He could not hear traffic noise nor could he see if the SUV had stopped. He knew from his training he was almost certainly in shock but needed to act regardless. His left arm was pinned, but his right arm dangled free. He tried to move it, found that he could. There was no pain, but he knew if the arm was injured he wouldn't feel it until later. He found his holster with the free hand, released the Sig Sauer.

Zack found he had a partial view through the blown-out windshield up the gradual slope to the road. Now he saw the black SUV backing, then stopping, its front fender crumpled. It took a huge effort to rotate his body enough to bring the Sig Saur to bear on the SUV. A pair of legs appeared near the fender just as Zack pulled the trigger. The legs disappeared immediately and the black SUV sped away.

The immediate danger over, Zack tried to assess his condition. As his shock wore away, pain washed over him. He hurt where the seatbelt constricted his ribs and waist, he saw blood seep from somewhere along his left arm, his head and neck throbbed from the ferocious whipping action, but most worrisome was a lack of feeling in his legs. His right hand felt for his phone and came away empty, then he remembered he'd left it on the passenger seat. God knows where it was now.

Zack wanted to try to rescue himself but worried he might have a spinal injury that could be aggravated by more movement, so he forced himself to wait for help. He re-holstered his gun; he wanted to keep it in hand in case the bad guys returned, but his pain was growing and the possibility of lapsing into unconsciousness loomed. If the gun slid from his hand, he would not be able to reach it again.

He began to smell fuel, realized he had smelled it from the time the engine quit but convinced himself it was a natural thing under the circumstances. The truck wasn't built to rest on its side. He didn't suspect a tank rupture or gas line leak, necessarily, because of the way the truck had landed. The fuel filler cap was on the driver's side, now the upper side, so fuel should be contained except for possible small leaks caused by the impact. All in all, he decided it was best to wait where he was until help arrived.

The wait seemed endless, however, with pain steadily increasing around his ribs. His neck and head had begun to throb in unison. His left shirt sleeve was completely soaked with blood. His phone rang several times, then stopped. He couldn't turn his head far enough to see where it was. It might as well be on the moon.

Above the ringing in his ears, he heard a car door slam somewhere behind where he couldn't see. He heard another. He heard gravel crunch, then a voice above him at his window. His neck pain screamed when he tried to angle his head around to look. He glimpsed a face peripherally but could not make out features. His right hand closed on the Sig Saur.

"Hey, dude, are you okay? What happened, man? Can I help?"

Zack could only whisper. "Call an ambulance…"

He heard the sound of a siren. Then came more voices, one commanding, "Please, move away from the vehicle.

Give us room to work." Another voice at the window. "Sir, we are going to remove you from the vehicle. Can you describe your condition?"

"I have whiplash, possibly a broken rib or two, a cut or cuts somewhere on my left arm. I cannot feel my legs."

"Thank you for that. We will take care not to aggravate your spine, just in case. But we will have to remove the door first." The voice was that of a professional caregiver, calm and reassuring. The man turned away and said something to another person. They were going to use the Jaws of Life to cut off the door. The first thing to enter Zack's mind was the look that would appear on Janice's face when she learned he had destroyed another FBI vehicle, a propensity for which he was fast becoming infamous.

Before they began, the man's voice was in his ear again. "I've got something here for the pain once we get you out. Hang in there."

Zack didn't. Once the hydraulic tool began tearing metal, everything went black.

When the call came, Sarah was seated in the living room of the safe house, Arlene across from her on the couch. Eagle Feather was perched on the couch arm. They had been this way for the last hour, wondering what was keeping Zack. As time crawled on, their concern had deepened.

LOST OASIS

They received the news from Janice. It was shocking. Zack had been run off the road by a person or persons unknown, was currently in Palo Verde Hospital emergency room in Blythe. He was being treated for whiplash, two cracked ribs, lacerations to his left arm, and contusions. The hospital expected to keep him overnight. Janice had arranged police protection but wanted Sarah to go to the hospital and pick him up within the hour. Eagle Feather could stay with Arlene.

"Here's the thing," Janice told Sarah. "We have a clear breach. Someone knew exactly where Zack was at the time. If they had planted a bug on the truck, the question is when? If it was before today, our safe house is no longer safe. We've towed the truck and are examining it. But I'm not yet ready to give up on the safe house until we know for sure it is blown."

"How will we know?" Sarah asked.

"If we find a bug, it may tell us. But I also need to interview Zack. I'm allowing four hours to get it all done. If we have nothing conclusive by then, we have to bail. Sarah, after you pick up Zack at the hospital, drive to the Best Western. Park next to a familiar bakery van you will see there. Wait for instructions. Any questions?"

Sarah had none. She explained the situation to Arlene and Eagle Feather.

Arlene was shocked. Her mouth hung open, her cheeks reddened. "How can this be? How can this happen? Aren't you the FBI?"

"I know it doesn't seem possible. Most people respect the authority of the FBI just as you do. But some do not. Yet they always underestimate us."

Eagle Feather had started for the door.

"Wait a minute," Arlene called to him. "Didn't you hear Sarah? You have to stay here and guard me."

Eagle Feather turned to look at her with a sympathetic expression. "When the fox comes after the hen, he does not come from inside the hen house. I go to watch for the fox." He turned and was gone.

Arlene stared. "What the devil did that mean?"

"I think he is saying he can guard you better from outside where attackers will not expect him," Sarah said.

"I sure as hell hope so." Arlene walked to the fireplace and picked up an andiron, weighing it with her big hand. "He'd better announce himself when he comes back in, though."

The pickup at the hospital went smoothly. Zack was in a wheelchair out front with a burly policeman on each side of him when Sarah arrived. She opened the door to the back seat. One of the guards rolled the patient toward the door but Zack stopped him and stood, a bit unsteady at first, and walked to the car and climbed in. Sarah was shocked by the difference in his appearance. His face was wan, he stooped like an old man, he moved gingerly with little gasps from time to time.

Sarah climbed behind the wheel.

"You look terrible."

"You, on the other hand, look beautiful."

Sarah grinned into the rearview mirror. "Well, you haven't lost your chutzpah, anyway." She told him Janice's instructions. "I'll pull up next to this van, once we identify it. Then we wait."

"No problem."

When they pulled into the Best Western parking lot Sarah spotted the van immediately. It was a white panel truck with a white and blue emblem painted on the side with a chocolate Hostess Cupcake broken open to view the cream filling. It made the mouth water to look at it.

Sarah pulled in next to it. Immediately the cupcake split open, a vendor in a white uniform and white billed cap leaped out, opened Zack's door, and helped him into the truck. The truck door closed and Sarah drove away. It all took less than a minute.

Sarah would go for a cup of coffee now, keeping an eye on her car from the café window to watch for surveillance. When she was sure there was none, she would return to the safe house.

Zack, meanwhile, belted himself into a single back seat in the van and the Hostess driver went forward and climbed behind the wheel. There were no cupcakes in the van, there were various electronic devices in bins along the wall and an impressive display of flack jackets and weapons. The driver drove out of the lot. It all happened so quickly that Zack, still foggy from pain drugs, barely understood what had happened. A pair of ice-blue eyes studied him in the rearview mirror. For a moment he felt he was still in Sarah's car with her eyes peering at him.

"Janice!" he said unable to contain his surprise.

"I need to see for myself if you are in a condition to continue this mission."

"And?"

"I guess you'll have to do."

Zack's brain was still fuzzy. "Why all the…"

Janice's eyes darted from the mirror to the road and back. "Our antagonist is privy to information that could only be accessed digitally. We have your phone. I've taken away Sarah's phone. There are two throw-away phones in the pocket behind my seat. My new number is already installed under the name Madame X on the blue phone. That one is yours. Sarah will share her new number with you. Give Eagle Feather the red phone. Your new number is in it. Tell him to leave his personal phone in a safe place. Any questions?"

Zack's brain was coming around. "You think a rogue FBI agent with access to our data and instruments is behind this?"

Janice's eyes flickered back to the mirror. "Not necessarily an agent. Remember, your original phone was compromised. It's possible someone who knows their stuff could have gained information from it. It seems likely the one who ran you off the road had eyes at the rest stop you were using with Eagle Feather. We could be dealing with someone in the FBI, someone at Santini & Marsh, maybe even someone hidden away with the Highway Patrol or local sheriff's office."

"Great," Zack said with a groan.

"We just don't know, Zack, but I have to consider the worst-case scenarios."

"Who is 'we'?"

"Slip of the tongue, Zack. 'We' is me. Everything from here forward, especially the location of the safe house, is known to four people, just you, me, Sarah, and Eagle Feather. That's all. The only numbers we can call on these phones, my new one included, is one of those four. Arlene Pettigrew is not to have access to any electronics whatsoever. We must tighten the circle as much as we can until we get more information."

"What's next?" Zack asked.

"I will deliver you to the safe house. Sarah will come along later. When she does, she'll have a new vehicle for you. My technician will go over both your phones to look for software intrusions. He is working on your truck right now. With luck, we might find something that will take us somewhere."

Feeling neurotic, Zack asked, "Who is your technician?"

"The technician I use is 'need to know only' and sworn to secrecy. I use him for private jobs. We are secure there." Blue eyes studied him. "That circle is tight. I intend to keep it that way."

The eyes continued to bore into him. "And Zack?"

"Yes, Janice."

"If you wreck another of my vehicles, you will be riding a tricycle from then on."

CHAPTER TWENTY-THREE

Janice helped Zack to the door of the safe house. Arlene was surprised to see him arrive on the arm of a Hostess Cupcake truck driver but said nothing. Janice left immediately, without introducing herself.

Zack's meds were beginning to wear off and pain from his ribs and back set in. The loss of feeling to his legs had been temporary, it turned out, apparently due to swollen back muscles compressing the nerve. A good dose of ibuprofen had helped with that, much to his relief. He could deal with the contusions and cracked ribs, he'd done that before. The lacerations to his left arm, while requiring stitches, did not inhibit movement. The doctor had sent him away with pain meds, but Zack opted to use them sparingly. He didn't want a fuzzy brain.

Then there was the matter of Libby, his wife, and their child. At the hospital, Zack had worried that word of his accident would reach them, that they might become unduly concerned. Fortunately, Janice had removed that particular anxiety by managing to conceal his identity. Her motive was to prevent the perpetrators from knowing his condition. If they believed they had incapacitated or possibly even eliminated him, they might drop their guard.

Arlene was relieved to have Zack back again at the safe house, regardless of his condition. Then when Eagle Feather drifted in from wherever he had gone and Sarah arrived driving Zack's new vehicle, Arlene was noticeably more relaxed. The Navajo and both FBI agents immediately began trying to solve the puzzle of how the driver of the black SUV could have known precisely where to find Zack's truck as he drove to Blythe.

"They must have known we used the rest stop," Eagle Feather said. "Suppose he went there after meeting Thomason and waited. He would have seen you get off my bike and get in your truck. He simply followed you."

Zack's attempt at a nod was suppressed by neck pain. "That explains why we couldn't find the black SUV after he met with Thomason. We didn't take the time to check the rest area." He tried to remember. "I don't remember seeing a black SUV when you dropped me off. I'd have noticed, I think."

"He may have parked among all the trucks."

Zack sighed. "Probably. I didn't take the time to look."

Sarah's eyes went back and forth between the two men. "We can draw some conclusions from this," she said. "We know Thomason is connected to the killers in some way, willingly or not. There are two vehicles involved; a black SUV, Zack thinks probably an Escalade and a motorcycle. Can we also assuming there are more killers?"

"We know there were at least two assassins until we killed the woman," Zack said. "Those two likely worked as a unit. The black SUV may have been their other vehicle. Our first sighting of the black SUV came this morning, and we heard the motorcycle departing last night." He started to shrug, winced. "Might be two killers, or a single, very active one."

"Speaking of multiple vehicles, your new truck awaits you outside," Sarah said. Then she gave a mischievous grin. "Janice is right pissed at you. I wouldn't even scratch this one if I were you."

"I already got an earful about that." He gave her an annoyed look. "It seems the apple doesn't fall far from the tree."

She chuckled. "The good news is, the bad guys won't know you are driving this new truck. At least until you put a dent in it."

"I do not wish to interrupt this little squabble," Eagle Feather said. "But I am ready for a beer."

"Ah, I almost forgot." Zack reached in a pocket and handed the red phone to Eagle Feather. "This is a gift for you." He explained how it was to be used. He turned to Arlene. "You are our only witness to attempted murder. You will remain safe only if you allow us to protect you. That means no internet, no phone, no trips outside the house, day or night. These people are determined and have every resource available to them. Let's not help them."

Sarah put a hand on Arlene's shoulder. "We know it must be difficult, but I'll be here and we will find ways to entertain one another."

Arlene looked haunted. "How long are we talking about here?"

"It all depends upon what Janice learns in the next twenty-four hours from her technician, from Interpol, and a few other sources. We are badly in need of a thread to follow." Zack turned to Eagle Feather. "Our best source right now is Ned Thomason, even though we can't trust him. As Sarah pointed out, he seems to have some connection with the other side, willingly or not. We should continue to watch him."

"He should be at his office now. I will go watch," Eagle Feather said.

"Eagle Feather and his motorcycle are known to the killers," Sarah pointed out. "He could take the truck."

"I'll drive," Zack said starting to rise.

Sarah put a restraining hand on his shoulder. "Oh, no, you don't. I have strict orders to see that you rest today." She took the truck keys from her pocket and tossed them to Eagle Feather. "Leave the key to the bike. I'll use that if I need a vehicle."

Eagle Feather nodded and dropped the bike key on the counter on his way out.

Zack did not object, happy to avoid the pain and effort. He knew his body needed time to rest. He couldn't help worry about Eagle Feather, though. The opposition had shown their hand. They would not hesitate to kill the Navajo if the opportunity arose.

Eagle Feather wasn't thinking about his danger when he drove away in the truck Sarah had delivered, a Ford Ranger Raptor. He was thinking he'd rather have his bike. Although he always preferred to travel through the landscape on his own two feet, he enjoyed the freedom the motorcycle offered as a second-best option. He least liked modern vehicles with strange screens and switches he did not understand, a conveyance that demanded a learning curve he had no desire to pursue. He did, however, like the truck's name, Raptor. He felt a little better about it because of that.

He decided to stop off at the rest area, knowing he would not be noticed in this truck. He parked near the place Zack's truck had been. He looked through tinted windows at the paved parking, the sandy desolate ground, the handful of palm trees, the few tables, and the restroom buildings stark against the endless desert panorama.

The truck parking area, as always, was packed with diesel-driven monsters. When a truck pulled out from among others, it left an alley where a smaller vehicle, even the large black SUV, could easily hide. In his mind, this confirmed his theory that the killer in the black SUV simply waited there for Zack. It came to his mind to wonder what would have happened if he had been last to leave. Would he have been the one attacked? Being sideswiped while on the motorcycle would have been deadly.

Eagle Feather put the thought out of his mind and drove on. Thirty minutes later he was headed down the off-ramp at Desert Center. His phone rang. He pulled over, checked both phones, saw it was his private one. It was from George Madrigal.

"Hello, George."

"Greetings, Eagle Feather. I hope you are well."

"I am. I hope you are also well." He waited.

"I hoped we could meet if it is convenient."

Eagle Feather glanced at his watch. "Right away?"

"If it is convenient."

"I can be there in just over an hour."

"That will be fine."

Eagle Feather bypassed the Kaiser Road turnoff and drove north on S.R. 177 next to the Coxcomb mountain range. It was hot and dry…and beautiful, by Eagle Feather's standards. At the junction with S.R. 62, he turned left and shortly arrived at Twentynine Palms. Madrigal met him at the casino door and walked him to the Oasis Grille. There he was surprised to see Dr. Silvia Mike at a table with a man Eagle Feather had not met.

Madrigal did the introductions. "You already know Dr. Mike, of course." Silvia smiled up at him. "This is Lucas Hanks Leivas. He is a tribal member and among other things, a private investigator."

Eagle Feather had been curious about this unexpected meeting, now he was even more so.

"Thank you for responding so quickly, Eagle Feather," George said. "I consider it a personal courtesy, particularly knowing how busy you must be."

Eagle Feather sat in a vacant chair and waited.

George sat, including the other two with a glance. "We became aware of a recent death, a killing, in Great Wash not far from our sacred site. We are concerned about this on many levels."

Silvia spoke up. "We are naturally always concerned about violence in our homeland, but we are particularly concerned by the proximity of this murder to a place of such cultural and spiritual importance to us."

"*Ta'va Ma'ma'u,*" Eagle Feather said.

"Yes."

"Why call me?"

"You are Native American yet you are associated with the FBI. You have been investigating the case of this scientist who went missing in that same location. We assume you must know something about this."

"What do you want?"

George gave a grim smile. "Right to the point. Okay, then." He folded his hands together on the table. "We want to know what is going on."

Eagle Feather's face was blank. "We do not know."

The other man, Leivas, stirred. He was a large man, with a massive chin and long jawline as if carved from rock. He put his fist on the table, pointed a chunky finger at Eagle Feather. His voice rumbled deep in his chest. "You were there, you were in that place where the killing happened."

"I was. More than once."

"You were there the same day."

Eagle Feather considered this man with new interest. "Are you are a tracker?"

"I am Chemehuevi," he said as if that answered the question.

Eagle Feather nodded and looked at Madrigal. "I think you know more than you have told me. What do you know about the disappearance of the scientist?" His eyes went back to Leivas. "So you are a tracker. What happened to the man?"

The big chest rumbled. "He flew away from there."

Eagle Feather studied the craggy face, looking for signs of humor. He saw none. "You know this, or you can explain the missing tracks in no other way?"

Leivas took a moment to study Eagle Feather in his turn. "You are a Navajo tracker, a good one, I have heard. What is your answer to that question?"

"I believe he was abducted somehow, taken into the air."

"Why? Because you could not find other tracks?"

"Because there were no other tracks."

Madrigal coughed. "We need to know about this killing."

Eagle Feather's eyes were still on Lucas. "You were out there. You are an investigator. Did you see the body?"

Lucas glanced at Madrigal, who gave a quick nod.

"Yes, I did."

"It was you who reported it."

Another glance. "Yes."

Eagle Feather looked from Madrigal to Leivas. "Who was the victim?"

"The victim was a professional killer, a woman," Leivas said.

"What was she doing there?"

Madrigal waved a hand. "Look, Eagle Feather, we aren't trying to keep secrets from you or your associate. We simply need information. I'll tell you what we know, but I want a quid pro quo."

Eagle Feather's gaze went to each of the three in turn. "I will tell you what I can without harming our investigation or endangering the people we need to protect."

Madrigal nodded. "That is fair. I can tell you my friend Lucas here was hired by the tribe when the important scientist vanished. We asked him to conduct an investigation on our behalf because we feared repercussions. We knew if this scientist was not found, fingers would point to the tribe. Our traditions and our sacred site would be violated. We hoped Lucas could find the answer quickly so we could put the matter to rest."

"It did not work out that way," Eagle Feather said.

"No, it did not. Lucas saw what you saw. The tracks ended. The man was gone."

"How?"

Madrigal leaned back in his chair, glancing at Silvia. "We do not know. We do know this company that is building the battery in the desert, EverSun, is very rich and powerful and has many, uh, capabilities."

Silvia lay a hand on Madrigal's arm. "Eagle Feather, we saw that the sheriff's deputies were unable or unwilling to solve the disappearance. Their investigation ended when they called in the FBI. But before that…" She hesitated, looking at Lucas.

The Chemehuevi tracker remained silent, his dark face still. Madrigal glanced at him, then spoke. "There is something you should know about Lucas."

Eagle Feather felt their hesitancy. He waited.

Silvia spoke. "Lucas is more than just a tracker. He descends from a long line of legendary Chemehuevi runners, those I described to you.".

"You mean, a flying desert runner."

"Yes."

The table was silent as this revelation hung like a forbidden spirit.

Eagle Feather spoke first. "I accept your understanding of this ability, even if I do not understand it myself." He looked at Lucas. "But this scientist…are you trying to tell me he flew?"

"I do not think that," Lucas said. "None but the desert people have this ability. When I first saw his tracks, I saw how they disappeared. I walked back along them and studied them for a long time. The distance between the prints grew, the heels lifted so that only the forefoot and toes touched the ground as if running swiftly, and then"— he looked at Eagle Feather—"as you saw, they disappeared."

"It is the same way Lucas' footprints appear in the sand when he flies." Madrigal had leaned forward, his voice almost a whisper. "I have seen them." He saw Eagle Feather's expression. "This is hard to believe if you are not Chemehuevi. But now we must tell you something you will understand. Before you and your FBI associate came here,

221

on the day Lucas studied the tracks and was returning up Great Wash, he was shot from ambush."

Eagle Feather stared at Lucas who lifted a thatch of straight black hair away from his forehead to reveal the angry red line of a bullet scar.

CHAPTER TWENTY-FOUR

Lucas' face was impassive as he told his story, although his jaw muscles bulged with anger. "I was lost in thought about the scientist's strange tracks one moment, and the world turned black the next. When I regained consciousness, I did not know what had happened. I think now I was unconscious for only a minute or two. I felt blood drip into my eyes. I then understood I had been shot. I lay still realizing I could be shot again at any moment. I lay there maybe an hour, but there were no more shots and no one came."

"You were lucky," Eagle Feather said.

"Yes, I was very lucky and was very careless. I returned the next day, I found the footprints of the one who shot me. I followed them to the place the shooter had left a motorcycle."

"Was it the woman?" Eagle Feather asked.

"The shoe size was small. When I found the body of the woman I learned it was the same person."

"Do you know who killed her?"

The Chemehuevi's face was blank. "Two men, one in moccasins who followed the woman into the arroyo, another who waited in ambush and shot her. The answer to your question is not difficult."

Madrigal's eyes went to Eagle Feather. "We know the FBI had been called off the case."

Eagle Feather said nothing.

Madrigal pressed. "I believe the woman was a professional hired by someone to keep people from learning the truth."

"Do you know who hired her?"

"We do not know. Someone is desperate to protect something in that area." He squared around toward Eagle Feather. "It is your turn. Quid pro quo, as you said. We know you and your FBI colleague are still investigating. What is so important in that wash a killer was trying to keep people out?"

Eagle Feather looked around the table. "We do not yet know all the answers to your question. We do know there is at least one more assassin. The female killer had a partner. We tried to catch him last night, but he was too smart. He almost killed my partner today. There could be even more killers. Very powerful people are trying to stop our investigation."

Silvia glanced at Eagle Feather. "After Lucas discovered the killer's body, he reported it to local law enforcement, but there has been no news about it." She raised her palms in question. "A woman was murdered no more than twenty miles from here yet it is not reported in the papers. How can this be?"

Madrigal spoke for Eagle Feather. "I think the same powerful people who hired the killers and were able to call the FBI off are responsible for quashing that news. Such a thing is not new."

"The sheriff called in the FBI to investigate the death of the woman," Eagle Feather said. "Local law enforcement does not wish to be involved."

Madrigal gave his head a shake. "I cannot blame them. There is a risk of physical and political danger to anyone who is involved." He pointed a finger at Eagle Feather. "This is why we asked to meet with you. Already some say the Tribe is involved in this. We wish to protect our sacred sites, but we do not hire professional killers."

"What do you want from me?"

Madrigal gave the Navajo a thin smile. "We have heard you and your colleague have a certain amount of autonomy within the agency. We want to work with you. We can help you and you can help us."

"Help you how?"

Madrigal spread his palms. "Help us help ourselves from becoming victimized. We want the truth to be known. In this, we share a common purpose, a common goal. If we unite our resources, it would not serve our purpose if particulars of the woman assassin's death were revealed."

Eagle Feather almost smiled. "I see we are not above using a bit of leverage. I will consult with my friend. Please give me a moment."

Eagle Feather stood and walked out of the casino into the warmth of the late afternoon sun. Its heat was welcome after the cold of the casino air conditioning. He took out his new red phone and called Zack to explain the circumstances.

He heard Zack's laugh. "You want to make a treaty with the local Indians, then? That's fine with me. We could use more players on our team."

Eagle Feather returned to the table in the Oasis Grille. He did not sit this time but extended his hand to Madrigal. "We accept your proposal," he said. To Lucas, he said, "Would you walk with me, please?"

Navajo and Chemehuevi walked side by side out to the parking lot. Eagle Feather turned to Lucas. "I go now to the Santini & Marsh project site to do surveillance. What is your plan?"

"I will go search for the other killer."

"How will you do this?"

"Our people have eyes in many places. I will ask around to find where he is hiding."

"How can I reach you?" Eagle Feather asked.

"I have a cell phone." The men exchanged phone numbers.

"Good hunting," Lucas said and walked away.

When Eagle Feather reached the Santini & Marsh parking lot, Thomason's blue pickup was gone. The parking lot was nearly empty. Quitting time had come and gone. Eagle Feather swung the truck around and headed back to the interstate. When he reached Blythe, he drove to Thomason's condo. The blue truck was not there, either. Eagle Feather went on to the safe house.

Zack was dozing on the couch and wonderful smells filled the room when Eagle Feather arrived.

"You are just in time, Eagle Feather," Arlene called from the kitchen. "Dinner is just about ready."

Zack stirred and looked up. "Eagle Feather? What's happening?"

Eagle Feather glanced at the kitchen and walked to the living room. He sat opposite Zack and spoke quietly. "Thomason's truck isn't at his workplace or his home."

Zack sat up, swung his legs around to the floor. "Maybe he stopped for some groceries."

Eagle Feather raised an eyebrow.

"When was the last time we saw his truck?" Zack asked. "Was it when you and I were looking for the black SUV this morning?"

"Yes."

"You don't know if he left the workplace early or at his regular quitting time."

"No."

Zack took his phone from his pocket and brought up the location app. In a moment, a map appeared along with a flashing red icon. Zack widened the map with his fingers. "I can't get a street name here. His truck seems to be in the middle of the desert." He reached for his briefcase and rifled through it and found a California map. He glanced between the map on his phone and the California map.

"His truck is on something called Wiley's Well Road." He yelled toward the kitchen. "Anybody know a Wiley's Well Road?"

"Isn't that the name of the rest area on the interstate?" Arlene called back.

"Yeah, that's right." Zack went to Google. "There's only one thing out there," he said, searching. "The Chuckawalla Valley State Prison."

Sarah came in from the kitchen. "I had no idea there was a prison around here," she said. She looked at the app map on Zack's phone. "What's this just down the road from the truck?"

Zack widened the view to look at the spot. "It says Wiley's Well Campground." He glanced at Sarah. "We better go out there and look, I think."

Eagle Feather was already on his feet, moving toward the door.

"Hold on a minute," Zack said studying the California map. "Let's be smart here. There are two ways to approach the area. If Ned is meeting someone, they could all be gone by the time we arrive. There's another road, Bradshaw Trail, off Route 78 south of town."

He glanced up at Eagle Feather. "Take the bike. That route takes you to the south end of Wiley's Well Road near the campground. I'll take the Interstate 10 route. There won't be many cars on that road. If we hurry we may trap them between us or at least see if anyone is with him." He closed the laptop and stood. He couldn't help emitting a groan.

"Are you in any shape to go?" Sarah asked.

"Cracked ribs are nothing new to me," Zack said. "The rest I've had has helped a lot. Regardless, we have to learn what's happening with Ned."

LOST OASIS

"I'll call Janice to let her know what's going on," Sarah said. She flipped the key to the bike to Eagle Feather. He flipped the truck keys to Zack.

The front door had just closed behind the two men when Arlene emerged from the kitchen. "Dinner's ready!" she called out in a cheerful voice. She looked around the empty room, saw Sarah on her phone. Sarah shrugged at her and had an embarrassed look on her face.

"Well, shit," Arlene said as realization dawned.

Zack loved the new truck. He loved the purr of the engine, the spurt of acceleration from the little four-cylinder engine, the nimble feel of the vehicle. The driver's seat was as comfortable as his favorite overstuffed chair at home. He played with the layers of electronic data on the large display as he hummed down Interstate 10.

He took the ramp for the rest area and drove slowly through it, looking for the black SUV or anything out of the ordinary. He knew Eagle Feather's route was longer and wanted to give him time to get close. If anyone came north on Wiley's Well Road, he'd see them from here. After circumnavigating the entire rest area and seeing nothing unusual, Zack checked his watch and decided to go on. He crossed over the interstate bridge.

Wiley's Well Road ran straight as an arrow south toward the horizon, even now tinted by sunset's orange and red flare. The area around him was desolate. His was the only vehicle on the road. When he came near the entrance to the prison, he pulled over and checked his phone app. The red icon still blinked in the same place. Thomason's phone had not moved.

Zack sent a text message to Eagle Feather and waited.

Several minutes later, his phone rang. "I am still several miles away from the intersection with Wiley's Well Road," Eagle Feather said.

Zack thought about it. "The campground is right at the intersection. Go there and wait, watch for anyone driving south. I'll go check on Thomason."

It was soon apparent Wiley's Well Road received less regular maintenance beyond the prison. Road ripples caused continuous vibration through the truck. After several miles without seeing any other vehicles, Zack pulled over and checked the app again. The icon still blinked, but it was behind him now. He had seen nothing. Zack turned around and retraced his route, slower now. He scanned the desert on both sides for anywhere a truck might have gone. When the app indicated he was in the right place, he pulled over and got out.

Far to the northwest, he could see the electric towers and taller structures of the prison. In between was nothing but sand and desert plants. In the other direction, desert stretched as far as he could see. There was nothing out there. It could mean only one thing.

Zack found Thomason's phone number and called his phone as he stood in the semidarkness by the side of the dirt road. He heard the phone ring, keep ringing. The sound was coming from a bunch of mesquites just off the shoulder. As Zack walked toward it he saw a light. Ned's phone.

It meant Ned and his truck could be anywhere. The question was, did he discover the locator planted in his phone somehow and throw it away or was he in trouble? Zack bagged the phone. It might have fingerprints. He called Eagle Feather.

The Navajo answered right away. "Hello, White Man."

"Where are you now?" Zack asked.

"I am at Wiley's Well Campground. I am standing next to Wiley's Well."

"So Wiley's Well is at Wiley's Well Campground on Wiley's Well Road. That is good information. However, we have a problem. Thomason's phone is not in Thomason's truck. I found it under a mesquite bush. Thomason and his truck are missing."

"Thomason's truck is not missing. It is right in front of me," Eagle Feather said.

"You mean Thomason's truck is at Wiley's Well Campground?"

"Yes, in front of Wiley's Well, which is—"

Zack hung up.

CHAPTER TWENTY-FIVE

Wiley's Well Campground consisted of isolated clusters of
Palo Verde, Smoke, and Iron Wood trees in a bed of sand.
It was not entirely primitive, saved from that distinction by
the availability of water from Wiley's Well, the very well
dug by hand by a Mr. Wiley over a century ago. Since that
time it had been deepened and reinforced. The campground was a nest of four-wheel-drive vehicles, trailers,
dune buggies, and a handful of campers. Although a sign
limited campers to one night, most camps had an air of
permanence.

Glances of mild curiosity greeted Zack's truck as he
drove in. There were friendly nods. Each campsite had a
table with a sun canopy and an enclosed fire pit. It was all
very tidy. Zack crawled along, keeping the dust down as he
idled through the campground. He came to an open area
and parked. He climbed out, keeping the Sig Sauer on his
belt under his loose shirttail. There had been too many
surprises lately, to his mind.

Beyond a smoke tree was a large wood sign telling the
tale of Wiley's Well. The well itself stood just beyond it.
Thomason's blue truck was parked near the well. There
was no sign of Eagle Feather or his bike. Zack walked
toward the truck. He could see the cab was empty. He
walked completely around it looking for prints in the sand.
He saw footprints at both doors, suggesting two people
had been in the truck and exited here. He opened the

driver's door and looked inside. Some spiral bound books, apparently geology reports of some kind, were tucked between the seats. A pair of worn leather gloves rested on the shifter platform. The keys were in the ignition.

Zack closed the door and looked in the truck bed. It was empty. He studied the prints in the sand, found where impressions of two people led away from the truck toward a gap among the trees at the edge of the campground. He followed them and came to a dry wash. Many feet and many vehicles had been up and down the wash. He had no way to know where the truck passengers had gone from here.

He stood, undecided. With the sun nearly gone and shadows long, he could do no more. But where was Eagle Feather? He called his number. The Navajo's phone was off.

Zack walked back the way he had come. Why would Eagle Feather have left instead of waiting? Something or someone must have drawn him away. He walked back to Thomason's truck. When they spoke on the phone, Eagle Feather had told him the truck was right in front of him and the well just beyond it. Lining the truck up with the well, Zack walked back from the truck searching the sand. A short distance away he found fresh tire tracks made by a motorcycle and a footprint pushed deep into the sand as if someone had balanced the bike with his foot.

Zack studied the view from there. The truck was in the foreground and beyond it the well. Trees marked the edge of the wash beyond the campground. Several gaps in the trees provided a view into the wash, but just one looked large enough for vehicles to pass through. Had Eagle Feather seen something there? Zack looked down at the motorcycle tire print. Beyond the deep footprint, the wheels had dug in where the bike moved off. Following it with his eyes, Zack saw the motorcycle had joined the confusion of vehicle tracks headed toward the entrance to the wash.

Zack went back to the Raptor, started it up, and drove through the gap into the wash. He dropped the truck into four-wheel drive and flipping a mental coin, turned south down the dry bed. The gravelly sand was firm and the ride smooth except for occasional drops over a shale ledge. Zack could follow the main track of previous drivers to avoid the worst pitfalls. He needed all the extra lights the truck provided to see the course before him.

After a short time, the wash intersected a graded road. Zack surmised it must be Bradshaw Trail, the road that intersected with Wiley's Well Road. Now he was stymied. With three choices, right, left, or straight ahead up the wash, he had no way to know where Eagle Feather might have gone. His search was over.

A moment later his phone rang.

"Where are you, White Man?"

"I am in the wash south of the campground, at Bradshaw Trail. Where are you?"

"That is good. Turn left and drive to Wiley's Well Road and go south. I will meet you along the road."

The call ended.

Relieved to know his friend was still alive, Zack followed the Navajo's instructions. When he came to Wiley's Well Road, he turned south and picked up speed. He found the bike and rider at a side road. He pulled over. A moment later the passenger door opened and Eagle Feather slid in.

"Hello, White Man. It is good you are here."

"I almost wasn't. I took a wild guess." Zack was frustrated.

Eagle Feather regarded him solemnly. "You seldom make wild guesses. It is not in your nature."

Zack gave up. "Why are we here?"

"Thomason is here," Eagle Feather said. "He is not alone."

"What is this place?"

"It is another campground, called Coon Hollow."

"Is he here willingly? Who is he with?"

"Whoa, White Man, one question at a time. I do not know if he went willingly. The one he is with is the assassin."

"Where are they?"

"I do not know. I know only that they are here."

"How do you know they are here, then?"

"A friend told me. We need to go to meet him."

Zack stared at the Navajo, then shrugged. "Okay. Where?"

"I do not know. He will find us. The campground is small. If we drive in this way, they will see us, maybe run. We must go another way."

"Okay," Zack said. "Lead the way."

Eagle Feather climbed out and returned to his bike. He went north on Wiley's Well Road with Zack following. They'd gone less than a mile when the bike slowed and turned off onto a rough trace across the desert. Zack followed, driving with just his parking lights. When the motorcycle taillight slowed and dipped, Zack saw they had come to the bank of the dry wash. Once in the wash bed, they followed it south, moving slow. The bed of the wash was rough here, with many snags and boulders to be avoided. When the tail light of the motorcycle ahead turned off, Zack turned off the truck parking lights. Their progress slowed considerably after that. Shortly, the bike stopped and Eagle Feather climbed off. He walked back to Zack's truck. "We leave the vehicles here," he said through the open window.

Zack slipped on his jacket. The temperature had dropped with the sun's disappearance. He was armed with his pistol and carried a rifle. He followed Eagle Feather down the wash. They made no noise on the firm sand. There was very little breeze in the shelter of the tree-lined wash and despite the deepening chill in the air, the exercise quickly warmed Zack. His recent injuries ached, he was unbelievably fatigued and extremely hungry. He pushed on.

A smell of smoke came to him. A speck of light appeared in the distance, grew as they neared. Zack felt Eagle Feather's hand on his arm.

"That is the campground," the Navajo said in a low voice. "We must move carefully now."

More specks of light joined the first, which by now Zack could see was a lantern on a picnic table. As they moved on Zack realized the campground stretched out along the dry wash, like cabins on a lakeshore. He saw only tents and small trailers here. All had lights of some sort on tables or hanging from guy wires. Many were cooking dinner over the fire or on a Coleman stove. Zack's stomach grumbled so loudly he feared it would be heard.

Eagle Feather kept moving down the wash. They were safe from view in the darkness so long as they made no noise and no one pointed a flashlight in their direction. Fortunately, all the campers were either chatting at their dinner tables or already in bed preparing for another day of four-wheeling or rock-hounding.

Eagle Feather stopped and waited for Zack.

"We will wait here," Eagle Feather said. "My friend will find us."

Several minutes elapsed. Zack's lack of movement brought back the chill and he zipped his jacket. Minutes later, a very large figure loomed out of the darkness, came close, and grunted a greeting to Eagle Feather. The Navajo made whispered introductions.

"Zack. Lucas."

The man Lucas grabbed Zack's hand, crushed it. He was huge, towering over him by a half foot.

"Lucas followed the assassin," Eagle Feather said. "I followed Thomason. We found each other at Wiley's Well and tracked them both here. Lucas followed them into the campground while I waited for you."

The voice of Lucas rumbled. "They are here. The ATV they used is near a small trailer. I could not see into the trailer."

Eagle Feather looked to Zack. "Your call, White Man."

"Let's go," Zack said.

Lucas led the way. They climbed up the loose sandbank, cut through a small grove of trees, and slid along the shadow outside the halo of light created by the camps. After skirting two campsites, the Chemehuevi stopped in the dark under some trees. Just in front of them was a small trailer. The two small side windows were curtained. No light showed from the inside. They were behind the trailer, the door was out of their view.

Zack touched Lucas's arm and signaled for him to stay on guard, then with Eagle Feather moved around to the front of the trailer. The area was gently illuminated by light from the next campsite. The trailer had a single step up to its aluminum door. The door was solid, but there was a small window to one side of it.

Zack pulled his pistol from its holster and crouched on one side of the door. He waited for Eagle Feather to move into position opposite him, then raised a fist and banged on the door. Tensed for action, they waited. There was no sound inside.

Eagle Feather raised a hand toward the door handle but Zack waved a hand to stop him. Something was bothering him, something was missing. Then he knew. It was the ATV. He had not seen one.

"Where's the ATV?" Zack whispered. He glanced around, searching. Behind Eagle Feather, in the tree shadows, he saw a reflection of light, a movement.

"Down!" Zack shouted.

CHAPTER TWENTY-SIX

Zack dropped to the ground, flattened his body next to the metal step and slid partially under the trailer in one instinctive move. He felt rather than heard the explosion, it slammed him hard into the ground, vibrated through him as if he were being physically beaten. He heard whistling sounds and then nothing but roaring in his ears. His eyes were left blind by the flash as if from staring into the sun.

But he was alive! Even in his shocked state, his first worry was Eagle Feather. What had happened to his friend? He needed to know, but he knew he might have new injuries of his own. He found he could move his head, his neck seemed to function. The gun was gone from his right hand, but he could move the fingers, then the arm. A methodical tally of body parts came up positive. Everything functioned, but everything hurt.

Moving just his right arm, Zack made a slow sweep of the ground with his hand. He remembered the reflection he'd seen of something metallic in the tree shadows just before the explosion. Someone had been there and might still be a threat and he needed his gun. His fingers touched cold metal, the Sig Sauer. He grabbed it. When it was secure in his hand, he turned his head to look for Eagle Feather.

A concussive noise still filled his head, his whiplashed neck had a whole new level of pain, but his sight was returning enough to see the outline of objects. He tried to sit. His ribs hurt too much. Instead, he crabbed his body along the ground until he could view the side of the trailer where his friend had been.

He wasn't there.

Zack glanced at the trees but saw nothing. There was motion elsewhere, though, where figures were moving in other campsites. They would soon be coming to learn what had happened. Zack had to be sure the danger was past, the killer gone. He had to get up.

Levering his arms on what once had been the trailer step, ignoring the pain, Zack hoisted himself into a kneeling position. He saw the gaping hole where the door to the trailer had been. Parts of it were all over the ground. It had blown outward, fortunately for them a directed charge with most of the force projected higher. Had he been in front of it, he would not be alive.

But there was no sign of Eagle Feather. Zack pushed up from his knees and regained his feet. His eyes blurred and he felt faint but kept his pistol trained on the trees as he limped past the blown out door to the side of the trailer. He turned the corner and encountered a huge shape. It was Lucas.

"Where is Eagle Feather?" Zack asked.

Before the Chemehuevi could answer, the voice of the man in question sounded at their feet. Eagle Feather crawled out from beneath the trailer.

"You should have warned me sooner, White Man," he said and came to a sitting position. "That was too close."

Lucas helped him to his feet.

Eagle Feather took some gingerly steps, moved his parts, and brushed himself off. He looked toward the road.

"We have company," he said.

Campers were approaching along the roadway, speaking in hushed voices. Zack went toward them. When they met, he spoke to them in low, calm tones.

"I am an FBI agent," he said. He showed his credentials as he spoke. "This area is now a crime scene. You will be perfectly safe if you return to your campsites and remain there. My colleagues and I are investigating."

There was a flurry of questions. "But what happened?" "How did you get here so fast?" "Is anyone hurt?"

Zack held up a palm. "Someone will come by to answer all your questions in a while. But I must ask you now to return to your campsites."

There was more mumbling and discussion as the campers turned away.

Zack limped back to where the other two men stood near the destroyed trailer door.

"Did you see who did this?" he asked Lucas.

"No, sorry, man," Lucas said. He pointed to the edge of the clearing in the back of the trailer. "I was over there in case anyone tried to run. After the explosion, I could not hear much at first. I started toward the front, then saw movement over there." He pointed toward the trees. "I stopped here. A moment later I heard a motor start up over there somewhere." He pointed toward the wash. "Maybe it was the assassin."

"It probably was," Zack said. "But we need to look inside the trailer to be sure."

As they turned to walk that way, Zack grabbed Lucas' arm. "I don't think the assassin was inside when the explosion occurred. Let's assume the bike you heard start was the killer and not waste any time. Can you follow him now?"

The big man nodded. "It will take longer in the dark, but I can track him."

"That's good. Please keep in touch with Eagle Feather."

As the Chemehuevi tracker turned and disappeared into the darkness, Zack and Eagle Feather walked to the front of the trailer. It was indeed evident the charge had been placed to blow the door outward, a trap that had been set by the assassin to kill or maim his pursuers. He'd waited in the shadows with a remote of some sort and set off the charge when his victims were in position. It meant the man had known they were close behind him. To Zack's mind, he was too clever by far.

Eagle Feather stared at the destruction. "What alerted you to the bomb?" he asked Zack.

"I happened to be looking the right way to see movement and a reflection of light off something metallic in those trees. Lucas had said he saw an ATV near the trailer but it wasn't there. So the man must have driven it away while Lucas was meeting us. But if he had, who was in the trees? That's when I remembered the bomb under my Jeep and I yelled. Sorry I didn't think faster."

243

The Navajo glanced at him. "Maybe next time you will do better."

Zack grinned. "Let's hope so."

But Eagle Feather was still staring at him. "White Man, there is something very different about you."

To Zack, it was one of the greatest compliments the Navajo had ever paid him.

But the gaping hole in the trailer that yawned open before them was sobering. A debris trail was strung out in a straight line from the door toward the road. The aluminum roof above the doorway was crumpled back, like a partially opened can of beans. The top aluminum step had been twisted and ripped apart. The charge had likely been fixed to the door. If the two men had not ducked under the frame of the trailer when they did, they could not have escaped.

"He may have set other traps," Zack said. "We need to be careful." He took his flashlight from his pocket and stepped into the trailer. The interior was strangely tidy beyond the immediate area of the bomb's destruction. Straight ahead was a larder and shelf arrangement. The wooden doors were split, food items were scattered and smashed. A small dining area was to his right. It was empty, undisturbed. Shining the narrow beam to the left, Zack saw a built-in couch. A man lay on it on his stomach, his hands tied behind him. Before moving toward him, Zack showed the flashlight on the couch and the cheap floor carpet looking for tripwires. The light shimmered on blood. A sweep of his flashlight convinced him no one else was in the trailer.

Moving a step at a time, ever conscious of booby traps, Zack went to the man on the couch. Without touching him, he leaned over the body and shown the light on his face. It was Ned Thomason. The scientist's throat had been cut. He was dead. Zack turned and looked at Eagle Feather, shook his head. They left the trailer.

"Thomason?" Eagle Feather asked.

"Yes," Zack said. He took his phone from his pocket and called Janice. When she answered, Zack described the situation.

"Have you touched anything?"

"No."

"Okay, I'll notify the locals to secure the site, but we will remain in charge. I'll send an agent and a forensic team right away. Stay there and guard the scene until you hear a siren approaching, then you should leave. I don't want local law enforcement to find you there. I need you free to move about. What about the killer?"

"We have a Chemehuevi ally, an investigator who helped us tonight. He is tracking the assassin."

"Another Indian who does not exist, eh? Can you make this any more complicated?" Janice rang off before Zack could reply.

The two men waited outside the trailer, saying little. The campers had dispersed as requested. Zack was glad for the quiet. His system was still in shock, but his brain was restless, chewing away at the mystery. Why had the assassin killed Ned? Or maybe the question was, why hadn't he done so sooner? His mind thus occupied, it seemed just a short time before he heard sirens sound out on Wiley's Well Road. They waited until they saw the red and blue flashing lights in the blackness before sliding quietly off into the shadows of the wash.

Eagle Feather followed Zack back to Blythe and the safe house. Both men were enormously hungry now. Arlene eyed them with her large hands on her hips, her lower lip protruding, but never said a word and went about reheating the refrigerated meal. But she must have been pleased when the men devoured it all with loud exclamations of happiness.

Zack recounted the night's events to both women.

Arlene was shocked at the news of Ned's death. "There but for the grace of God go I," she said. "Poor Ned. He was so innocent, so naïve."

"That's true," Zack said. "In the end, his nature did not serve him well. I doubt he saw the end coming."

"He seemed to go willingly with the killer," Eagle Feather said.

"We know he met with someone on the highway yesterday in that black SUV. Do you think it was the killer?" Sarah asked.

"It could have been," Zack said. "It certainly looked like the same vehicle that ran me off the road. But it could have been someone else, too, maybe even the person who hired the assassin."

"Janice has local law enforcement looking for a large black SUV, likely an Escalade, with damage to the passenger side," Sarah said. "But my guess is the vehicle has already been flattened at some junkyard."

Zack's phone rang. It was Janice.

"Zack, our people are at the trailer and will get samples to the lab quickly. What we do know, Ned Thomason's throat was cut cleanly and professionally. The examiner found no other wounds, such as torture would leave, so if it was information he wanted, he didn't need to use force. The initial examination of the trailer suggests the killer wore gloves and was very careful, no surprise there. He had been using the trailer for a while, they believe. The bomb materials, at first glance, correspond with those used in the bomb attached to your Jeep. They'll check that at the lab as well."

"Any luck tracking down that black SUV?"

"Nothing yet, Zack. We checked with Santini & Marsh and found that no one there owns such a vehicle. We are still checking with EverSun, and the Riverside County Sheriff's deputies are looking for it as well."

"Anything on our agency leak?"

"No." Janice did not seem to want to enlarge on that topic.

"How about the truck Arlene described when she was almost abducted?"

"Yes, we found it dropped over the side of a deep ravine. But as you might expect, we found nothing helpful there." She paused. "Anything else?"

"Guess not."

"How are you doing, Zack? Do you need some time off?"

Zack laughed, then reacted. "Ooh, that just hurt. But no, I can manage."

After concluding his call with Janice, Zack relayed the news to the others. They sat in silence in the living room, drinks in hand, watching the clock climb toward midnight.

Zack asked the question on everyone's mind. "Where do we go from here? We hope Lucas can track down the killer again, but even if he does and even if we catch him alive, which is doubtful, he won't tell us anything. Where else can we go?"

Everyone was silent for a moment. "I think the black SUV is important," Sarah said after a while. "Even people with money to throw away don't generally use Escalades or the like to smash into other cars. One of our parties of interest may have owned it. We need that car."

"I agree," Zack said. He paused. "We know what we want, the black SUV, the assassin. But what do they want? If you think about it, they've managed to eliminate every witness to Dr. Scheidecker's discovery except for one." He looked at Arlene.

"Thanks for the comforting word," Arlene said.

"Sorry, not a nice subject. However, you are perfectly safe here. They won't find you." He looked at the others. "And that's the problem, do you see? It's a stalemate. Neither side can move without more evidence. We need to find the FBI leak. To do that, we need someone who can

248

lead us there. But so long as they can't find Arlene, they don't have anything else to try and won't expose themselves. Their efforts died with Ned. Stalemate."

"Unless…" Sarah leaned forward.

"Unless they find Arlene," Zack said.

Sarah nodded. "Then they'll make a move." Her eyebrows rose in surprised realization. "You want to…"

"I want to give them Arlene."

CHAPTER TWENTY-SEVEN

The silence in the room throbbed with tension. Everyone looked at Zack and avoided looking at Arlene. Sarah's eyebrows were still arched in surprise. Arlene stood smoothing her apron, a look of petulant defiance on her face. Eagle Feather showed nothing, but his eyes had a curious look.

"Don't worry." Zack spoke in a rush. "Of course, I have no intention of actually handing Arlene over to these people or even bringing her close to them. Arlene will stay right here in the safe house and this house must remain secure, no matter what." He glanced around at the attentive faces. "We need to create an illusion. We need to make them think she is somewhere they can get their hands on her so that they will make an attempt."

"A subterfuge," Sarah said.

"Exactly. A trap."

"Who is they, White Man?"

Zack glanced at Eagle Feather. "Well, yes, that is the difficulty. We don't know who they are, we only know about the assassin they hired." He looked at Arlene. "Sit for a moment. We need your thoughts here. Let's put the assassin aside for now. Lucas is on his tail and will report when he has news. Let's treat him as a separate job. Besides, I think the killer's contact with his employer is infrequent, it feels to me like he is on his own. He'll make a mistake, we'll nab him sooner or later." Zack turned his gaze back to Arlene. "We need to think of everyone who has an interest in concealing Scheidecker's discovery because I believe that is what this is all about. We need a way to send a message that will reach all of them. We need them to believe Arlene will be in a certain place at a certain time, a place where they believe she will be vulnerable and they can get to her. And, we need to be able to identify the players who act upon our message." Zack threw his hands in the air. "I just don't know how or where."

"You mean somewhere like a boardroom or a CEO's office, maybe bug the room after we get the message out?" Sarah asked.

"Maybe."

"But you want somewhere they might be forced to show their true colors, or even confess," Arlene said.

"That would be ideal."

"But it could be anyone," Sarah said with her arms out to encompass the world.

"Within certain limitations," Zack said. "These globetrotting assassins don't come cheap. It needs to be a person or group with money or access to money. It needs to be a person or group with a critical interest in this desert generator project. It needs to be a person or a group with enough power to turn off an FBI investigation."

Sarah tilted her head, looking thoughtful. "Within any group of people, you'll find the wicked, the greedy, the desperate but also the kind, the fair, and the thoughtful. What I'm trying to say is, it's unlikely we are looking for a group of people of any size that would engage in abduction and murder. And of course, the more people involved, the greater the risk of discovery. I think we are looking for just one or two people, most likely a single individual."

"It also has to be someone who knows enough about Scheidecker's volcanic intrusion theory to believe it could sound the death knell of the project," Arlene said. "No one had any idea what Scheidecker was up to out there. He kept to himself."

"That's good," Zack said. "Let's start with that. Who could have known?"

"As far as I know, the only person Scheidecker told his suspicions to was Thomason," Arlene said.

"You don't think Scheidecker could have revealed it to a colleague elsewhere, maybe someone he worked with on a former project, maybe a family member?" Sarah asked.

Arlene shook her head emphatically. "That was not his style. Scheidecker never gave his hand away until he was ready to play his cards. He liked to play the genius, he would never reveal a theory until he was absolutely sure of his facts, then he'd lay it on you as a fait accompli. He wanted the reaction he got from people. He talked about it with Thomason only because Ned was a world-class geologist and could verify or dispute what Scheidecker believed he saw."

"You're saying it had to be Thomason who gave it away," Sarah said.

Arlene nodded. "I guess that's what I'm saying."

"So he could have been the first in a long chain of people who learned of it," Zack said. "Arlene, who do you think he might have told?"

She gave a wry smile. "Well me, for starters. He'd been sworn to secrecy by Scheidecker and only told me after Scheidecker had been missing for a while, and he became worried."

"So if we assume Scheidecker didn't tell anybody else, Thomason had to have leaked it before Scheidecker went missing, or Scheidecker wouldn't have gone missing, right? Or am I missing something?"

"Maybe someone knew about it before Scheidecker."

Everyone swung around to look at Eagle Feather. He had been perched on a kitchen stool like a vulture on a limb, listening and watching but saying little.

"Like…who?" Sarah asked.

"People who have been here all along. People who know this land."

"The Chemehuevi," Zack said.

Eagle Feather nodded. "Or prospectors, miners." He shrugged. "Take your pick."

Sarah looked excited. "Wait a minute, what about the Kaiser group who did open pit mining there during World War II? They would have had geologists all over the place."

Zack could feel his inner excitement rise. "So we might be looking for someone who was connected to previous mining or prospecting operations in the Eagle Mountains who is now involved in some critical way with the desert generator."

"That narrows it down, I should think," Sarah said.

Zack looked at Arlene, who shrugged. "I don't know of anyone offhand who fits that description. I'd need to do some research."

"No, not you," Zack said. "You need to stay here and stay off the internet. We'll handle the research. We'll need you to look at lists of names and pictures of people we bring you."

"What about the Chemehuevi, or other tribes?" Arlene asked.

"They do not care about the generator. The spirit of Eagle Mountain was disturbed long ago. That bird has flown," Eagle Feather said.

"Nor do I think it likely any of the tribes have the power to stop an FBI investigation," Zack said. He glanced at Eagle Feather. "We need to go find a place to jump on the internet where no one can trace the activity to this safe house."

"I know a place," the Navajo said.

They left the truck for Sarah to have should an emergency arrive and took Eagle Feather's motorcycle. It was well after ten o'clock when they entered the Coachella Valley on Interstate 10. The freeway seemed just as crowded as during the day. The air was warm with the strangely pleasant aroma that the desert breathes out at night, along with occasional fast food smells. Riding behind Eagle Feather, Zack kept his helmet visor up and allowed the wind to swirl across his face, cooling it. Bright lights everywhere indicated when they were nearing Palm Desert. High rise casinos like Spotlight 29 and Agua Caliente Resort appeared like sparkling vertical bridges up to the sky.

Zack did not know their destination, nor had he inquired when Eagle Feather offered a place, but he was surprised when they turned off the highway at the Morongo Casino complex. Eagle Feather steered the bike through a network of small roads and alleyways and dropped down a ramp into an underground garage and a parking place marked Guests Only.

"We are here, White Man," he said over his shoulder and turned off the engine.

Zack climbed off, enjoying the coolness of the garage. He saw it was full of expensive cars.

"Are we crashing someone's party?"

"We are our own party," Eagle Feather said. He led the way to the elevator and pressed the button to the top floor suites.

It was a long ride. When the door finally opened, they stepped into a glass hallway with a view down to tiny cars and roofs far below. Beyond that, the glittering highway of lights on Interstate 10 ribboned off toward Palm Springs. Eagle Feather took a card from his pocket and flashed it near the huge mahogany door. It clicked open. Inside, the ornate furnishings, thick carpet, luxurious drapes, and windows with magnificent views took Zack's breath away.

His face showed nothing, but Zack knew Eagle Feather was enjoying the moment.

"So friends in high places?"

Eagle Feather nodded. "The Wi-Fi works well here."

"I'm not surprised," Zack said. He removed his laptop from his satchel and set it down on a coffee table. As he set up, Eagle Feather phoned down to room service for a late snack. Then he called Lucas. The conversation was brief. Following it, he came and sat down.

"Lucas will get some sleep now and continue in the morning," Eagle Feather said. "He was able to follow the man's quad north up the wash. He lost it somewhere near the prison. He will look again in the morning light."

Zack nodded. "He must have another place to hide away or he would not have destroyed his trailer so readily."

"He may have many."

"Yes, he would want several holes to crawl into."

"The food will be here soon," Eagle Feather said. "I have calls to make. I will make them in the bedroom."

Shortly, Zack heard the murmur of Eagle Feather's voice in the distance. The food came, was eaten, and the men worked on into the night. It was well after midnight when Eagle Feather emerged again from the bedroom.

"I have ordered breakfast for tomorrow morning at eight," he said. "Your bedroom is through there." He pointed.

LOST OASIS

Zack worked another hour before closing the laptop and trudging off to find the bedroom. When he crawled under the blanket in the luxurious king bed, he went right to sleep. The next morning, after coffee, which he found waiting for him, he went back to work. Eagle Feather had gone out already. By the time the Navajo returned, Zack was working his way through the assortment of breakfast items room service had brought earlier.

Eagle Feather came and joined him.

"Have you had any word from Lucas yet?" Zack asked.

"No. Not yet," Eagle Feather said, reaching for toast. "What have you learned?"

Zack sighed. "There are too many possibilities. Prospectors crawled all over those mountains before Kaiser Steel Corporation came in. They took over the Eagle Mountain area and mined iron ore to ship out to Kaiser's steel mill. They built the town of Eagle Mountain, that fenced-in ghost town we pass to get to the Santini & Marsh project site, to house the workers and their families. After World War II, production diminished, became sporadic, and finally the mine closed in 1983. Now here's an interesting bit. In 1986, the California Department of Corrections decided to put a private prison of low-risk prisoners in there. They converted the town's shopping mall into a prison. The experiment ended in 2003 from a combination of budget problems and a fatal riot." Zack chuckled. "Get this—the riot began while the prisoners were watching the World Series game that year. Talk about soft time!"

"Lucas said he lost the assassin's tracks near the Chuckwalla Prison."

Zack glanced at Eagle Feather, then drummed his fingers on the table. "There could be a connection. Let's file that one away to investigate."

Zack sipped some coffee. "To continue, after the prison experiment, the remaining years on that site involved just two entities—the Los Angeles Sanitation Department trying to organize a landfill there, an effort ultimately lost to red tape many years later, and the hydraulic generator project which was initially dreamed up and started by a local company called SolarVenture. They were soon bought out by EverSun."

"You do need geologists and other specialists for a landfill project," Eagle Feather observed.

"Yes, you do. I plan to concentrate my efforts on any common employees among the landfill project, SolarVenture, Santini & Marsh, and EverSun."

Eagle Feather stood, wiped some crumbs from his leather pants. "I need to see a shaman about a rock," he said. He walked to a side table, picked up a set of keys, and tossed them to Zack. "If you need to go anywhere while I am gone, that vehicle comes with the room. Just go down to the basement and use the remote to find it."

CHAPTER TWENTY-EIGHT

Jason Selder looked up from his desk at Lucy's knock. He had an open file in his hand and a stack of similar ones on his desktop.

"Yes, Lucy."

"Deputy Hagen to see you, sir," she said.

Jason put down the file, sighed, and nodded. Immediately the room was filled with the presence of Sheriff's Deputy Cliff Hagen. The deputy was a large man, a former boxer turned policeman whose muscle had softened and midriff enlarged from hours of sitting in patrol cars. His nose was flattened and knocked off-center by his former profession, but his big cheeks and blue eyes had crinkle lines from smiling. He wasn't smiling now, however.

"Always good to see you, Deputy," Jason said.

"Maybe not always," Cliff said. "I'm afraid I've got more bad news for you."

"How bad can it be?" Jason asked. He pointed to the stack of files. "These are all candidates for a temporary position for someone to ride herd on my corral of scientists. My former supervisor suddenly left on an emergency visit to some sick relative or other, leaving me with her job and mine. That comes after losing Scheidecker, wherever the hell he went. Meanwhile, without Arlene, I don't have the answers to some critical questions from those scientists and we can't move the project forward until I do! And you say you've brought more bad news?" Jason had worked up a head of steam in his short rant.

Deputy Hagen was placid. "I'm afraid so. One of your scientists, a geologist, I understand, was killed last night. His name is Ned Thomason."

Jason's jaw dropped. "Ned? Killed? Christ!"

"Murdered, in fact. We got a call from the campground out there, Coon Hollow. He was found in a trailer with its door blown out, lying on a bed, his hands tied behind him and his throat cut."

"Jesus! What's going on around here? Ned? Ned Thomason? He wouldn't harm a fly. He wouldn't know how to."

"Well, someone sure as hell didn't feel the same way toward him. I got to ask if you have any idea why someone would want to kill him? Maybe he had valuable information or something like that?"

Jason was up out of his chair now, unable to sit still. He paced a few steps back and forth in front of the file cabinet thinking about it. The deputy sat still in his chair, calm, waiting.

"Everyone here has access to delicate information regarding our project, but nothing to kill anybody over. What was he doing out at some campground?"

Hagen grunted. "We don't know, we were hoping you might know. Coon Hollow is a popular place with rock hounds, you know, people who like to collect and study rock specimens. Maybe your guy was out there for that."

"A trailer? I thought he lived in Blythe."

Hagen took out a small notebook. "You got that address?"

Jason turned back to his desk, checked a Rolodex. "Yeah, here it is. Two Four Five Zero East Hobson Way."

Hagen wrote it down. He looked up, smiled. "You should know the FBI guys are working this case. The sheriff's office is working with them, meaning we're running around doing their errands for them. But you can for sure expect a visit from one of their guys."

Jason sat down in his desk chair, suddenly very tired. "Yeah, no doubt. Thanks for that, Cliff. Keep me posted, would you?"

Hagen stood, put away the notebook, shook Jason's hand. "Sure enough will, Jason."

Even before the deputy had left the room, Jason's finger was on the intercom button. "Lucy, get Blair for me, would you? I want him here now."

Blair Schäuble was ushered into Selder's office a few minutes later. Jason didn't pull his punches.

"Ned has been murdered," he said.

"Ned? Ned Thomason?"

"We got any other Neds?"

"My God, that's terrible."

Jason stared at Schäuble. He seemed surprised, but he didn't jump out of his seat.

"What's going on in the consultant department, Blair? First Scheidecker disappears, did a runner, you thought, then Arlene abruptly rushes off to some relative's bedside, now Thomason is murdered? That's your bailiwick, Blair. You are in charge of R&D. What's going on?"

Schäuble shook his head, a slow sad movement. "It's a puzzle to me, too. At first, I thought it was just coincidence, an accident of bad timing, losing Scheidecker, and then Arlene. But now? I just don't know."

"We got any geology experts left?"

Schäuble shook his head.

"We got to have a geology expert. That's what we're messing with out there, geology." Jason's face was turning red.

"I'll get someone, Jason. I know some people. We can borrow a topnotch guy on short notice."

"Do it. I'm working on a temporary replacement for Arlene, at least I hope it's temporary. This could put us behind by weeks. By the time I get Arlene's replacement in, then get him or her up to speed, who knows how long that will be?" He leaned toward Schäuble. "Listen, Blair, I need you to work with that team of specialists right now. Okay? Top priority. We got to get this liner problem resolved."

Blair Schäuble stood and nodded. "I got it, Jason. Don't worry. I'll handle that team and I'll find a geologist."

Jason sighed. "Thanks, Blair. That makes me feel better. Keep me posted." He turned back to the stack of files on his desk and picked up the one he had been reading.

Zack was scanning newspaper articles from an extensive period covering the emergence of SolarVenture, looking for notices of appointments and hiring done by the company. He'd found this to be the best way to learn something about company personnel. He was hoping to find a familiar name, some connection to current employees at Santini & Marsh. It was slow going. He was almost relieved when his phone rang. He glanced at it, picked it up.

"Hi, Janice."

"Hello, Zack. I've got some answers to your questions about SolarVenture. I gave the assignment to Blessing, over at corporate. He did some digging and came up with some interesting facts. On the surface, SolarVenture appears to be its own entity, a Limited Liability Company. It's stated purpose is to initiate climate-friendly energy resources for sale or development. Which is exactly what they've done in this case, purchase the site, develop the plan, and begin the design of a hydropower plant. When EverSun began to show interest, they courted them and eventually sold, but retained a small interest."

"So nothing is amiss."

"Well, there's more. Blessing peeked into the structure of the company and found it had the exact same board of directors as another company, a California utility company called San Francisco Power & Light."

"Yes, I know about them. They've been in and out of bankruptcy court as a result of wildfire death and damage suits. They hadn't maintained their infrastructure, according to complaints, much of which traverses forested areas. So, you have high winds, downed lines throwing sparks in extremely dry conditions leading to fires. This inadequate maintenance comes even after they were awarded a sizable price increase a few years ago for that very purpose."

"Blessing says they are on the brink," Janice said.

"Hasn't SFP&L invested heavily in futures with EverSun?"

"That's what Blessing tells me, so those futures plus their small portion of ownership in this hydroelectric storage facility project is their lifeline. I'd say they have a pretty sizable motive for keeping secret the fact there is a potential problem near the site."

Zack agreed. "Maybe someone during the earlier days at SolarVenture discovered this geologic anomaly while designing the plant and kept it a secret. Later, after selling, they learn Scheidecker is prowling around out there and decide they have to stop him."

"That makes as much sense as anything else," Janice said. "I'll have Blessing look for personnel in common to both companies." She rang off.

Zack leaned back and thought about things. A large utility company in danger of going under could affect many people, not just employees or administrators. Stockholders, lobbyists, statesmen, politicians—the list was endless. But who would have the power to stop an FBI investigation and hire an expensive assassin? It had to be someone with a huge investment in the project, the kind of investment that could bring them down if it failed. Zack picked up his phone and called Janice back.

"Let's look at stockholders in both EverSun and SFP&L. Have Blessing get the names of the top ten in each."

"Will do."

While waiting for a response, Zack turned his mind to people who might have had reason to study the geology of the place, the prospectors, and scientists. He called Arlene. Her voice sounded drowsy when she answered.

"Are you sleeping in?" Zack asked.

Arlene snorted. "I'm afraid I could develop some bad habits with this kind of life. What happened to you last night?"

"We started working and, well, just never stopped. I'm still at it."

"Have you turned up anything?"

Zack could hear liquid pouring in the background, imagined the cup of hot coffee. "Nothing solid yet, but we may have found a company with a sizable motive to keep that ancient oasis a secret. Do you know if anyone currently working at Santini & Marsh, particularly one of your scientists, ever worked for either SolarVenture or San Francisco Power & Light?"

"Umm, I'd have to think about that. Can I use the internet to access my work files?"

"Absolutely not, Arlene. No internet, no telephone calls on that phone except to one of us. I hope that's clear."

'Yeah, yeah, it's clear. Sorry. Okay, I have some stuff in my briefcase that might stir my memory. Give me a while to wake up already. I'll call you." She hung up.

Zack grinned. Here was a woman who couldn't stand *not* to be doing something productive. He figured she was compelled to either work hard or sleep, but nothing in between.

As he turned back to the computer, he remembered SB 772, the California Senate bill that had been tabled, waiting for just the right pork barrel to drop in. The senator who authored that bill was pushing hard to mandate California to purchase a minimum of reserve power by the end date 2023. The bill was worded in such a way to make it a criminal offense not to meet the time limit. Although the bill had been set aside, the wording, in Zack's opinion, suggested the author was strongly motivated to force the state to purchase a lot of additional energy.

Zack leaned back in his chair. A lot of political power resided in the California Senate, he mused. Was it enough power to, say, call off an FBI investigation? Maybe, if the people behind the bill were well enough connected. Zack googled California Senate Bill 772, found the name of the author, and almost fell out of his chair. The name was Edwin Marsh.

Could this Senator Marsh be related to the Marsh of Santini & Marsh Construction & Design? Zack never doubted it for a moment. He tapped his fingers on the table. Still, did it really matter? Other than a bit of shady self-interest, something not unheard of in politics, he couldn't prove anything criminal going on here.

Zack thought through a possible scenario. Suppose you owned a large construction company with the capability to design and build large, seldom attempted projects. There weren't that many around, but if you could find one, it could potentially send your company to the Fortune 500. Suppose you look around, you see shortfalls in energy in your state where wildfires have knocked out infrastructure forcing electric cutbacks, a major utility company is in danger of going under, and what is California to do? Maybe a large energy storage facility was needed, one that Santini & Marsh was eminently qualified to build.

Zack puzzled over the next part. How could Marsh have known of the old Kaiser Mine Site and its potentiality for a massive generator? Then it came to him. What if Santini and Marsh had been bidding for the LASD landfill project contract, wasting lots of time and money, watching a great opportunity slowly fizzle. What if, because of his close watch on the situation, not to speak of inside information available to him in his political post, Marsh figured out this upstart SolarVenture company, the one that bought the old Kaiser site, was in actuality a shell company invented by San Francisco Power & Light? What if Marsh saw an opportunity to get in on the ground floor, knowing SFP&L had no intention of building the plant but instead wanted to sell the idea of the project to a huge corporation that actually could afford to build it and in the process cut out a piece for themselves and assure access to a large source of future supplemental power?

If I were Marsh, Zack thought, and I was a California State Senator, I could contact a huge corporation like EverSun with its clean fuel energy projects, bring in SFP&L, cut a deal, and then author a bill such as SB 772. Even if it never passed, it might get several readings over the years, might stay alive just long enough to ensure the start of a project like the EverSun hydroelectric battery. Of course, the Santini & Marsh bid on the project would win.

Now Zack needed to connect the Marshes. As a public figure, Edwin Marsh was discoverable. It seemed he had a wife of twenty-four years and three children, two girls and a boy. His father, deceased, had been an architect of some renown. He had two sisters and one brother, who was...*here it comes*...Ervin Marsh, co-owner and CEO of Santini & Marsh Construction & Design.

So far, Zack's theory was holding together. There was no doubt in his mind Edwin was a silent partner with his brother Ervin. It was a family business.

Next Zack looked up the corporate record of Santini & Marsh, found the company had been started when Santini Construction merged with Marsh Design, apparently old man Marsh's outfit, then run by the two sons, Marsh senior having died. It was a natural marriage of two different yet supportive capabilities. The original Santini passed some years after the merge, but the name, and undoubtedly the family stockholding, were kept. Meanwhile, the Marsh brothers took over the day to day running of the business. It would have been natural for one of the brothers to enter politics, after visibly disengaging from the family business to prevent any conflict of interest complaints.

Pieces were falling into place. But questions remained. Who knew about the geological timebomb at the lost oasis? And who among all these possible candidates was so desperate to conceal a potential project-ending flaw as to resort to kidnapping and murder?

CHAPTER TWENTY-NINE

Eagle Feather felt the phone buzzing in his pocket, saw he was adjacent to a Starbucks store, and pulled into the parking area. In his mind, it was fortuitous the call had come when it did, for he had decided a Grandé coffee with a splash of sugar was just what his spirits needed. Seeing the call was from Lucas, he postponed the coffee momentarily and called the Chemehuevi tracker right back.

"Hello, Eagle Feather. I have some news."

"What is it, Lucas?"

"I believe killer man entered the Chuckawalla State Prison and spent the night there."

"That is surprising."

"I, too, was surprised. He left early this morning."

"Have you tracked him?"

"Yes, but only to the freeway. It is impossible to know if he went east or west. I have put out the word among my people to watch for him. Now I must wait."

"I am on my way to see George Madrigal," Eagle Feather said. "I will call my boss and ask him to learn how this man could enter and leave a prison at will."

"I, too, am on my way to the casino. I will see you there."

Eagle Feather walked into the Starbucks and went to the counter. The young woman took his order and flashed a wide smile. Eagle Feather often stirred such reactions with his black leather pants and vest and his reservation hat adorned with a single eagle feather. Many people assumed he was a movie star by his costume. The coffee du jour, Pike's Place, was his favorite and after adding sugar, he brought it out to the Yamaha and filled a thermos he kept in the saddlebag. He then continued his ride down Twentynine Palms Highway. It was a beautiful day for a ride, the sun just hot enough in this early edge of the morning to assuage the cold wind and the air quality pure as spring water. The desert's heaped boulders and Joshua trees stood out in bold relief. It must have been on such a day as this First Man and First Woman emerged from the lower world, Eagle Feather decided.

Twenty minutes later, he pulled into the parking lot of Tortoise Rock Casino. He removed the thermos from this saddlebag and enjoyed a long sip of the hot beverage. Inside, he skirted the one-arm bandits and walked to the cashier counter.

"Is George Madrigal available? I am Eagle Feather."

The girl picked up a phone, spoke, then smiled. "Go on in, sir."

Eagle Feather walked to the manager's office and knocked. He heard George's voice call him in. When he entered, he saw that Lucas was already there. The big man was sprawled in a leather chair, his leg hanging over the arm. He gave Eagle Feather a big smile.

"Lucas has been telling me about your near-miss last night," George said. "This man...this killer...must be caught and dealt with."

Eagle Feather slid into the chair next to Lucas. "It was as if he knew we were coming," he said.

"Why do you say so?"

Eagle Feather ticked the points off on his fingers. "The phone with the location app was by the side of the road when Agent Tolliver arrived, but the scientist and his truck were gone. Who threw it away? The scientist or the killer? One of them must have known the location app was in the phone." He put up another finger. "I went a different way to Wiley's Well Campground, and I believe I surprised them there. They were out in the wash ready to escape on an ATV. Yet they waited. I believe their escape was timed for Agent Tolliver to pursue them." Third finger up. "How did the man know Agent Tolliver would come to find the scientist in the first place? Again, he must have known about the location app."

George frowned. "So you are saying the killer knew about the app, knew when the scientist went off course Agent Tolliver would come to investigate."

"Yes," Eagle Feather said. "How did he know about the app? I believe only Zack and I and the FBI knew about it."

"Well, it wasn't you and it wasn't Agent Tolliver who told him. That means the leak had to have come from the FBI," George said. The three men sat quietly for a moment, considering the implications.

Finally, Lucas said, "I do not need to tell you how difficult this has become. Who can we trust?"

George agreed with his investigator. "No offense to you, Eagle Feather, but perhaps we need to go back to two separate investigations."

Eagle Feather peered from under creased eyebrows. "Yes, you can not know how much of what you tell me will end up at the FBI and be leaked. That is fair. I can tell you this. Zack Tolliver is not an ordinary FBI agent. When he learns of this, he will stop sharing with the FBI and will act alone. He has done so before."

"Can you rely on that if your life depends upon it?" Lucas stared at Eagle Feather.

Eagle Feather nodded. "I can. And I have." His gaze went to each man in turn. "Let me invite him to meet with us. I think he will convince you."

The two Chemehuevi agreed to a meeting. Eagle Feather called Zack to explain the situation. Zack immediately agreed to come to the casino.

Eagle Feather and Lucas wandered off to the café for a late breakfast while they waited for Zack, and left George to his casino tasks. The new meeting was set for eleven a.m. The intervening hour rolled by quickly. Eagle Feather found Lucas to be a most interesting man, a former Special Forces sergeant who had traveled widely, but also a Native American whose instincts and abilities kept him close to nature and spirituality. They had much in common.

On their way back to George's office, they saw Zack at the main entrance and went to greet him. The FBI agent was standing there bemused by the amount of business at that hour, with people crowding tables, machines making a constant din with their bells and dings, and occasional whistles.

Lucas shook Zack's hand. "I am happy to see you looking well this morning," he said. He noticed Zack's look. "The noise seems loud now, but after a while, you do not hear it."

Zack grinned. "It amazes me so many people have so much time and money."

"Maybe they do not but pretend that they do," Eagle Feather said.

Madrigal's door was open. They walked on in.

George rose to greet Zack and ushered him to a seat. Lucas and Eagle Feather found two other chairs and the meeting began. Madrigal leveled his gaze on Zack.

"I have a serious concern," he said.

"Go on."

"We do not allow other casinos to advertise in our parking lot."

Lucas and Eagle Feather were startled by this, but Zack simply chuckled. "You need to blame him," he said, pointing at Eagle Feather.

George beckoned Lucas and Eagle Feather to his window. In the parking lot close to the door of the casino was a car painted in wide yellow, orange, and blue stripes, with large letters proclaiming the Morongo Casino. The colors were so bright they almost seemed to be a light source of their own.

Eagle Feather glanced at Zack, shrugged. "Sorry, man."

"It's the perfect ride for an FBI agent wishing to be inconspicuous," Zack said.

When everyone was seated again, Zack spoke. "Eagle Feather has explained your concerns to me. I understand your hesitation to confide in us now. However, before we decide how we will go forward, may I ask you some questions?"

"Of course," George said.

"You believe the assassin knew about the app I placed in Ned's phone. You think everything that happened last night was predicated on that fact. But what if the assassin simply followed Ned and captured him along the road, threw his phone into the brush where we later found it so he could not call for help, then forced Thomason to drive to the campground where they left his truck. He then forced Thomason onto his ATV, where Eagle Feather and Lucas consequently saw them." Zack glanced at the Navajo. "Eagle Feather will tell you I am not one to readily accept coincidence, but in this case, it may well have been just that."

"You present a convincing story," Madrigal said. "But I must tell you, it was your colleague Eagle Feather who convinced us otherwise."

Zack looked again at Eagle Feather. Eagle Feather did not return his look.

Lucas spoke instead. "Let me ask you a question," he said to Zack. "How did the assassin know this Thomason would be driving down Wiley's Well Road at exactly that time?"

"Maybe he didn't accost Ned on Wiley's Well Road, but at the rest stop, or along the interstate where he knew Thomason would have to pass on his way home from work."

Madrigal leaned toward Zack. "Without some kind of prearrangement, it would still have been difficult to time an abduction along the highway or, for that matter, to bring it off without attracting a lot of attention. And where was the assassin's other vehicle? He would have needed one to do that. The ATV was in the wash, remember. He couldn't stand out there like a hitchhiker waving a gun. The second vehicle problem holds for the rest area as well, even if he had some idea Thomason would stop there, which he had little reason to do while heading home from work. But he would not have needed a second vehicle to leave his ATV at Wiley's Well Campground and walk out to the road at the point we found Thomason's phone. It's not all that far, from what I understand. But he would have needed to know exactly when Thomason was coming. Someone told him not just about the app, but about Thomason's movements."

Zack was silent, lost in thought. He stirred. "You're right. I see no way the killer could have known where and when to intercept Thomason unless"—he paused and looked at the other three men—"unless he was in collusion with the killer."

"Wait. What?" Madrigal scratched his head. "Why would a man be in collusion with his own killer?"

"He didn't expect to be killed, of course," Zack said. "But in the killer's mind, Thomason's usefulness had come to an end. The killer had one final job for him, to lure me to my death."

"Why would Thomason work with the assassin?"

"He may have had no choice. Remember how Eagle Feather caught him watching him in Great Wash? It could be the killer, or perhaps whoever hired the killer, had something they held over Thomason's head."

"And the phone in the brush?" Lucas asked.

"You are right there. The killer must have known about the app and once he met Thomason on the road, made him throw the phone away. We know Thomason didn't know about it or he would not have exposed his meeting with the black SUV. Someone fed the information about the app to the killer." Zack sighed. "It could only have been someone in the FBI. I have told no one but Eagle Feather."

Madrigal studied Zack's face. "Why not let Thomason keep the app and lead you directly to the campground? Why throw it away sooner and risk the chance you wouldn't go there?"

Zack gave a rueful smile. "I suspect that's the genius of this man, the subtlety. He knew we'd check out the area on a map before going there. We'd see the phone and presume Thomason was sitting in the middle of nowhere. He knew that would galvanize us into action. Once we located the phone all by itself, we'd see the campground within a reasonable distance. Of course, we'd go check out the campground."

"That man wants you real bad," Lucas said.

"Which may help us in the end," Zack said. "I sense the loss of his female colleague, maybe someone close to him has unhinged him a bit. He could have quietly eliminated Ned and left him in that trailer with no one the wiser for a long time. But he wanted vengeance on me and took extra risks to try to kill me as well."

Madrigal shifted his body in his chair. "So? Other questions? Where do we stand?"

"In a dung heap, from my perspective," Zack said, his voice quiet but intense. "The app I transferred to Thomason's phone is an FBI tool, but because it intrudes upon personal freedoms its use is restricted. I had to order it through my superior who followed a lengthy protocol. To put it simply, a fair number of people higher up in the judicial branch of the FBI would have known about it and its purpose."

"And you think one of them may be your leak. You now see our concern, Agent Tolliver."

Zack nodded. "And you propose we each go our own way with our investigations."

"Unless…" Madrigal glanced at Eagle Feather. "Unless, as Eagle Feather has suggested, you can keep the FBI in the dark about our progress."

Zack glanced at Eagle Feather, gave a wry grin. "I cannot deliberately mislead the agency. And I trust my immediate superior implicitly."

"So…where are we?" Madrigal asked.

Zack laughed. "My superior refers to Eagle Feather as the 'Indian who does not exist' meaning she maintains deniability that he works with me. It has served a purpose in the past and may do so again." He looked around the group. "I propose Eagle Feather continue to work closely with Lucas. They can choose what to tell me, what they think I need to know. My reports to my superior can include only what I know. Is that sufficient to allay your concerns?"

Madrigal looked at Lucas, who nodded. "I can work with Eagle Feather," he said.

"Done, then!" Madrigal said. "What now?" he asked Zack.

"I may have a way to draw out the assassin. I will need your support for it to work. I cannot tell you the details yet, but as the plan develops, Eagle Feather will keep you informed."

"Fair enough," Madrigal said. "And what about your FBI leak?"

"We intend to root it out."

CHAPTER THIRTY

Agent in Charge Janice Hooper was not a happy person. She had been the one to convince Zack Tolliver to rejoin the agency in the first place. She understood his unusual gifts, his ability to cross many cultural divides, his willingness to adopt methods outside the sometimes confining, scripted practices of the FBI. She believed such independence of mind was critical to the agency and had fought to create a Department of Special Cases and place Zack in charge, reinstating him with the rank of Supervisory Agent. Yet Zack had resisted, protesting he needed more time with his family to heal a developing breach in his marriage. Then Janice had promised he could work from home with a minimal caseload at first, even allowing him to decide which cases he would take. But it wasn't until she revealed to him that his wife Libby had already given her support to the idea, that he had agreed.

Initially, he had turned down more cases than he had accepted, cases he felt did not tap into his special talents, cases sent his way by agents who simply wished to be rid of them for one reason or another. But those few cases he accepted had been success stories that had expanded his reputation in the agency, not to speak of her own. Janice was confident no agent other than Zack Tolliver could have reached beyond the strange and improbable circumstances in those cases to draw out the truth. No one but Zack and his Indian friend. Gradually the agency had come to see the wisdom of Janice's choice.

But now Zack, his department, and Janice herself were being undermined by someone cloaked within the agency. Someone over her head, privy to details of this case, was doing everything possible to obstruct her progress. She had promised Zack near perfect working conditions to bring him back, and now someone was undermining his safety, her credibility, and, so far as she was concerned, everything the agency stood for.

She was not about to let it go. She leaned across the shimmering surface of her nearly empty desk and plucked a Cross silver and gold plated ballpoint pen from its slender holder. She turned to the bound moleskin notebook open on her otherwise empty desktop, and wrote "who?"

That was a difficult question. Janice necessarily worked with a myriad of people on every case. She needed all sorts of specialists—forensics, firearms, explosive device experts, experts in language, culture, biology, and so on, and so on. This case was no different. Up until she was made aware of the breach in this case, she'd engaged firearm experts, explosive experts, fingerprint and identification experts, trolled Interpol, searched out FBI safe houses, engaged vehicles, sent questions on up the line. Anyone within the agency who wanted to know about the case could easily have satisfied themselves.

But once the Scheidecker case had been terminated somewhere far above her pay scale, she realized she had a big problem. She'd learned from Zack that almost every move he'd made against the assassin had been anticipated as if the killer had been informed in advance. He'd pointed to the cell phone listening app she'd authorized for him, claimed the assassin had to have known about it, and possibly even used the information to his advantage. It was Janice's job to support her agent in the field and with leaks everywhere, she was failing. Yeah, she was pissed.

Janice perched forward on the edge of her leather office chair, her legs together under her tidy plain gray skirt, her back straight as a rose trellis, and considered the problem. She knew she had to tighten the circle of those who had information about the case to a small, easily controlled number. Her first step had been to reassign her niece, Sarah, to Zack's case. Sarah had been assigned out of the academy to the St. George office at Janice's request and although an agent of just two years experience, the girl showed strong potential and maturity beyond her years. But Janice's foremost reason for choosing her for this mission was she could trust her, pure and simple. Next, she had found a safe house in Blythe not yet on the Agency lists, known only to her. Fortuitously, she had been the sole purchasing agent and had not yet advanced the paperwork. It was the perfect place to deposit their one and only witness still living, with Sarah there to guard her. She had purchased throw-away cell phones, limited them to calls to team members only, calls that would be concealed from the Agency. The app she had authorized for Zack to use had predated these precautions, and now the damage was done, including the death of a potential witness. She hoped there were no more hanging chads such as that to worry about. While the damage was contained, the danger was not eliminated.

Now Janice looked at the question she'd just written in her notebook. "Who?" Who indeed? She decided to think about a mid-level administrator, someone with sources on the ground but higher access within the agency. She began with a hypothetical question—how might one go about shutting down an FBI investigation? Although such an action in itself was not unprecedented, it tended to occur in high politics, when a sitting president needed to control an outcome, for example. Not so much perverting justice in some minds, perhaps, just not following the thread to the end. At least that was the rationale. And the Scheidecker case had not been the usual sort of investigation for the FBI, the grounds were tenuous. The case had been taken up due to local politics in the first place, which made it that much easier for the agency to dismiss.

Regardless, Janice knew the pressure had to have come from the very pinnacle of politics. No one else could cause the FBI Director to dismiss a case so swiftly, so abruptly, no matter how insignificant it might seem in the scheme of things. That kind of pressure would have come from a large lobby or corporation or group to which POTUS owed a political favor. EverSun potentially fit that description.

But someone must have facilitated the process from within, someone with the ear of the director. That same someone had access to details of Zack's work in real-time, was aware of the phone app, maybe part of the approval chain, and had enough technical knowledge to reverse the app to reveal Thomason's moment to moment location for the assassin. This person might also be the assassin's operator. Janice needed to find a way to uncover this person.

One thing still nagged Janice. She couldn't quite square the matter of motive. Of course, it was vitally important to EverSun to prevent knowledge of a geologic flaw that had the potential to render the entire project useless. If word of it got out, EverSun would probably have to give up the project, at a great loss. Still, she thought, it wouldn't be the first time a huge corporation faced such a circumstance, nor would it be the last. No doubt they were heavily insured against such possibilities. Janice was familiar with EverSun's financial status. The corporation owned two utility companies that poured revenue into the communal chest and easily balanced the ebb and flow of EverSun's research and development corporate arms. Somehow, murder, kidnapping, hired assassins just didn't seem to fit the picture for EverSun. Janice thought about the other company involved, Santini & Marsh, and decided they didn't have the political clout to influence POTUS.

Her head was spinning. The possibilities were overwhelming. Janice needed to simplify her approach. She walked to her window and stared out. Clouds sailed timelessly in a perfect blue sky. The forecast was for heat, lots of it. The people far below traversing the campus had already shed their sweaters and jackets. Inside, though, it was cool and comfortable.

Janice decided to start by tracing her request for the surveillance cellphone app she had obtained for Zack. She would track the identity of everyone involved in the process, person by person, moment by moment. She walked back to her chair, sat down, and turned to the side table where her laptop awaited her.

Her burner phone rang.

"Hello, Zack."

"Hi, Janice. Do you know a California State Senator named Edwin Marsh?"

"No. But I'm sure you will enlighten me."

"He is a very influential man. More to the point, he is the author of Bill #772 in the California State Senate which, had it passed, would mandate California to invest heavily in reserve energy by a fixed date which corresponds neatly with the completion date for the Eagle Mountain project. Oh, and his brother's name is Ervin Marsh. He is CEO and majority owner of Santini & Marsh Construction and Design."

"But the bill didn't pass?"

"No, but it hung around long enough for the project to be launched."

"I see." Janice paused to think. "Do you think this Senator Marsh has enough influence to cause POTUS to pressure the director to call off the investigation?"

There was a short silence. "On the surface, I'd have to say no. But he certainly knows people who do. By the way, you've no doubt discovered by now that SolarVenture, the company that originated the project at Eagle Mountain and then sold to EverSun, is a shell for San Francisco Power & Light?"

"Ah, the California utility that's facing bankruptcy from wildfire suits?"

"The same."

'Zack, I think you've just solved my motive problem. Thank you."

Janice hung up. She had no doubt now that SFP&L was behind the coverup. She had heard enough about the company problems, even knew agents who had investigated the company for various dodgy acts in its attempt to stay alive. If this California utility was involved with the EverSun project, and from what Zack had just told her it certainly was, it had enough motivation to satisfy her. She turned back to her computer and began to search for links between SFP&L and FBI agents assigned to the Information and Technology Branch. She remembered she had an ace in the hole in Agent Kent Schmidt, a former colleague who admired more than just her intelligence. She knew he still carried a fairly large torch for her.

He answered at the first ring. "Janice, how nice."

She chuckled. "That will depend, I suppose."

"Don't tell me you didn't call just to whisper sweet nothings in my ear."

"I called to ask you to whisper some sweet somethings into my ear, in fact."

Kent gave an exaggerated groan of despair. "It's always business before pleasure with you."

"Whoa, there, boy, it's always business."

"So I have nothing to dream about. Alas! I'll just have to carry this burden. But meanwhile, how can I help?"

"Kent, this needs to be on the QT. Big brother is looking over my shoulder."

"Of course, Janice. Since it's you asking."

"I was hoping you'd feel that way. I need to know anyone in your department who may have any kind of connection with San Francisco Power & Light. Any connection at all."

"Hmm. SFP&L, eh? Can I call you in ten?"

"You have my number."

"Wish that I did!"

When Schmidt rang off, Janice turned back to her computer screen. She searched for cases involving SFP&L over the last decade. There were many, far more than she expected for a single company, even though the utility company was large, servicing most of California.

She sighed. This was not going to be as easy as she had hoped. A glance at the company's history surprised her. It had been in existence in one form or another literally since the gold rush. Following the 1906 San Francisco earthquake, nearly every competitor had been eliminated while SFP&L managed to survive through remote facilities and a lot of capital. In 1999 the company reorganized as a holding company maintaining the regulated utility, and adding a non-regulated energy business. At about the same time, the company sold off most of its gas plants, and in so doing limited its own electricity generating capacity, which caused them to have to purchase it from other energy generating sources.

It was during this decade SFP&L was found responsible for a series of damaging fires linked to poor vegetation management and insufficient infrastructure maintenance and found guilty of criminal negligence, up to eight hundred counts for one fire alone. Drought and the subsequent reduced hydroelectric power available for purchase, new regulation of consumer prices, and rolling blackouts all caused SFP&L to purchase out of state energy at great cost without contracts until the inevitable bankruptcy filing in 2000. The utility entered into another bankruptcy proceeding following more fires later in 2019. The list of fires and disasters attributed to the utility company during this time marched across Janice's monitor like bird tracks in creek mud. There were investigations of collusion, 'judge shopping,' violation of state laws, falsification of records, illegal dumping, and dodging taxes. At some level, FBI agents had been involved in investigations involving SFP&L in dozens of cases over the decade. Where to begin?

She decided to begin at the end. She looked at the most recent investigations. These included falsification of "locate and mark" records, forms created then predated in an attempt to hide the lack of warning signs in locations where near-surface gas lines were vulnerable to digging. The investigation had involved hundreds of hours of record checks by a team of auditors, overseen by FBI agents. Why FBI, she wondered? This should be a state province, not federal. Digging deeper, she found people had died from explosions caused by digging into unmarked gas lines on systems bringing gas from other states, crossing state lines. It was a morass. She listed every FBI agent involved in this case over the years. It took her an hour to search them all out. The result was a list of twenty different agents.

Janice sighed. At this rate, the prospect of weaning the list down to a single agent most connected to SFP&L was looking hopeless. Then her phone rang. It was Agent Schmidt.

"I've got something for you," he said.

"Thank heaven," Janice said. "What have you got?"

"It's a who," he said. "The who is Special Agent Carl Santini."

CHAPTER THIRTY-ONE

"You're damn right I'll do it. All I ask is a shot at the guy before you take him away." Arlene's nostrils flared like a charging bull as she glared across the lunch table at Zack. A plate of sandwiches cut into quarters with a variety of fillings adorned the center of the table.

Sarah and Arlene had been busy that morning with their mini think tank, peeling back Arlene's memory to the days before Scheidecker's disappearance. After both admitted exhaustion from the effort, they had gone into the kitchen to prepare a late lunch. They never knew how many people to expect for a meal, so they erred on the side of bountiful. Meanwhile, Zack had returned the vividly colored Morongo Casino vehicle to the casino garage and arranged a ride to Blythe, where Sarah had picked him up in the truck just in time for lunch.

Now Zack nodded, not surprised at Arlene's response. He had expected nothing less but was gratified she was willing to risk her life, at least on paper, to trap the killer. The plan was still hazy in his mind, but it was important to confirm all the players would be in place. Eagle Feather was not with them for lunch, having said something about visiting a shaman after their meeting at the casino, but Zack knew he could count on him. Sarah's role would be backup and extraction if it proved necessary.

After a dessert of cupcakes, Arlene cleared the table, and Sarah and Zack adjourned to the living room to discuss the morning's findings. Sarah opened her notebook and looked at Zack. "What would you like to know?"

Zack was again struck by the similarities between Sarah and Janice, niece and aunt, the sparkling curious eyes, brilliant smiles, and poised trim figures. "I guess I'd like to have a sense of how Santini & Marsh operated at the project site, you know, in terms of personnel relationships. Who seemed most connected to upper management, who held the company line, which manager was closest to Arlene's consultant group, that kind of thing."

Sarah didn't need to glance at her notes. "Arlene said Blair Schäuble was the man directly above her. He was responsible for the consultants and he reported directly to the project manager, Jason Selder. Schäuble's other responsibility was to the construction crew. Arlene says he spent more time with the job boss, a man named Ed Fitzgerald than with her, although lately, he'd been checking on her more frequently and even attended one of her morning consultant meetings, a rare appearance, apparently. But it was not uncommon for Arlene to go directly to Selder with news or a problem. He pretty much demanded to be kept current with her department news, no matter what."

"A hard-ass?"

"She says not so much that, he just wanted information in hand in real-time as much as possible."

"Did she get along with Selder?"

"Yeah, basically. He could blow when things went south, but mostly he was a good boss, to her mind."

"And Schäuble? What did she think of him?"

Sarah smiled. "A weasel. Arlene didn't hide the fact she didn't like him. She saw him as sneaky, underhanded, never said what he really meant, that kind of thing."

"She didn't trust him?"

"Not at all."

Zack scratched his head. "Selder has an administrative secretary, I recall. What does Arlene think about her?"

Sarah had to check her notes this time. "Her name is Lucy Martin. Arlene didn't say much about her. She was just kind of there, you know?"

"Good at her job?"

Arlene happened to be passing by. She paused and answered for Sarah. "Real good. She guarded her boss well, kept you out if he was too busy, ushered you in if she felt he wanted to see you. One of those mind reader type administrative secretaries. She would take the initiative when she had to. Very polished."

"You liked her."

Arlene perched on the couch arm. "Not so much that I liked her, more like admiring a piece of equipment that functions well."

"What about the CEO, Erwin Marsh. Did you know him?"

Arlene raised her eyebrows. "Mr. Marsh? He might have visited two, maybe three times during my entire employment there."

"Any time recently?"

Arlene nodded. "Yes, he showed up a couple of days after Scheidecker disappeared."

"Who did he talk to?"

"Well, Selder, mostly. Schäuble was lurking about the whole time, trying to be noticed."

"Did you see him arrive?"

"No, I didn't. He probably arrived while I was holding my consultant meeting, which was pretty tense at the time. I learned later he was there."

"Who told you?"

"The weasel, Schäuble. He came to my office and told me I'd better be on my toes, the big boss was here."

"So Mr. Schäuble tried to be noticed, you say?"

'He sucked up big time. But Mr. Marsh didn't seem to notice him, much to his disappointment."

"Mr. Marsh spent most of his time with Jason Selder, then."

Arlene nodded. "Yeah, except when he toured around the place. Then Lucy escorted him."

Zack's head came up. "Isn't that unusual?"

Arlene shook her head. "Not really. She knows everything about the business. I guess Jason figured if she played tour guide the people with real work could keep at it."

"Sounds like he trusted her completely."

"We all did," Arlene said.

Zack leaned back in his seat, thinking. After a moment he said, "Arlene, if I wanted some information to get to

Mr. Erwin Marsh's ear on the QT, from someone he'd believe enough to take it seriously, who would I tell?"

Arlene stared at Zack, considering. "You mean unofficially?"

"Right."

She grimaced. "Well, if he thought it would benefit him, the little rat Schäuble would try to contact him in a heartbeat."

'Bypass Selder?"

"Absolutely. But the question is, do you want Mr. Marsh to believe the information? He probably wouldn't even read Schäuble's email."

Zack shook his head. "No, we need him to have confidence in the source."

"But it can't be Selder, right? Because that would make it official."

"Right."

Arlene raised an eyebrow. "I know where you're going here. You're thinking about Lucy. You think maybe she has a connection with Mr. Marsh."

"What do you think? By your account, she spends a lot of time with him when he visits. I assume she talks to him or his administrative assistant a lot as part of her job."

"I'm sure she does."

"Would she pass information to Marsh without telling Selder?"

Arlene shrugged. "I'm sure it would depend on the information."

Zack tugged his chin. "But she might share gossipy information with Marsh's admin secretary. People in those jobs sometimes establish their own connections."

Arlene grinned. "And his admin secretary just might mention it to Mr. Marsh."

"Exactly."

Arlene stood and put her hands on her hips. "Okay, Mr. FBI man, don't you think it's about time you told us what information you want to be passed along?"

Dr. Silvia Mike said she'd be delighted to meet with Eagle Feather, and would one o'clock work for him? She had appointments up until that time. They agreed to meet at the Oasis of Mara, a short distance from her office. For Eagle Feather, it was also a short distance from the Tortoise Rock Casino where he'd just met with George Madrigal, and now with a half-hour to kill, he stopped in at Denny's, a favorite spot. His lunch there wasn't far different from the breakfast he'd had less than two hours previously, and if he had his way, dinner would be similar as well. He was a breakfast man. The half-hour disappeared, and by the time he was climbing back on his motorcycle, he was in danger of being late.

Dr. Mike was waiting at the shaded entry to the park. Eagle Feather almost missed her in the throng of tourists. Like them, she wore jeans and an embroidered white blouse, a straw hat with flowers in the headband, and sandals. She clutched a leather pouch with drawstring closure in one hand and put the other hand in the air as a gesture to Eagle Feather.

"You did not seem to recognize me," she said.

"It took a moment," Eagle Feather said. "I last saw you in your dental office. You looked different."

She smiled. "A look for every environment. Perhaps I am like the chameleon."

They walked side by side past the visitor center entrance and out into the bright sun of the desert.

Silvia waved an arm. "This once was the soul of my people." She pointed across the oasis sand. "The casino over there is now the soul of my people, I fear."

"Yet it sustains you."

She nodded. "It does, in the manner white people like to be sustained. The native people are capable of sustaining themselves."

"But not in a white man's world."

A shadow passed over her face. "Yes, that is so."

They walked along the concrete path. Ahead loomed the first palms of the oasis, but where they walked was dry sand dotted with cacti and cholla. Far in the distance across the level barrenness Eagle Feather could see homes, a church, and other buildings of the reservation. To the south, outlined in gray, were the hills that guarded the canyon and highway leading to Great Wash.

Silvia glanced at Eagle Feather. "Did you go back to Great Wash after we last spoke?"

Eagle Feather nodded. "I did. The tracks were no clearer. They might have been as you say, or they might not." He shrugged. "The ground was hard and many people had been there." He did not mention the attempt on his life. Did she know, he wondered?

Her face gave no sign. "What did you wish to discuss?" she asked.

They had arrived at the oasis and the shade of the first palms. Here there was a bench. They sat in silence. Eagle Feather listened to the light breeze rustle through the palms, smelled the dry sweetness of decay. He peered up at the palm crowns. Some were withered and brown.

"These palms are dying. Few of the original twenty-nine palms planted by my people are still here," Silvia said. "It was not always like this." She reached her hand out and lay it gently on Eagle Feather's arm. Her fingers were long, delicate, graceful.

At her touch, a change came over Eagle Feather. His heart pounded and his blood surged. A new scent came to his nostrils, fresh, musty, vibrantly alive. New sounds came to his ears, growing, a babble, children's voices far away, adult voices calling to them in words he could not understand, distant chopping sounds, splashes, bustling, noisy living sounds. The palm crowns upon which his gaze was fixed grew full and green, others appeared where none had been before until the intense blue sky was but a small island through the swaying green. He looked down. The mud and dust and choked rottenness had become a large pool of emerald green water where skitter bugs and

297

dragonflies played. Eagle Feather was overcome with a feeling of wellbeing, a fullness, a sense of gratitude.

He felt the light touch on his arm removed.

"The younger palms are replacements," Silvia was saying. Her voice seemed tiny and distant, then grew until it came stronger in his ear. "Just as my people are dying and being replaced."

Eagle Feather glanced at her. "I think you have adapted well to the change. You walk two paths." He looked back at the Oasis of Mara and saw it was as he had first seen it.

She gave a sad smile. "Not with gladness, through necessity."

"What would you wish for your people today?"

"My people must not forget what we are. We must keep our language alive. We must remember the old songs, passed down from the very beginning. When our ancestors call to us, we must hear them." She shook her head. "Many of the young people today forget this. That"—she gestured in the direction of the casino—"draws them away. Drink draws them away."

Eagle Feather regarded the tall palms before them pensively. "The Navajo young people also seek new roads. They resort to alcohol and often choose the dark road. But we too have the casinos. The money the wealthy whites spend there helps our schools, where we teach our culture and language, and it helps to build museums, where we have displays that reestablish pride in our heritage." He looked at her. "The casino is not a bad thing in itself, it can be a means to those things you wish for."

Silvia stared ahead. "It could be so, but only if those who lead us remember why it was built." She turned her face toward Eagle Feather abruptly, as if discarding her last thoughts. "You are a spiritual man, I think. It is time for you to witness a *tavan'nawigyah,* a Calling of the Sun. It will happen tomorrow morning." Her eyes caught his. "Do you have the courage?"

"What is it?"

"It is a ceremony of healing. I have a patient. He was struck blind by sun exposure during a daytime drinking bout. He was sent to the hospital, where he recovered from all aspects of alcohol poisoning except the blindness, which the doctors have told him is permanent damage to his retinas. He has come to me."

"You can heal him?" Eagle Feather's tone was not one of surprise for he had seen Navajo Singers do as much.

She smiled. "Hopefully. I can call on the power of the sun to undo what it has done to the boy. If my familiar comes to me and is willing, this can happen."

"I am honored. I would like to see this."

"Meet us at *Ta'va Ma'ma'u,* the ancient Sun Pillar in Great Wash." She smiled again. "I think you know where it is. The ceremony will begin in the early hours, with just my patient. The relatives will come one hour before sunrise. You may come then."

She stood.

Eagle Feather also stood. "You asked me if I had the courage? Why?"

Silvia had begun to walk away, stopped, turned back to him. As she stood in the contrasting light of palm shadow and unfiltered sunlight, her face appeared as a dark mask with her eyes and teeth glistening strangely from behind it. "You never asked me what you came to ask. If you attend the ceremony tomorrow, and if you have the courage to witness all that happens, you will have your answers."

CHAPTER THIRTY-TWO

"What information do you want me to pass along?" Arlene had asked. Zack knew the answer to this was critical. It must be important enough to draw the assassin to some remote location where they could apprehend him. It needed to be something the assassin wanted above all else. But what? A lot of money, perhaps? More than he was already making? How much might that be? Probably more than Zack or the FBI could raise. What else?

And then it came to him. Zack suddenly realized what it was the assassin wanted more than anything else in the world right now.

His phone interrupted the thought. He glanced at it. It was Janice.

"You've caught me at an auspicious moment," Zack said.

"Hello to you, too," Janice said. "I have auspicious news."

"You show me yours, I'll show you mine."

Janice chuckled. "Okay, then. We have found our FBI leak."

Zack sat up straight. "Well, that is auspicious."

"I asked an agent I trust implicitly in the Information and Intelligence Branch to look for any particular agent who dealt largely with San Francisco Power & Light criminal cases. It was a huge task because SFP&L have been very bad boys for a very long time. It would have been overwhelming for him but for one name that stuck out: Special Agent Carl…wait for it!… Santini."

It took a second to sink in, then Zack couldn't restrain a gasp. "No. That would be too simple."

He felt Janice's smirk over the airwaves.

"Every once in a while the gods send a gift," she said. "This one is ours, wrapped in ribbon made from high tension wire. Agent Santini is a son of the late lamented partner to Santini & Marsh, and still owns considerable stock in the company, enough so that when it began to diminish after the landfill fiasco, he would have been ripe for exploitation by his father's friend and partner Erwin Marsh to pass along information from time to time. Nothing much at first, I'm sure, just a hint of what was transpiring in the SFP&L cases, likely. Between brother Edwin in the California Senate pushing forward his reserve energy bill and tidbits of information from Agent Santini hinting at the desperate needs of SFP&L, the Marsh brothers were able to put together a pretty good plan to construct the hydroelectric storage facility at Eagle Mountain where the failed landfill would have been."

Janice took a breath. "But they couldn't afford to build it themselves, so they searched for a partner and found EverSun, probably arranged for a large contract in futures between EverSun and SFP&L, offered their services for design and construction, and bingo—the huge gamble in the desert is off and running."

Zack's head was full. It was such a twisted rope but all of it made perfect sense. "What about Santini?" he asked.

The enthusiasm in Janice's voice dropped, and she resumed at a lower pitch. "That is a delicate matter. Senator Marsh has very influential friends, it seems. I've no doubt it was he who was able to find a way to influence POTUS to pressure the director into dropping the Scheidecker case. Based on the information we now have suggesting collusion and the leaking of confidential information, I've been able to put together an investigative committee to look into the affairs of Agent Santini. Meanwhile, we have arranged to intercept further information he may try to pass along." She sighed. "He's toothless now, but with his connections, the road to conviction will be long and convoluted."

"Is there any evidence connecting him to the assassins?"

"We have not found any. And I think it quite unlikely. I see this as a case where he was drawn deeper and deeper until he was in over his head and could be blackmailed into espionage, including the information about the location app in Thomason's phone. Someone else hired the assassins, I think, someone quite desperate." She continued in a bantering tone. "Now that's mine, show me yours."

"I have a plan to trap the assassin. Now, I need you to trust me with the details but be ready to loan assistance."

"Right. You want backup but you won't tell me what for?"

"Well, I guess that's right."

"So what else is new? Can you at least give me a time frame?"

Zack looked at Arlene. He could see she was pumped and ready. "Within the next twenty-four hours."

"I'll be waiting."

As he was ending the call, Eagle Feather walked in the door. Zack looked at him and smiled. "Have some lunch. There are tons of sandwiches left."

"I have eaten two meals already today. I cannot eat another." The Navajo came on into the living room.

"You're just in time," Zack said. "I just spoke with Janice and she has found the FBI leak."

Eagle Feather dropped into the armchair. "That is good news."

Sarah and Arlene spoke in one voice. "Who is it?"

Zack smiled at the response. "Obviously, the information may not leave this room. Janice is working with an investigative committee, but the process is tedious and delicate. However, we've identified the leak as one Agent Carl Santini."

There was a general intake of breath. "Santini," Arlene said. "Agent Santini. I work for the company but I had no idea."

"No one knew," Zack said. "The FBI is a private club for all intents and purposes, and its membership is not readily published. Nor would it serve Santini & Marsh to advertise the connection as we now know."

Sarah did not look happy. "So everything we shared, everything we reported to Janice, was vulnerable."

"Yes, until we realized and 'tightened the circle,' as she says."

Sarah sighed. "Well, at least we've identified the leak and can move forward. Which is to where, exactly?"

Zack leaned forward, his words soft but firm. "Our concern right now is to eliminate this assassin. We believe he is no longer answerable to his employers and operating on his own schedule for his own reasons."

"Why do you think that?" Arlene asked.

"His attempt on my life. We don't believe that was ordered by his client. It wouldn't make sense. It's too risky, too high profile to murder an FBI agent."

"How can you be sure it was the assassin who drove the black SUV?"

Zack raised palms. "I can't. But considering the elevated status of likely participants in this entire scheme, it would make more sense. Anyway, the assassin threatened Eagle Feather and me in no uncertain terms. And that brings me to our next step, which we need to discuss."

"The entrapment," Arlene said with a glimmer in her eye.

"Exactly." Zack cocked an eye at Eagle Feather. "We are considering a plan using bait,"—he glanced at Arlene——"pardon the expression, to draw out the assassin to capture or incapacitate him. But I need help with how and where. We think we have a way to pass information to the assassin's employer who hopefully will bite and get word to the assassin." Zack flashed a look at Eagle Feather. "Arlene has agreed to participate."

"I do have a time and a place," Eagle Feather said. He described his meeting with Dr. Silvia Mike and her challenge to him to attend the sun healing ceremony the following morning. "She expects me an hour before sunrise. Very few people will attend, just the family of the patient."

Zack grew excited about the idea. "I like this. It is remote, we can isolate ourselves from the family so they are not hurt. There are limited places the assassin can conceal himself within rifle range of the rock pillar." He turned to Eagle Feather. "Will anyone be there earlier?"

Eagle Feather checked his smartphone. "Sunrise will be at 5:36 a.m. People are expected to arrive at four-thirty. Before that time, only Dr. Mike and the patient will be there."

Zack jumped up from his chair. "We have very little time to put this together. Everything depends upon getting the message to the people who hired the assassin in time for them to respond." He looked at Arlene. "If we miss this window of opportunity, it is okay. We will have wasted time but no one will be hurt. But if we are lucky, we can end all this tomorrow." He glanced at his watch. "Arlene, how might you ordinarily reach out to Lucy if you were out sick. By phone? Messaging? Email?"

Everyone except Eagle Feather was standing now, caught up in the excitement.

"I would telephone her," Arlene said.

"Good. Use your own words. Make the overt purpose of your call an explanation of why you have been away, your sick relative and all that, ask what's new, then ask if she happens to know why this Agent Tolliver wants to take you to the lost oasis in the Great Wash where Scheidecker disappeared. Ask it as if you believe Selder or someone at Santini & Marsh might know the reason, and why at such an early hour." He put a hand on Arlene's shoulder. "Can you do that and make it seem convincing?"

"You bet your ass I can," she said. "I just want a shot at the bastard."

"Okay. Use Sarah's throwaway phone. They can't trace that here."

Arlene took the phone Sarah offered and went into her room to call.

Sarah looked uneasy. "I must confess I am not happy about placing the witness I was assigned to protect in such danger."

Eagle Feather spoke from the depths of his armchair. "Maybe there is better bait."

They looked at him.

"This killer wants us dead," he said, pointing to Zack and then himself. "For him, that is personal. For him, Arlene is just a job."

Zack thought about it and agreed. "That's true. But we need whoever hired the assassin to get word to him. Without Arlene, the killer's employer wouldn't care."

"Arlene doesn't need to go, though," Sarah pointed out. "We can say she will be there, even if she isn't. They won't know that."

"Yes, you are right," Zack said. "This could work."

Eagle Feather looked at Zack. "You are thinking you will be the bait in the trap for the sniper, but you were not invited to the ceremony. It must be me. He wants to kill me as much as he wants to kill you. I will be the target."

Zack grinned at his friend. "So you would trust my marksmanship?"

"I will trust my luck," the Navajo said.

"I qualified as Expert at Quantico, thirty-eight out of forty targets," Sarah said.

Zack looked at her with eyebrows raised. "That's very impressive. But what is your experience with live situations?"

"I've worked two incidents as a backup sniper in each." Then she gave a lame grin. "Never had to fire, though."

"I think she should come with us," Eagle Feather said.

Zack raised an eyebrow and grinned at Eagle Feather, then said, "Let me see what I can work out." He picked up his phone and called Janice.

Arlene returned while he was calling and handed Sarah her phone.

"Well?" Sarah asked.

"It's done. Lucy has the information, for what that's worth."

"How did she react?" Sarah asked.

"She seemed eager to hear everything I had to say." Arlene shrugged. "We'll see, I guess."

Zack put away his phone. "You won't," Zack said. "You'll stay here."

"Wait a minute. What was all that about, then? I told her I'd be at the oasis. They'll be expecting me."

"We want them to think you'll be there," Zack said. "But you won't."

Arlene's nostrils flared. "I told you I wanted a shot at that scum."

"Maybe after we've captured him we can find a little room and put you two in it. Meanwhile, though, you stay here. You are a valuable witness."

"By herself?" Sarah asked.

Zack shook his head. "As I said, she's a valuable witness. Janice herself is coming here to stay with her while the operation is in progress."

Sarah looked at Arlene. "Wow! You rate the queen."

"Like I need a damn babysitter."

"When will Aunt Janice arrive?" Sarah asked.

Zack looked at his watch. "Around midnight, I expect. It will be a long day. Meanwhile, we can spend the remainder of the day planning and resting."

"That sounds good," Eagle Feather said. "Anyone for a game of poker?"

CHAPTER THIRTY-THREE

Janice arrived at the safe house two minutes after midnight. She announced her arrival by phone to Zack, who let her in a side door. Despite her full day at the office followed by the long drive, there was no hair out of place as she slipped past Zack into the darkened hall.

Everyone was in the living room, most having napped through the afternoon, except for Eagle Feather and Arlene, who had played an intense game of head-to-head poker, ending only when Zack, up from his nap, insisted on borrowing Eagle Feather to go over their plans. Now everyone sat around the dining room table fortifying themselves with cake and coffee.

Janice's greeting for Zack had been a nod and her usual brilliant smile, but when Eagle Feather rose to his feet she walked over to him and gave him a hug. She leaned down to Sarah and gave her a peck on the cheek. Then she stood with crossed arms, looking at Arlene.

"So this is the amazing woman I've heard so much about."

Zack had known many impressive women in his life, but none so much so as those in the room with him right now. Janice's trim figure was enhanced by jeans and a flannel shirt with a bandana worn around her neck like a silk scarf, a Western-themed outfit she somehow managed to project into formal dress. Her natural air of authority was on full display, her posture straight as a column, yet somehow managing to seem at ease.

Arlene was undeterred by formality and rising from her seat extended a beefy hand, her expression open and frank, her large body moving with unconscious grace.

Yin and yang, Zack thought.

"So you are the big wheel at the FBI," Arlene said, vigorously shaking Janice's hand. "When Zack mentions you, it sounds like he's talking about the Virgin Mary."

Janice responded with a serene smile. "Mary, maybe." She turned to Zack. "Is everything in order?"

"Fundamentally," Zack said. He invited her to take a seat at the table and resumed his own. He gestured toward the cake, she smiled her refusal.

Zack unrolled a topo map of the Great Wash quadrant where the lost oasis was located. "This is the ceremony site." He put a finger there. "From our visits, Eagle Feather and I surmise the most likely place for a rifleman to position himself is either here or here." He pointed out two spots above narrow contour bands suggesting greater elevation changes. "Anywhere else will cause him to be too exposed, or out of reasonable range. Sarah will be our backup sniper. She will take a position here"—Zack placed a finger on the map—"where she will have a line of sight within range of both possible locations. In the pre-dawn desert light conditions, she should have excellent visibility to those targets."

Janice leaned close to the map. "Won't she be out of rifle range of the ceremony?"

311

Zack nodded. "Yes. But I will be here." He pointed to an arroyo closer to the site.

Janice studied the map. "If you are there, you are subject to this potential sniper position."

"Yes, if I expose myself. My job is to protect against an unexpected attack from a closer position. I will hunker down and wait." He glanced at Eagle Feather. "I think my friend feels safer with Sarah on the long gun."

Janice turned her attention to Eagle Feather. "You will attend the ceremony?"

Eagle Feather nodded.

"You may become the target."

He nodded again.

"If our message got through to the assassin, as hoped, he will be expecting to see Arlene at the ceremony," Zack said. "He won't, of course, but by then it will be too late, and we think he'll consider Eagle Feather a suitable prize and that will keep him there. In any case, he can't be allowed to shoot. That is why we need to be in place early, well concealed so that the moment he arrives and begins to prepare, Sarah can take her shot."

"It would be nice to capture him so that we can interrogate him," Janice said.

"You promised me time with him in a small room," Arlene added with a pout.

Janice raised her eyebrows at that.

Zack grinned. "It is more important to protect the innocents," he said. "Sarah will go for her most certain shot. But if we get lucky, who knows?" He glanced at Janice. "By the way, did you bring the ghillie suits?"

"They're in my car," Janice said. "When do you leave?"

"We'll leave shortly. This assassin is a careful man. He will be on location early to scout." Zack checked his watch. "Dr. Mike and her patient are most likely there already."

Janice looked at Eagle Feather. "Will she have a fire for the ceremony?"

Eagle Feather nodded. "Yes. Silvia and her patient go there by evening light. She will build a pinyon fire, let it reduce to hot coals. It will be outside a three-sided shelter near the rock tower. The patient will sit in it during the healing. It will open to the east, toward the rising sun. Dr. Mike will recite prayers and pass smoke over the patient and apply special herbs and tonics. The healing will happen as the sun rises and grows strong."

Janice stared at the map, then glanced at Zack. "Okay. I think the plan is good. If the assassin doesn't show up, you will have a long night but at least you will observe an interesting ceremony from the sound of it."

"Okay, then." Zack stood. "It's time." He looked at Eagle Feather, who left his chair and headed to the door. "Eagle Feather will go first and be on watch, in case our man arrives early. We will all be on the communicators. Sarah, let's load the equipment in the truck."

Zack and Sarah had prepared a pair of H-S Precision Pro 2000 HTR bolt action rifles with night scopes during the afternoon which now lay in cases on Zack's bed looking very much out of place next to the silk pillows.

313

The two were already dressed in fatigues and shoes appropriate for a long night of walking in sand and gravel. Now they grabbed the water and a pair of jackets against the cool of the desert night and made several trips to the truck with rifles, ammo and gear, and the ghillie suits from Janice's SUV. One more trip to the house to stuff their jacket pockets with high protein snacks, and they were ready to go.

Arlene crushed Zack with a bear hug, then Sarah. "You two are putting yourselves on the line for me and I love you to death for it."

"Remember, Zack," Janice said, "if things go south you'll be on your own." Then she flashed her brilliant smile.

Zack grinned back. From Janice, that was the equivalent of a hug.

The drive was long and they traveled with silence between them, both preoccupied with their thoughts. Large numbers of trucks passed heading east in the opposite lane, appearing first in the distance as twinkling lights then roaring by leaving abrupt darkness in their wakes. Once they were in the National Park there was nothing, just blackness and brilliant stars and chaparral rushing by momentarily washed by the headlights.

At the turnoff for Black Eagle Mine Road, Zack slipped the truck into four-wheel drive and they slowed. Bugs appeared as particles in the headlights. At the park boundary gate, Zack exchanged the truck headlights for fog lights. It almost didn't matter, the moon and stars were so bright.

They turned north and followed the boundary line road. Great Wash was just to the east. They would parallel it on this road to a position just north of the lost oasis, then cross over on foot.

Zack glanced at his watch. "We're in good time, but this road is not kept up. It could be slow going."

It did prove to be slow and also full of nasty surprises. Craters and gashes remained hidden in shadow until the last moment, some rugged enough to throw them forward against their harnesses. A boulder forced them off the road and around through brush. Steep downgrades led to abrupt hill climbs littered with ruts and protruding rocks. The road would have been difficult even in daylight.

Sarah kept track of their position on her smartphone. When they reached the correct GPS location, Zack stopped and turned off the truck. Their trek would begin here.

Outside the truck, it felt cool. Both agents prepared in silence, making last-minute adjustments to footwear, tucking ammo, water, and snacks in packs, helping each other with the ghillie suits, unpacking and slinging their rifles. They would proceed without lights, counting on the stars and moon. The synthetic ghillie suit of jacket and pants weighed just six pounds, the front was made of Cordura material that resisted snags and thorns. Despite this, they had to unsnag their netting from mesquite bushes more than once.

Zack was guided by his GPS positioner, but in the dark, the terrain was difficult and rough. Once a snake's rattle sounded and reminded Zack that such creatures hunted at night and he stepped even more carefully. Near Great Wash, they encountered a field of large boulders they had to slither around and over. Sarah kept pace easily, moving silently and capably despite the obstacles. When Zack came to the steep descent into the wash, he waited for Sarah to come beside him.

"We will be exposed crossing this arm of Great Wash," he said. "Give me a ten-yard head start, then keep low and move smoothly and steadily. You okay?"

At her nod, he lowered himself down to the wash surface and moved across. The travel was easier here, but well lit by the moon and Zack's shadow moving on the wash surface appeared huge to him. If the killer was here, they were sitting ducks. He forced himself to move slow, keep his motion smooth. He came to the base of the opposite bank without incident and Sarah soon joined him.

They were close now. Something moved in the shadows. He tensed until he recognized Eagle Feather.

The Navajo spoke softly. "He is not here yet. I will lead you to your positions."

They followed him. Three shadows, they moved across a moonscape of brush, boulders, and sand. The ground steepened before them. Eagle Feather stopped and tapped Sarah's shoulder. Zack heard her whisper "Good luck" and watched her disappear up into the shadows. Eagle Feather moved downslope and Zack followed.

LOST OASIS

They came to a gully and dropped down into it. The arroyo was narrow, its far side steep.

"This is your location," Eagle Feather said in a whisper. "Down here you are hidden. From above you can see the ceremony site." There was a pat on Zack's shoulder and he was alone.

Zack glanced at his watch. Two forty-five a.m. Lots of time yet. He put in his ear pod and adjusted his mic. "Testing…"

"Loud and clear." It was Sarah.

Zack set out his gear in the gulley. He reconnoitered the slope, found the best position for a shot, then slid back down. He settled his back against a smooth rock in the arroyo bed, his ears adjusting to the rhythm of the night noises. The chill began to creep in, but the suit was comfortable enough. He rechecked the load in his rifle by feel, peered through the night scope picking out objects here and there along the ravine. Satisfied, he sat back and waited.

Sarah used the image from the topo map in her mind to guide her as she climbed the boulder studded hill to her assigned location. The hill was substantial, rising fifty or sixty feet above the surrounding terrain, but once on top would give a panoramic view of the landscape to the south and, she hoped, the sniper's most likely position. She took her time on the climb, careful not to dislodge rocks. The effort warmed her inside the suit and she paused frequently to cool down and to minimize her motion. Once the slope before her gave way to nothing but starry sky, she knew her climb was over. She looked for a protected place, a comfortable prone position, and a good line of sight. She found the right place, settled into position making a myriad of minute adjustments until satisfied. Next, she positioned the rifle and adjusted her aim with the night scope on the place she expected the assassin to appear. She had just finished when her earpiece sounded with Zack's quiet voice. She was happy to hear him, the voice quality so clear he might have been next to her. The sound of it brought her comfort.

Sarah kept her scope trained on the target area and settled in to wait. Many thoughts came to her mind in her lonely vigil, including snatches of stories her grandfather had told her of the great sniper standoffs in Stalingrad during the German offensive there during World War II. She remembered hearing how the great Russian snipers would wait for their quarry to finally reveal himself, scarcely moving, sometimes for twelve to fifteen hours. She took comfort that her wait would be much shorter and far less cold.

CHAPTER THIRTY-FOUR

Eagle Feather intuited rather than sensed the arrival of the killer. One moment he was alone in empty darkness, the next moment an entity was nearby. The Navajo didn't understand how he knew this, perhaps it was a wisp of scent, maybe a lull in night noise, or maybe just a nuance of a new being in the atmosphere, but he trusted this instinct. At that moment he was lying prone on his stomach near the edge of a precipice studying the land below, searching for movement, his eyes looking for the slightest flicker of motion. He never suspected the object of his search was so close.

He knew he should not be surprised. He came here by emulating the moves he guessed the assassin might make. Should he be surprised to be so accurate? The killer had followed the same path for the same purpose, to gain an overview of the ceremonial site. He might next creep out onto the very slab where Eagle Feather now lay.

He resisted the impulse to move. He must be patient, first determine precisely where the killer was now. To do that, he must wait for the man to make the first move. At last, he heard a sound, just the slightest scrape, leather or cloth on stone, but enough to tell him the killer was just yards behind him and creeping forward.

Eagle Feather thought about attacking. If he succeeded, the matter would be done once and for all. He rejected the idea at once. The advantage was all on the side of the killer.

Eagle Feather would be outlined against the sky, his only weapon a knife, his back to the precipice.

He could only retreat, but even then his options were limited. The killer was too close for Eagle Feather to move laterally to either side along the cliff edge and avoid notice. He knew the man was highly skilled and would detect him.

That left the cliff edge. Eagle Feather inched forward, keeping his weight on fingers and toes until he reached the verge of the slab he was on. It was smooth on top but cracked at the face where it fell away. He angled sideways, then inch by inch like a human snake slithered over until he found a protruding ledge a foot and a half beneath that would support him. He was out of sight from above but if the killer peered over, he would be exposed. He steadied himself with one hand and grasped his knife in the other. He did not know what was beneath him. If he was discovered, he would attack and trust to luck.

Eagle Feather knew the killer was there when he heard his slight breath, just a whisper above the night noises. He visualized the man in his mind, prone on the slab where the Navajo had just been, scanning the terrain beyond. Sarah was down there somewhere. Eagle Feather willed her not to move, for even in her ghillie suit this man would detect her and her end would be swift.

Hunter's genes and years of practice endowed the Navajo with the patience to remain still for long periods. He became aware the killer had moved away only when his sense of the man's presence dissipated. Still, he waited. When he wormed his way back up on the slab, he caught the subtle yet distinctive scent of the man, one he would remember and identify in the future.

Eagle Feather took his communicator from his pocket and spoke into it. "He is here."

Sarah's mind leaped into focus when Eagle Feather's detached voice sounded in her ear. She wished the man wasn't always so cryptic, she'd like to know exactly where 'here' was—behind her? In front somewhere? She had to content herself with believing Eagle Feather would warn her if the killer seemed to be stalking her. She acknowledged with a simple "10-4," heard Zack respond similarly and felt her pulse quicken. The party would begin soon.

Zack heard Eagle Feather's warning and responded. He wondered if the assassin had just arrived or if Eagle Feather had just now located him. He was glad to hear Sarah's voice sound so calm. For one so young, she had turned out to be a real trooper so far. He shivered. The predawn cold had turned the stone on which he reclined into an ice cube. What was the saying? It's always coldest just before the dawn? Or darkest? Whatever. That brought his mind back to the assassin, wondering why he was moving into position this late. The guests would arrive for the ceremony soon. Likely the killer had been scouting, checking things out. This was the real test of the ghillie suits and the ability of those wearing them to remain still.

After hearing Eagle Feather's message, time passed in dentist chair minutes for Sarah. Her aim was on the small hillock where they believed the killer would appear. But there was a second possible site, to the right of the probable target. She knew not to move, not even to twitch, but that meant she could not swing the rifle scope back and forth to check both targets. Instead, with the slightest tilt of her head she used her right eye to look there, each time adjusting to the darkness and a new focal length, then returning her eye to the rifle scope and focusing all over again, an exercise both awkward and time-consuming. Her adrenalin was up, the hair on the back of her neck was also because she could not dismiss the idea she could be discovered at any moment and know it only from the punch of the bullet in her back. Or worse, the killer might choose a path through her location and trip over her. Her handgun was buried somewhere under the ghillie suit, and she would have no chance. Sarah had begun to sweat despite the cold. She tried to push all of these thoughts into the background of her mind. To override them, she mentally rehearsed the mantra of her firing sequence, over and over.

She saw him just after returning her right eye to the scope, a shadow that hadn't been there before and now was. She studied the shadow, gradually a human figure became clear. She breathed out, whispered into her mic, "I have a target."

Zack responded. "Hold until you see a rifle. Then fire when ready."

Sarah did not see a rifle, she didn't even see an arm. She saw a form, a person crouched with back to her, body black against a dark background. The person appeared to be working at something she couldn't see. She breathed, kept steady on her target, and waited.

Zack was relieved the killer had chosen the site they predicted. Sarah was set up perfectly for her shot, so long as no one gave themselves away. Zack had moved above the arroyo after Sarah's message came. He was close enough to the ceremony site to see the tiny glow of the fire under the pinnacle rock. Some figures stood in the ancient oasis. They had come on foot down the wash, likely following an ancient traditional route. It was too far away to see if Eagle Feather was among them.

The minutes stretched since Zack had permitted Sarah to shoot when ready. She must still be waiting to see a rifle. She should have plenty of time to fire her round before the assassin could set up for his shot. She should be able to see the rifle even if it was camouflaged. Still, as the minutes ticked by, Zack agonized.

He waited, covering the killer's location with his rifle. He had no target, his view blocked by rocks, but if the killer stood or tried to move to a different place, Zack would have his shot.

It came then, the percussive sound of a rifle. Zack's peripheral vision caught the muzzle flash from Sarah's rifle. After a moment of silence, Sarah's voice spoke in his ear. "He's down."

It almost seemed too easy. They had set their trap, the killer had walked into it, the trap had been sprung. Zack kept his rifle trained on the killer's position and waited. He heard loud voices from the oasis, questions, sounds of alarm.

Another minute went by. Zack kept his rifle on target, waiting. At last Sarah's voice came again, excited, confident. "He's not moving. He's down."

"Keep him covered," Zack said. "I'm going over there."

He began to climb to his feet.

Sarah's voice came again, now sounding shocked, touched by panic.

"Wait! He's moving, he's up…"

The flash and sound of Sarah's rifle came again. Zack heard the ping of the bullet off of rock. He was kneeling, in the act of lifting his rifle and folding the tripod. Looking out, he saw a figure leap up from the assassin's position. Zack hastily raised his rifle and fired from the hip but knew at once he had missed. He jumped up and with rifle in hand, ran recklessly down the brush and boulder-strewn slope after the killer who was sprinting directly toward the small crowd at the lost oasis. Zack knew he would not catch him in time. He stopped, knelt, and aimed but could not shoot. The killer was directly between him and the crowd. He pressed the button on his communicator, yelled a warning into it.

Eagle Feather was conversing with the patient's wife. The family stood together facing southeast toward the pinnacle rock, now outlined against the dawning sky like a tall dark needle. A reddish-yellow glow on the far eastern skyline foretold the rising sun.

The loud report of a rifle sounded. Everyone turned, startled, to face the sound. They stared up the boulder studded hillside where the shot still echoed.

"Who could be shooting out there?" an old man asked.

The sun peeked incrementally above the horizon, igniting the sky around it with a profusion of red, orange, and purple streaks. A horn sounded from the rock pinnacle, summoning everyone to the ceremony. The gathering turned that way.

Another shot sounded from the hillside. Then a third.

Everyone stopped, stared toward the hill, uncertain.

Eagle Feather saw motion on the slope, a figure running down it toward them. He could not tell who it was. He heard Zack's voice in his ear pod.

"Eagle Feather, he is running toward you. I have no shot."

Eagle Feather now saw a second figure, angling as if to cut off the first. He knew it must be Zack and that he would be too late. The first runner was close now, coming fast. He was dressed all in black, hooded. He ran swiftly, easily, in great strides, seeming to float above the ground. He held a rifle casually in one hand at his side. A glitter of black eyes under the hood looked directly at Eagle Feather. Without haste, without missing a step, the assassin raised his rifle in the one hand like a pistol and pointed it at the Navajo.

Eagle Feather twisted away, sweeping his right hand behind his back under his leather shirt, and pulled his knife from its sheath. As the knife came free, he used the torque of his twisted body to accelerate the swing of his arm toward the killer, now just twenty feet away, coming fast. At the full arc of his swing, he released the knife. He felt a great punch to his shoulder and was slammed backward onto the ground. He rolled as he hit and felt rather than saw the assassin pass by him. From his back, his head tilted, he watched the man run, his great loping strides seeming to grow longer with each step. Eagle Feather groaned with disappointment and the first flowering of pain.

The sun exploded over the horizon, a great fiery ball in Eagle Feather's eyes, directly aligned with the rock pinnacle before him, casting it in silhouette like a black needle to heaven. The entire flat expanse of the table-like plateau became visible in the sun's shimmer and the running man was a stick figure against the fierce light, made somehow taller and larger despite the distance.

Another man came into the Navajo's view, a huge familiar figure, running with the same easy loping stride in pursuit of the first, accelerating without effort, steps growing longer and longer, higher and higher. To Eagle Feather's bewilderment, both figures began to soar as they ran, each stride seeming less shackled to the earth.

Eagle Feather's gaze was pulled toward the rock pinnacle. It had changed, was beginning to radiate like a slab of steel in a mill furnace, its center turning orange and then pulsating red and now an all-red fiery glow with an intensity that forced the Navajo to avert his eyes. As he did, he caught a last momentary view of the Chemehuevi runner and the assassin, both dark specks in the sky now, then erased from view by the widening glow of the sun's needle.

It all ended as suddenly as it began. The sun broke free of the horizon and shrunk to its normal size, illuminating a few streaks of cloud. The stone needle shriveled to what it had been, just a chunk of vertical rock on a flat plain.

Eagle Feather saw nothing more.

CHAPTER THIRTY-FIVE

A shadow across his face brought relief from the intense light that burned Eagle Feather's eyes even through his closed lids. He opened them, waited for the blurred image to sharpen into recognizable features, and smiled. At least, Zack later insisted that had happened.

"Ho, White Man, it is good to see you."

"Eagle Feather, lie still. You have been shot."

"White Man, you always surprise me with your keen observations."

There was lots of movement around them, people standing, helping one another, children crying. Eagle Feather tried to rise, but Zack restrained him.

"Just hold on there, my friend. Let me take a look at that shoulder."

Another shadow passed over Eagle Feather and he saw Sarah's concerned face. She looked miserable. "Oh, Eagle Feather, I am so sorry. I can't believe I missed him. I thought I had hit him. I'm so sorry."

"You did not miss," Eagle Feather said. "When he was close, I saw he was wearing body armor."

Zack swore quietly. "I should have known." He slipped open the Navajo's leather shirt and inspected the wound. "It seems to be a through and through. You are lucky."

"I do not feel lucky, White Man."

Zack moved aside and another face peered at him.

"Let me look," Silvia Mike said. "I have some training in this kind of thing."

Eagle Feather tried to sit up again. "What about your patient? You should see to him."

Zack gently eased the Navajo down again. "Just wait," he commanded. "You're all a twitch."

Silvia smiled at Eagle Feather. "My patient is cured. That's what this was all about. He is with his family. Now we will cure you."

"Do not put me near that fiery pillar."

Silvia laughed, her eyes dancing. "I think we can use more modern methods for your injury." She removed a purse from her belt and set it down. She removed several antiseptic wipes and cleaned the entry wound. Then after Zack eased him to a sitting position, they helped him out of his shirt and Silvia cleaned the exit wound. She dusted both wounds with a white powder and taped bandages over each and with her palms on both wounds sent healing energy through him.

Eagle Feather watched her face as she worked. "That pinnacle seems to draw great power from the sun."

"The ceremony of *tavan'nawigyah,* the calling of the sun, is a powerful thing," she said. "I am but a tool to the will of other powers beyond our understanding."

"And the blind man?" Zack asked.

"Can now see," she said. "But he has gauze on his eyes and must be careful to use very dark sunglasses for a time." She stood and looked down at Eagle Feather. "Just as our

329

patient here must refrain from moving this shoulder for a while to allow it to heal."

Eagle Feather's shoulder throbbed and his head ached. But he still had questions. His eyes searched the ground around him.

"What are you looking for?" Zack asked.

"My knife. I lost it after I was shot."

Sarah and Zack went to search for it.

Eagle Feather seized his moment and said to Dr. Mike, "I saw the killer escape into the sky."

She searched his face. "The killer must be of the blood of the ancient desert runners to do such a thing. But he will not escape. Lucas will catch him, somewhere, sometime. You will see."

"Did others see what I saw?"

Silvia helped Eagle Feather to his feet. "Only those who are spiritually aware, such as yourself." As she turned and went to speak with family members, Eagle Feather heard the soft jingle of bells and saw she was dressed in a beautifully embroidered white deerskin dress with tiny bells at her waist and on her moccasins.

When Zack and Sarah returned to Eagle Feather, they were empty-handed.

"Someone may have picked it up," Sarah said. "We can ask Dr. Mike later if anyone found it."

"Sorry, Eagle Feather," Zack said.

Eagle Feather nodded. The knife was special to him, but its loss raised more questions than he had answers. The Navajo insisted he was able to walk up the wash to where he'd left the motorcycle and ride it back to the safe house, but the others were firm in denying him this. He was to wait with Dr. Mike and her patient for the helicopter the Tribe had arranged.

Sarah left with Eagle Feather's directions for how to find the motorcycle and ride it back. Zack would carry both rifles and the extra gear back to the truck. It would take him a long time to return to it and drive the tough terrain. He could then give Eagle Feather a ride from the Twentynine Palms airstrip back to Blythe.

By the time they all arrived back at the safe house, everyone was exhausted, their bodies aching. Arlene had a huge pot of coffee on, and there was a pile of donuts on a platter. Everyone made a great fuss over Eagle Feather, who immediately became grumpy. They put him in Zack's bedroom and with the aid of strong pain killers Dr. Mike had given him, he slept.

The mission debrief was not pleasant, made terse by the fact no one had gotten any sleep.

"This was not your finest hour, Zack," Janice said. "We've got a wounded man and the perpetrator got away."

Zack shook his head. "I know."

"It's my fault," Sarah said. "I missed the shot. I should have realized he might be wearing body armor."

"What could you have done about it?" Zack said. "You couldn't risk a headshot at that distance in that light. You did what you could."

"Zack is right," Janice said. "The fallacy lies in the planning. I approved it, ultimately it is my responsibility."

"We have underestimated this man all the way along," Zack said.

Sarah stared at Zack. "Someone else went after him when he ran off. Who was that?"

Janice darted a look at Sarah. "What do you mean?"

"I thought I saw someone run after the assassin while I went to help Zack with Eagle Feather."

Janice looked at Zack.

"It may have been Lucas Leivas, the Tribe's Chemehuevi investigator," Zack said. "I thought I saw him too."

"Who is this man?" Janice demanded.

"I'm sure I mentioned him to you," Zack said.

"You didn't mention an investigator hired by the Chemehuevi people." Janice's gaze was cold.

Zack sighed again. "Janice, by then we all knew there was a leak somewhere, almost certainly within the FBI. George Madrigal didn't want his investigation at risk and we agreed to keep our inquiries separate, but with Eagle Feather as the bridge. He would decide what was important for me to know without compromising the Tribe's progress. Lucas and Eagle Feather work well together."

"So we now have two Indians who don't exist and an entirely separate investigation."

Zack shrugged. "That's about right, I guess."

Janice was not amused. "The cart is leading the horse here, and I am not happy."

Zack was tired and felt defiant. "Sometimes that way works best. Remember, when you first put me in charge of this department, you knew I wouldn't use standard methods."

"It's all about results," Janice said. "And we don't have any."

Sarah spoke up. "We know who the FBI informer is now. If the leak is stopped, there is no reason to separate the investigations anymore, is there? And poor Eagle Feather won't be in shape to help us for a while."

Janice looked at Sarah, her expression softened. "You're right. What's done is done, and we need to move forward. Swiftly." She turned to Zack. "We are searching documents, emails, messages, phone records, everything Agent Santini touched in hopes we will find the person to whom he was passing information. Do you have other ideas?"

"In fact, I do," Zack said. "We did successfully move a message through Lucy, Jason Selder's administrative secretary at Santini & Marsh. That's how we brought the assassin to us. And that is how we will set a new trap. But we need to act now before someone connects those particular dots and realizes what we have done."

CHAPTER THIRTY-SIX

"I don't understand," Sarah said, reaching a long arm toward the donut platter. Sarah's love of chocolate had become legendary among them, and it was easy to guess the particular pastry she wanted resided on the far side, a crème filled, chocolate-slathered beauty. As everyone watched, entranced, she moved the plate in a counter-clockwise direction with two fingers with such delicacy it remained in its exact position relative to the tabletop, revolving inch by inch like a Lazy Susan, the desired donut riding closer and closer to its doom. Meanwhile, Sarah carried on speaking without pause as if nothing else was happening. "We sent Arlene's message through Lucy Martin, Selden's admin secretary, hoping she'd pass it on to someone who was connected to the assassin. It seemed to worked. Or maybe it was just coincidence that the killer showed up. But, either way, we don't know specifically where the message went, who it went to, you know?" By now her mouth was full of donut and her words became muffled. "Show how do we know who to set a trap for?"

Zack had watched Sarah's unconscious drama of conquering the donut with great amusement. "Granted, it is another gamble, but again one with little fallout if it fails, other than a short loss of time. And in the absence of anything else right now, other than the hope that Lucas will catch the assassin, which Dr. Mike seems to believe, I think it's worth a try. We know the perpetrator is someone high in the ranks of one of the involved companies. If we think of that person as the spider in the center of the web it has woven, we can put names to radiating strands of the web. For instance, the political strand that is Senator Edwin Marsh, the internal spy strand that is FBI Agent Carl Santini, the strand that is the shell company SolarVenture, the strand that is San Francisco Power & Light, the strand that is EverSun Energy Company, and, of course, the strand that is Erwin Marsh, president and CEO of Santini & Marsh. All these strands lead back to the spider, who I believe is a substantial player in one of the companies, certainly someone with a vested interest." Zack paused to sip his coffee.

"So how does that help us figure out who to trap?" Arlene asked.

Zack set his coffee cup back down. "To continue the analogy, last night we tugged a strand in the web. We tugged the Santini & Marsh strand through Lucy. Now, as you know, I am not a believer in coincidence, so I do not think the assassin showed up on his own. If we assume Eagle Feather picked up on his presence fairly soon after the killer arrived, I'd say he came rather late to the party for one who plans so meticulously. That suggests to me he received his notice late, which suggests he did get our message."

Sarah nodded. "So let's say the message goes from Lucy to her counterpart at Erwin Marsh's office. If so that person either told her boss about it, or called someone. If we look at your spider web construction, it would make the most sense for that person to twitch the strand running directly to the spider."

Zack gave a thoughtful nod.

"What the hell are you two talking about?" Arlene was lost.

Janice lay a hand on her arm. "What it all means was there wasn't much time for the conspirators to act last night to have the assassin in place before dawn."

"Exactly," Zack said. "The spider, our chief conspirator, sits in the middle of the web and feels every twitch of every strand. He's in control. He would have been called directly by the first of his fellow conspirators to get the message. Since a decision on action was needed quickly, I think someone called the spider directly last night."

Sarah was excited. "We can check phone logs."

Zack shook his head. "That could take a long while and probably be a dead end. I think it likely the spider has a burner phone."

"I agree," Janice said. She aimed an arched eyebrow at Zack. "You want to send another message along the same strand and listen to calls in real-time."

Zack nodded. "Exactly. Even if it is a burner, if we can catch it live, we can get a location."

"Okay, what phones do we tap?"

Zack looked around the table. "Well, let's see. It is obvious we need to tap Lucy's phone. She might even have called the spider directly. Then there's Erwin Marsh and his administrative assistant. We need both of those."

"Jason Selder?" Sarah asked.

Janice wrote it down. "Best not leave anyone out. Other ideas?"

"Blair Schäuble, Assistant Supervisor at Santini & Marsh," Arlene said.

Janice wrote the name, looked up, waiting.

"Anyone connected to Solar Venture, EverSun, or SFP&L?"

Arlene thought. "There's Nicolás Constantine at EverSun. He's the only name I've heard Jason mention from that company." She shrugged. "But I have no reason to suspect him of anything."

"We'll add him anyway," Janice said.

Zack stretched and stood, speaking through a half yawn. "Janice will get our taps authorized. Arlene, I'll have a message for you to plant with Lucy later today. Everyone get some sleep now. We'll begin operation spider as soon as Janice is ready."

No one had to be asked twice. Sarah headed out the door to her little cottage, taking Janice with her. Arlene put dishes in the dishwasher and went to her room. Zack went to the spare bedroom to find a blanket and pillow to throw on the couch but soon found his plan unnecessary. Eagle Feather was on the floor, sleeping, wrapped in a blanket. Eagle Feather generally preferred sleeping on the floor. He had once remarked, "Why search for the world's firmest mattress when terra firma is always available?" Zack wasn't going to argue, even if the man was wounded, and he crawled into his bed and was asleep before his head hit the pillow.

Zack was chasing some vaporous elusive figure on a barren sandy landscape among mesquite trying to catch up to it but fearing to do so at the same time. When he rounded each mesquite bush the figure would just be disappearing behind another, close, but just out of reach. Suddenly he heard the buzz of a rattlesnake and felt something touch his left leg. He leaped to one side but his legs snagged in something heavy and held him back and meanwhile, the buzzing sounded louder...

"White Man, wake up. Your phone is ringing."

Zack sat up to find his legs wrapped tightly in the blanket and his phone vibrating on the bed beside him. Eagle Feather was in a sitting position on the floor, watching him.

"You have exciting dreams, White Man."

Zack grabbed for the phone and answered it. It was Janice.

"Hello, Zack. I'm sorry if I woke you. I just received authorization for the wiretaps and have an agent setting them up now. We need you to tell Arlene what message to forward."

"Now?" Zack's mind struggled to keep up.

"Now."

"Okay, I'll do it now." He dropped the phone on the bed and swung his legs around, yawning. He looked at his friend and smiled sheepishly. "Sorry to wake you." He glanced at his watch. He'd slept just four hours.

Zack went to splash water on his face. In the bathroom, he stared in the mirror. His dream still haunted him. He felt as if he should recognize that fleeting figure, it was important, but he just couldn't.

When he left the bathroom he was happy to see Eagle Feather had to all appearances gone back to sleep. Zack slipped on his trousers and trod barefoot into the living room where he found Arlene and Sarah. Sarah was working on her laptop.

"Hail, the conquering hero arises!" Arlene said.

"Wish it were so on all counts," Zack said with a smile. "Are we ready?"

Sarah nodded.

"Where's Janice?" Zack asked, looking around.

"She had to get back to St. George, left right after you crashed this morning."

"Oh." Zack had assumed she was calling from the next room.

"She said to tell you she's arranged for extra agents to be on standby, she's putting in for the wiretaps, she'll have everything ready to go."

"Doesn't surprise me a bit." Zack thought for a moment, looked at Arlene. "For your message, just tell Lucy your sick relative is much better and you are coming home."

Arlene frowned. "Coming home? What do you mean, coming home?"

"Home. You know, home to where you live in your apartment here in Blythe. That's all."

"But the safe house, my protection?"

"We want them to think we have caught the assassin and believing you are now safe, have released you from protective custody. But just stick to the story about the sick relative, and now the relative is better, and you are coming home."

Arlene didn't look happy. "But they know I've seen this guy, the one who tried to kill me, that I know things."

"That's right."

"So they'll come after me."

"Right again."

"Oh. I see. Here we go again."

"How do we know the spider himself will come?" Sarah asked.

"If the assassins he hired are both unavailable, he has to come himself to see the job is done." Zack turned to Arlene. "Go ahead. Make your call. Use Sarah's phone."

Arlene took the phone and went to her bedroom.

Sarah's eyes followed Zack's face. "What if the assassin got away last night and is actually available?"

"We fervently hope Lucas is keeping the killer too busy."

Zack looked at the coffee pot, saw the carafe was still half full, and poured himself a cup. He had just had his first sip when Arlene reappeared and handed Sarah her phone.

Zack raised an inquiring eyebrow.

"All set," Arlene said. "Lucy sounded happy about the news."

"What did you say, exactly?"

"I said I was driving home tonight and would come into work tomorrow."

"Excellent."

"How will you know when and where they will attack me?" Arlene asked, unable to hide a slight shudder.

"Don't worry," Zack said. "Our wiretaps should give us all the information we need. In any case, you'll still be right here."

"What if we don't get any information?" Sarah asked. "What if nothing happens? Does Arlene just go back to work?"

"I thought about that," Zack said. "We'll decide how to handle that when the time comes. It seems to me it's about time something went our way for once."

"I do not think that will happen, White Man."

They all swung around in their seats to look at the bedroom door. Eagle Feather stood there, one arm in a sling, the other holding his phone.

"I just had a call from George Madrigal," the Navajo said. "They found Lucas Leivas dead in the Oasis of Mara this afternoon with a knife in his heart."

CHAPTER THIRTY-SEVEN

Eagle Feather came to the table and sat down. He held his upper torso rigid, but if he was in pain his face did not show it. "This means the assassin is still alive," he said explaining as if to school children.

Zack felt bitterness sweep over him. "That means we accomplished exactly nothing last night except endanger everyone at the ceremony."

"Who is investigating Lucas' death?" Sarah asked.

"George says the San Bernardino County Sheriff's Department is investigating."

Zack grabbed his phone and called Janice.

"Zack?"

"Hi, Janice. We've had a complication arise regarding tonight's operation." He told her about the Chemehuevi runner's death. "It means, of course, the assassin is still out there. It also means our message route through Lucy may be compromised."

Janice did not comment, but promised to call back as soon as she knew more. "Don't do anything more on tonight's mission until you hear from me."

Zack agreed and hung up.

"Again and again, we underestimate this man," Zack said. He regarded Eagle Feather. "How are you, my friend?"

"Well enough, but I could use some coffee."

"You should be lying down, or at least reclining on the couch," Arlene said, starting to rise to help him.

Eagle Feather gave a hard shake of his head. "The sling is comfortable when I sit upright."

"How does this change things?" Sarah asked.

"The assassin knows we tried to trap him," Eagle Feather said.

Zack nodded. "He knows we must have leaked the information that Arlene would attend the ceremony. He knows she was not there. He will be wary next time."

"Do you think the assassin has had time to warn his employer of that fact?" Sarah asked. "If not, the wiretaps may help us regardless."

"That is my hope," Zack said. "Meanwhile, we need to wait for Janice to get back to us."

She did, an hour later, after the team had enjoyed what felt like an early dinner.

"The signal waves have been humming," she said. "I have calls from Lucy Martin to Karen Bockwith, Erwin Marsh's secretary, to Blair Schäuble, to Ed Fitzgerald, and Sheryl Hunter. I don't know those last two people. Immediately upon receipt of his call, Blair Schäuble called Nicolás Constantine at EverSun, in Florida, who was on our list, who immediately called a cell phone. We do not have that phone listed. No one answered. I suspect it was a burner phone. No one else Lucy called and who is on our list called any third person within the frame of a half-hour. A lapse of a half hour suggests to me a lack of urgency and

343

therefore not important to us. I have no information about Fitzgerald or Hunter."

She paused. "As to the murder of the Chemehuevi man, the county sheriff has taken jurisdiction and sees no connection to our case. However, he was willing to share information anyway. The time of death is fixed between five and six this morning. Death caused by stabbing, a large bladed knife directly into the heart. The knife is now in their possession. There were no tracks, prints, or other clues at the scene. The coroner believes the murder was committed at the scene in the Oasis of Mara. The sheriff sent along a photo taken at the crime scene." She paused. "That is all the information I have at the moment, Zack. Call me when you have decided what to do with it."

Zack scrolled to the photo Janice had sent, looked at it, and raised his eyebrows. Without a word, he slid the phone across the table to Eagle Feather. The Navajo looked at it, grunted, and slid the phone back to Zack.

"Your knife?" Zack asked.

"Yes, that is my knife."

Sarah looked at Eagle Feather. "Did you just say that is your knife? The knife you lost last night is the knife that killed Lucas?"

"I did not lose it, exactly," the Navajo confessed. "I threw it at the killer to save my life at the same time he shot me. I thought I had missed him. Maybe I did not."

Arlene broke in. "Wait, you are saying you threw your knife at the man and he caught it? Or picked it up from the ground? I don't understand."

344

"He did not catch it," Eagle Feather said. "I threw it low, at his legs, because as he ran toward me I saw he was wearing body armor. He could not have caught it."

"Do you think you might have wounded him?" Arlene asked, her eyes wide. "Do you think he ran with your knife in him?"

Eagle Feather shrugged. "I do not know."

"That is not the only strange thing," Zack said. "The coroner gives the time of death between five and six this morning. We all saw the assassin at the ceremony at four-thirty this morning." He looked at the faces at the table. "How is that possible?"

"Two assassins," Arlene said in horror. "Christ, we have two assassins."

Sarah was slowly shaking her head. "But that doesn't explain how Eagle Feather's knife was used for the murder. And Eagle Feather says he saw Lucas at the ceremony."

"Lucas ran after the assassin after I was shot," Eagle Feather said.

"Maybe you were mistaken." Arlene's lower lip was pushed out pugnaciously. "Or maybe the knife just happens to look just like Eagle Feather's knife."

Zack shook his head. "No, I think we have to believe both men somehow reached the Oasis of Mara in a very short time. If they had access to motorcycles it might have been possible, and the coroner could be mistaken on the early side." He shrugged. "Let's look at the other

345

information we have from the wiretaps." Zack shared Janice's information.

"This activity seems to point to Blair Schäuble," Sarah said.

"The snake! I never did like him," Arlene said.

"Isn't he your immediate boss?" Zack asked her. "It does make sense for Lucy to pass information about your return to him."

"Well, yeah, I suppose so. But what about that unknown cell phone number he called?"

"We have no information about it, Janice says, but she intends to try to locate it. She mentioned two other people Lucy had called. One was Fitzgerald, the construction boss, and the other was someone named Hunter, Sheryl Hunter." He looked at Arlene.

"Oh, she's one of my consultant team members. She's a climate specialist, a very bright girl. She probably ran the group in my absence."

"You think calling her would be a natural thing for Lucy?"

"Yes, I do."

Zack paused, shrugged. "Well, that leaves Schäuble and Constantine as our only possibles. If we extrapolate, we might suppose the unknown mobile number belongs to the assassin. If so, Constantine did not reach him. That may help us."

"What now?" Sarah asked.

Zack thought about it. "If I were the one concerned about what Arlene might say, and to whom, I'd not want her to get to the office tomorrow where she could talk to all kinds of people, would you?"

Everyone shook their heads.

"If the perp is Schäuble, he has failed in his attempt to reach his assassin so far. Is he desperate enough to do something about it himself? If so, it probably would be tonight."

Sarah nodded. "We'll set a trap at Arlene's house tonight."

Zack smiled. "I have a plan."

At ten that evening a yellow convertible Volkswagen Bug pulled into Palm Drive Apartments and drove to the parking area at 200 North Palm Drive. A large, weary-looking woman climbed out of the car and reached into the back seat for a suitcase. She locked the car, extended the handle on the suitcase, and rolled it across the parking area to the sidewalk, then along the sidewalk to the entrance of number 200. She took keys from her pocket, fit one into the lock, and opened the door.

A light went on in the house and the woman stepped inside, dragging the suitcase after her and closing the door. Another light came on behind curtains in a downstairs room. All was quiet outside now but for the occasional crackling sound of the cooling VW engine. There was a light breeze, the air just starting to cool from the hot day.

After ten minutes, the large downstairs light turned off. A light came on upstairs and the second downstairs light went off. A second upstairs light came on. After another ten minutes, the second upstairs light went off. Five more minutes and the remaining upstairs light went off. The house was dark.

A car door creaked open and clicked closed. A figure in dark clothes ghosted across the parking lot and slipped to the front door of the apartment. There was a metallic noise and after a short time the front door opened, the figure slid inside, and the door closed without a sound. The house stayed dark, all was silent. Five minutes later, two quick flashes lit up the upstairs room, each followed by two muffled reports. Just as the echoes died the interior of the apartment lit up like a used car lot at night. There was the sound of shouted voices inside the house, commanding, demanding.

Sarah's radio came alive. "All clear. Come on in."

Sarah waved a group of agents from bushes and nearby doorways and they all rushed to the house. Sarah swung open the unlocked door and ran up the stairs. The bedroom door was open. Inside, Zack stood by the bathroom door, still in his wig and dress, his firearm pointed at a masked man standing in the center of the room. A silenced pistol lay at the man's feet, the barrel still smoking. On the bed was a mannikin wrapped in a blanket. A wig lay next to the mannikin's head, which was shattered.

"You can remove that mask," Zack said, keeping his weapon trained on the figure.

The man reached up with one hand and pulled off the ski mask. The weasel-like features of Blair Schäuble were revealed. He was so angry he was spitting. "It was all that damn Scheidecker's fault," he screamed. "He just couldn't keep his damn mouth shut. We offered him a king's ransom, for Christ's sake, and he still couldn't keep his mouth shut."

Schäuble was still choking and spitting with indignation as the agents cuffed him and took him away. Zack looked at Sarah and sighed.

She grinned back at him. "You look mighty pretty, there, lady."

Zack pulled off his wig, then dove inside the bosom of his dress for his phone and pushed a button. "Hello, Janice. Good news. We have him, caught in the act. Two big holes in our expensive manikin." He listened, then said, "Yes, it was Schäuble. You can act on Nicolás Constantine now."

CHAPTER THIRTY-EIGHT

Eagle Feather stood near a window in the large hall, away from the crowd consoling Lucas Leivas' mother, and found refuge looking out at the sunlight just beyond the glass pane. Everyone was standing around awkwardly, it seemed to him. The native people here looked out of place in the setting of a Mormon church hall, although many were members of the church. The larger number of those present probably belonged to the Peyote Church, Eagle Feather guessed.

He felt a touch on his arm and his reverie faded. He looked into the face of Silvia Mike.

"Lucas would find this strange, I think," she said, her eyes moving around the crowded room. "Young as he was, he still mostly adhered to the old beliefs. Lucas was a sky person. He knew the souls of the departed reside in the sky. I suspect he even visited them there when he flew." Her dark eyes locked on his. "You saw him fly."

"I did," Eagle Feather said. His eyes crinkled, almost smiling. "White Man saw it also, but won't let himself believe it."

Silvia smiled. "White men use denial their entire lives, even when that which they do not believe is right in front of their eyes."

"But another man flew as well." Eagle Feather searched her face.

Silvia Mike stared out the window. Her words were soft. "Who knows what lies within us? Even those who begin life's journey inseparable can grow in opposite directions, as branches of the Palo Verde tree never follow the same path."

Eagle Feather studied her face. "I knew when he flew that the killer must have his roots here. I think you know him."

She didn't speak, her eyes were distant.

Eagle Feather was insistent. "You must have known all along, but said nothing. Why?"

"I did not know, I suspected." She took his arm. "Come. We will walk."

The morning was cloudless, the sun's warmth a balm after the air-conditioned formality inside. They found a small garden behind the hall with dirt paths among flowering bushes. Silvia walked for a while in silence.

"Lucas was a twin," she said at last. "Both boys were sons of a famous Chemehuevi runner. The gift was passed to both." Silvia turned her face toward Eagle Feather. "The only way you can become a special desert runner is to be born to it, it must be in your blood. Their father was a legend, but well past his prime when he married. He died when the boys were still babies. Their mother drank too much and could not care for the twins and they were placed in the white man's foster care." She gave a small, helpless gesture. "It is a common story. They were split apart, taken in by two different families and given other names, other lives. Lucas' new family was here, in the land of his ancestors. But those who took his twin took him far away, half-way around the world to some foreign land, I have heard. I know nothing of his life there."

"But you knew he was here now."

"Lucas came to me. He was hired by the tribe to track this assassin and followed him through the desert. He sensed something about him and came to me to ask about this feeling he had. I believe he somehow knew he was tracking his own twin." Silvia stopped walking, turned to Eagle Feather, and looked up into his face. She pointed to her heart. "I knew in here. I counseled him to stop tracking this man, that there would be death at the end of that road." She shook her head. "But of course he could not stop. The call of his twin was too strong."

Eagle Feather looked off at the horizon where brown hills met blue sky. "The killer must have known, do you think? He must have known it was his twin tracking him. He killed him anyway."

Her eyes met his. "They both flew. Of course, he knew."

Janice sat in a wing chair in the living room of the safe house. She had flown down from St. George to officially congratulate the team for bringing the conspirators to justice in what was being called by the media the Lost Oasis case.

"I knew that scumbag Schäuble was involved," Arlene said. "I always knew something was wrong about that man."

Janice smiled. "Well, you were right, Arlene. But he wasn't the chief conspirator, although he stood to gain substantially from the scheme. He served as the eyes and ears for Nicolás Constantine, who was the spider in the web, as Zack would say."

"Who is that guy, anyway?" Sarah asked.

"Nicolás is, was, I should say, the project director for the Desert Energy Storage Facility at EverSun. EverSun is a huge corporation with many irons in the fire. The project here is just one of them. Constantine was the company's link to the project and had full control. Of course, he had his regular reports to file and higher-ups to satisfy, but they were all easily pacified, particularly since the project was almost without controversy, except for the usual groups of environmentalists."

"Did he get greedy?" Arlene asked.

"I think he was always greedy, but saw his really big chance with this project. He was handed the project, I'm told, based on his success with another smaller project he had completed for EverSun. He dug into the history of SolarVenture and saw right through the shell company, tracing it to its roots at San Francisco Power & Light. He immediately recognized the game SFP&L was playing and the illegal, under the table conspiracy with Santini & Marsh Design & Construction. So he dealt himself in, probably for large amounts of cash and stock in both companies.

For their part, this alliance with a controlling player at EverSun had its own advantages. Win, win."

"So a flaw in the game was revealed when Scheidecker discovered the rock pillar at the lost oasis and examined it closely. He realized the significance of the igneous material that constituted it. What then? Did he tell the wrong person?" Zack asked.

Janice held up her palms and shrugged. "We may never know for sure, but undoubtedly he told someone and it got back to Schäuble somehow."

Sarah looked puzzled. "Why was Schäuble so concerned about the mineral content of rock ten miles away?"

Zack explained. "It wasn't the rock pillar so much as the significance of how it got there. It meant a massive intrusion up through the earth's crust meaning a weakness through the entire area, much like what is under Yellowstone National Park. It meant an instability that could not be tolerated if you are building such a large project dependent upon hydrology right on top of it."

"And that depended upon containment of huge amounts of water," Arlene said.

"Without leaks," Zack said.

Janice smiled. It was her first relaxed gleaming-toothed smile in quite a while. "So there you have it. Both Constantine and Schäuble suddenly saw their fortunes begin to slip through their fingers once this information became public. Scheidecker's mouth had to be closed or they stood to lose everything. He couldn't be bought, so

Constantine contracted a very expensive global team of professional killers to erase Scheidecker. They almost got away with it."

"Do we have any clue where Scheidecker is now?" Sarah asked.

Janice waved an arm. "Somewhere out there under tons of rock and sand, I imagine."

"What now?" Arlene asked. "What happens?"

"I think both Nicolás Constantine and Blair Schäuble will become guests of the United States for a very long time, despite an array of very expensive lawyers likely to appear on their behalf. As to EverSun, San Francisco Power & Light, and Santini & Marsh Design & Construction, I'm sure it's business as usual."

Maria favored both men with a flashing smile, grabbed two menus, and her festive dress swaying sauntered in front of them into the dining room. She took them to a table in the corner. She put a menu at each place and with both hands on cocked hips and an impish smile said, "We seem to be in a celebratory mood tonight. Two house margaritas?"

They agreed without argument. A day had passed with Eagle Feather resting and recovering in his suite at the Morongo Casino while Zack helped his team tie up loose ends.

Zack saw Eagle Feather watch Maria sway away. "See something you like?"

"She has a strong presence. There is something different about her."

"Hmmm. No doubt."

Eagle Feather ignored his jibe. "Will you go home now, White Man?"

Zack smiled. "Yes. And you? Back to Elk Wells and the Reservation?"

"It may be wise not to go home just yet, White Man."

Zack stared at the Navajo. "What are you talking about?"

Before he could respond, Maria returned with the drinks. The margaritas looked particularly large and fancy tonight. She placed one in front of each man.

"The drinks are on the house, gentlemen, in recognition of the accomplishment of your mission."

Zack looked up. "Mission?"

Maria laughed. She had a particularly pretty and resonant laugh. "It's all over the news, you know. You two are heroes." She waltzed away.

Zack stared after her. "How could she…?"

"I think she is very, very special," Eagle Feather said.

Zack's eyes narrowed. "Why did you say I should not go home?"

Eagle Feather lifted his glass. "First we drink. Ahóá!"

Zack was puzzled but lifted his glass. "Uh, yes, Cheers!"

After a slow sip, Eagle Feather put down his glass and sighed. "It is not over, White Man."

"Okay, spoil my night, my drink, my meal. Go ahead."

"White Man, I fear there is unfinished business, and if you go home to your family it will follow you there."

"The assassin." Zack's heart sank. "I was certain he was long gone back to where he'd come from. The entire state is looking for him."

"He made a vow to kill you that night in Desert Center."

"I thought it was you he vowed to kill," Zack said. "And you are the one who wounded him."

It was Eagle Feather's turn to look surprised. "You know this for certain?"

"The forensics people did a complete analysis of what they found on your knife. There were two different fingerprints and two different blood types on it. One print was not in any file, the other was yours. One blood type belonged to the victim, the other did not."

"Will I get my knife back?"

Zack laughed. "Not soon. But I'll get it for you eventually. But before you slide away from taking credit here, my reading of the evidence suggests your knife hit home when you threw it at him. Wherever it struck, it lodged deep enough to stay in the man as he ran. Possibly Lucas would not have caught the assassin had your knife not wounded him. Unfortunately, the assassin was apparently able to overpower Lucas, maybe because he had a knife handy."

"Now I am to blame for Lucas' death."

"I do not think that will burden you." Zack thought about it. "It would take a strong man to run on as he did with such a wound."

"He must have flown to reach the Oasis of Mara where he killed Lucas."

Zack carefully set his drink down, his eyes narrowed.

Eagle Feather waved a dismissing hand. "We will not pursue that now. Both Lucas and the assassin possessed special powers. I have never seen a tracker as good as Lucas. His strength, eyesight, hearing, intuition, and endurance were beyond most men."

"Okay, but Lucas is dead. Now you are warning me about the assassin."

Eagle Feather paused. "The assassin is his twin. Silvia told me this."

Zack stared. "Did the killer know he was killing his own twin?"

"That is what Silvia believes."

"Cold bastard," Zack said. He slumped in his chair. Somehow the joy of the evening had evaporated. "But if he is that cold, he should be interested in collecting his fee and getting back to his very lucrative business, not chasing me around."

"You might think that."

"I choose to," Zack said. "How about another one of those outrageously wonderful margaritas?"

CHAPTER THIRTY-NINE

Sobered by the thought of a master hunter lurking in the shadows, if only in the recesses of his mind, Zack found it hard to maintain his mood, despite margaritas that seemed to grow in strength as the evening progressed under the guidance of the beautiful Maria. Eagle Feather, for his part, could not take his eyes off the waitress. The Navajo had indulged well beyond his usual strictly managed code of imbibing and lapsed into silent moodiness.

It was Zack who called a halt to the evening, worried about his friend's recent wound.

"I'm done. The meal is on me, my friend, or should I say my expense account."

"By that you mean the American people, I think," Eagle Feather said. "But I thank you anyway. I will stay for just one more drink."

Zack raised his eyebrows, then peered out toward the hostess counter where Maria was working. "Are you sure it's just one more drink you want?"

"White Man, your total wisdom wouldn't fill a thimble."

Zack gave up, raised his glass saying, "Here's to that!" and drained the remnant. He took a wad of bills from his pocket and counted out a generous number of twenties. "This is from the good people of New York," he said after the first. "This is from the Flower Children of San Francisco," he said of the second. "This is from the forgotten people of Yuma, Arizona, this is from the ever suffering citizens of Blythe…"

Eagle Feather reached out and grabbed his arm. "You'd better stop before the United States goes broke. That's enough money. The people of the Navajo Nation are grateful." He held on to Zack's arm. "Where will you stay tonight?"

"Not far from here. I need to return the truck and rifles to the first safe house before I go home. I'll sleep there."

Eagle Feather let go of his arm but looked concerned.

"Are you worried about me, old friend?" Zack said, smiling.

The Navajo waved him away. "White people take longer to leave than they do to arrive," he said.

Zack stopped at the counter on his way out. Maria was not there. A man Zack knew to be the proprietor greeted him. Zack explained he'd left money with his friend to pay for the meal and a tip. He walked through the screen door, letting it slam behind him and stepped out into the darkness. He knew he was a bit tipsy. The moon had risen, the parking area was a mosaic of shadow patches and light. The white FBI truck gleamed next to Eagle Feather's old rusty red one. Zack fumbled for his keys, pressed the lock release as he came near, opened the door, and stumbled into the driver seat.

"Are you sure you are okay to drive?" A familiar low voice came from the rear seat.

Startled, Zack glanced in the mirror. He saw the barrel of a silenced pistol.

"Actually, maybe not," Zack said and reached for the door handle.

The cold pressure of the gun rested against his neck. "I think you will be fine for the short distance we will travel."

"Where are we going?"

"Where were you planning to go?"

"To the casino to play a few hands of Black Jack."

There was soft laughter. 'Oh, I think not. I think you are going to the safe house. Would you like me to remind you of the address or do you think you can remember the way?"

Zack started the truck. "Wouldn't you like to ride up front? It's much more comfortable."

More laughter. Maria did have the sweetest laugh. "I'm sure you will drive carefully for my benefit."

Zack did as he was told. His brain was foggy, but Maria helped him with turns. Zack's mind thrashed like a bird caught in a net. How could Maria know the way to the safe house? He tried to remember his conversations with Eagle Feather at Garcia's. How had he given it away? He gave it up realizing he was living moment to moment now and needed his brain as clear as possible.

Maria guided him as promised. When he turned in the drive next to the cabin, she instructed him to stop the truck and turn off the engine and with his left hand on the steering wheel, to use two fingers to remove his handgun and lay it on the passenger seat. That done, they stepped out of the truck in careful sequence, Maria always unseen behind him. They went around to the rear of the house and entered with his combination for the security system. Once inside, she directed him to the living room.

"Sit down on the couch, please," Maria said.

Zack did as he was told. He watched Maria sit on a stool facing him, the silenced pistol in her lap. She looked relaxed and confident. Even now she looked incredibly beautiful, so graceful and refined. Zack simply could not grasp the reality of what she truly was—a cold-blooded killer.

She smiled impishly. "You have questions, I'm sure." She watched him. "Or would you rather work it out for yourself?"

Zack's brain could not stop racing through bits of information and experiences, struggling to bring the scattered puzzle pieces into some kind of picture.

Maria watched him with amusement.

"Perhaps it is better if I tell you my story. We have some time before the silent alarms you set off here bring the posse."

Zack could only shake his head in wonder. She seemed to be ahead of him at every step, as indeed the assassin had been all along. But he still wasn't sure.

"Please," he said.

She put the pistol's suppressor barrel against her chin like a finger in a gesture of thinking, in itself a disturbing paradox. "Yes, I think we should start at the beginning. I was born thirty-three years ago right down the road at the Oasis of Mara Reservation. I have learned I had a twin, that my father and mother were Chemehuevi, that my father was a legendary desert runner, all things I learned later in life, because, after all,"—she shrugged—"as far as I knew, I was the only child of a ruthless but successful smuggler who lived in Moldova. I could give you the Cinderella story, say that life was harsh, but really, that was not true. My adopted father was a hateful man, but he raised me to be his heir and gave me everything. But when I crossed him, his punishments were severe." Maria pulled her dress up along a shapely leg to display an angry purple scar shaped like a vee. "One of his little tools, a red hot poker." She let the hem of the dress down, shrugged. "That's the one that shows best, the others are in here," she said, pointing to her head and then her heart. "Anyway, none of that is of interest to you, I'm sure. Suffice to say my daddy taught me many of the skills I needed to become who I am today."

"An assassin for hire," Zack said.

'An odd jobs manager, an obstacle remover, a problem solver." She gave a modest smile. "I try not to limit myself."

"And this job?"

"This job interested me greatly. I had recently met someone of similar interests, formed a new association, and felt an urge to learn about my roots, a curiosity that often follows new relationships. It would not be our first trip to the U.S., but imagine my excitement when I learned this job meant I would be returning to the land of my birth. And it paid very, very well." She gave a little peal of delighted laughter. "How perfect! Of course, I accepted. I spent the intervening weeks doing background research."

"You made Scheidecker disappear."

"Yes. Once they offered him money to keep quiet about that geologic anomaly in the desert and he refused, they recognized they were up against a principled man. No one is more dangerous than a principled man." She winked at Zack. "Much like yourself. There was only one solution for such a person. But what fun! Using my supposed talent I chose to have the scientist disappear abruptly in the very area he had hoped to expose: poof! As if by magic. Fooling, I believe, even your skilled sidekick."

Maria gave a shake of her head as for a naughty child. "We truly thought that would be the end of it. No one seemed to care the man was gone." She snorted. "Certainly not the local cops. We were paid promptly and prepared to leave the area. I had no desire to remain in this place, despite my heritage." She let out another unrestrained peal of merriment. "And then you came along. What fun! And your Indian! A team, just like us! Our employers were ready to pay us vast amounts to make you go away, but I think we would have done it for free."

"You planted the bomb in my Jeep."

"Oh, not me. That was my partner. She is…was very good with explosive devices. A simple, yet effective idea, using the exhaust heat to melt the plastic around the igniter to set it off. She was such a genius!" For a split second her eyes became hard as agate, then softened. "How did you know?"

Zack shrugged. "A lucky accident. I had the window open, heard the plastic rustle in the wind, thought something had caught under the vehicle."

She pouted. "Who rides around in the desert with the windows open? Good luck for you, bad luck for us. It could have ended right there."

"And Dr. Scheidecker's thumbprint on the bomb?"

"Oh, yes. We had to borrow his thumb, but we did put it back."

"I'll guess it was you who ambushed Eagle Feather in the desert."

"Yes. He is a very skillful and resourceful man. He caught my motorcycle with his little sand trick and got away that time."

"It must have been your associate who entered my motel room and used my phone to call Eagle Feather."

She giggled. "Yes, wasn't that cute?"

"Then your employers managed to end the FBI investigation," Zack said.

She pouted again. "That was a mistake. I never thought it would end the problem, but we were paid sufficiently for our time and expense and that was that."

"You left?"

"No, of course not. The fun had just begun. We'd come to know you, in a way. I, for one, never believed you'd give it up." She smiled, almost affectionately. "And you didn't disappoint me."

Zack confessed. "I might have left as directed, but Eagle Feather had already gone to Great Wash to track you. I couldn't leave him out there."

She gave a grim smile. "As I said, a principled man. You went to save your friend. What happened?"

Zack studied her a moment. "You weren't there, were you? You don't know what happened." For the first time, Zack felt a measure of control.

She gestured with the pistol. "Tell me."

"Your partner blew out my truck window. Missed my head by inches. Pure luck, again. But she had me pinned. I had to scramble and was trapped in the hot sun until Eagle Feather found me."

"I don't know whether you two are that good or just plain lucky. Go on. How did you manage to kill my partner?"

"Do you want a drink?" Zack asked. "Since we are going through all this?"

She laughed. "You've had plenty to drink for one night, big fellow. Go on. How did you kill my partner?"

Zack studied her, shrugged. "Eagle Feather had a good idea of the terrain. He had seen where your partner was positioned and guessed she'd use the next arroyo to get to her vehicle. He followed her to drive her toward the road."

"Like herding cattle."

Zack said nothing.

"And?"

"I drove the truck out and set up my shot where the arroyo emptied toward the road."

"And she waltzed right into the ambush." Maria stared at Zack. He couldn't read her expression. "So, to recap, my partner had a shot at you and missed, you had a shot at her and didn't miss."

Zack said nothing.

"And you just left her body there. I'm guessing you never even reported it. You couldn't, could you? Zack Tolliver, FBI agent, called off the case yet killing in cold blood from ambush. How are you and I different?"

Zack pretended it was a rhetorical question and said nothing.

Maria studied him in silence. When she spoke again, her manner had changed.

"After my partner died, the amateurs got involved. They tried to hijack the witness on her way to work, totally blew it. She made them look like what they were—clumsy amateurs."

Zack looked at her, his eyebrows raised. "So that wasn't you?"

She sent him a withering look, disdained to answer.

"But it was you later who shot at Eagle Feather at the project site."

"Just a message to let him know I was still there. My employers were going off the deep end. Once my partner's body was found, you can imagine the concern." Maria pealed off one of her merry laughs. "They must have thought we were done, kaput! And now the FBI is back in it again!" She studied Zack. "You set that all up, leaving the body there. You figured it would go that way, didn't you?"

Zack sighed. "I had hoped."

Mariah seemed like a happy child now, reminding Zack of a little girl humming a tune as she dressed a doll. "This is my favorite part," she said, with a smile. "I come home to my refuge for a few hours sleep at Desert Center and what do I find? The two of you ensconced in my deserted motel office. How did you know which building I was using?"

Zack's head had begun to ache, the night of drinking was catching up adding to the strain of intense focus and great care in his answers. Here was a psychopath of enormous proportions, of incredible power. Who knew what might set her off?

"We simply chose the best building for our purpose. Our choices aligned, it seems."

"Luck again! Don't you ever worry your luck will run out?"

Zack shrugged. He seemed to be continually shrugging. "I do the best I can and hope for the best."

Her laughter came, completely unrestrained. Her joy in the moment lent her incredible charm. Zack had never met someone so charismatic…and so deadly.

She eyed him with fondness, then said, "Now we've got the amateurs out in full force, their next great act is an attempt to use that geologist as a spy to learn your plans. But by now you've got your clever little app in his phone, and you broke up their highway meeting."

"But we didn't catch them." He glanced at her. "How did you know about that?"

"I was watching you from the rest area. "

"It was you who ran me off the road."

She nodded modestly. "I borrowed their SUV. But again, you were lucky."

He groaned, remembering. "I didn't feel lucky."

Maria seemed to grow impatient, her mood had changed yet again. "It's time to end all this."

Zack watched her face, looked for clues. "You don't want to talk about Lucas, do you?"

A look of wonder crossed her features. "What an amazing thing, to find a twin after all these years." Her eyes were wide. "You actually feel it, you know? I knew who he was when he began tracking me. He was so good! It was a challenge to stay in front of him." She giggled again. "But it was fun, so much fun. But my employers were panicking. I knew they would crack. I knew it was time to sever all my connections to this job. I had hoped to wrap it all up at the trailer in Coon Hollow. You figured it out. The scientist was my bait. I got all three of you there, but something warned you. Did you see me there in the trees?"

"Yes."

"Luck, luck, luck. You have such incredible luck. And then you set me up at the sun healing ceremony. "

"I had a feeling you'd come."

"That was a mistake," Maria said with a low shake of her head. "I knew it was a big risk. But it was so much money! I had to take the chance!" She looked like a sad little girl whose ball of ice cream had fallen off her cone. "I wore body armor, though. I don't like to wear it, but this was too chancy. Your sharpshooter hit me square in the back, knocked me unconscious for a moment, in fact. I had expected the ambush, but I thought I'd find you first. But I didn't. Strange. Like destiny, almost."

"You were smart to run toward the crowd, no one could shoot."

"That was my only chance. I knew your Indian friend was there, I knew I'd have to take him out. I was surprised he didn't shoot me, then realized he didn't even have a gun. So I shot him, but he did this amazing little twisting move and this knife comes out of nowhere." Maria carefully lifted her skirt from her other leg. There was an angry horizontal wound in her leg adjacent to her pelvis, four inches long, stitched with black thread. She dropped the hem. "I had to run with his knife sticking out of me." She laughed, a long rippling musical sound. "He looked fine tonight. He seems to heal well."

"He's had a lot of practice."

"Yes, well the knife slowed me down. That's the only reason Lucas caught me." Her look was smug, happy even. "But it was meant to be. We bonded. There had been a piece missing from me—I always knew it." She waved an arm across in front of her, tracing an imaginary path, elegant, graceful. "The breeze against my face, running, bounding, floating, nothing felt real except the two of us. He was behind me but part of me, we connected, shared

370

the secret of who we are, all while moving through this unreal landscape, like a dream."

Zack saw her turn inward, live it all over again.

"We came to this place of palms and grasses and pure water and faced each other, looked into each other's eyes, looked into each other's hearts. Here were our missing pieces, found, whole again. I pulled the knife from my leg and put it in his heart." Her eyes were dreamy. "It was the final, perfect act. It was the completion of my life's cycle. I can leave here now, a whole person."

She stood in a single graceful movement, the gun pointed at Zack's heart. "There really is no more to say."

CHAPTER FORTY

Zack waited for the impact of the bullet. The imminence
of his death felt strange rather than frightening or sad. It
was ever there in the back of his mind, this knowledge he
would die someday, obscured by the veil of everyday
reality. He had thought he would hate it, fight it, not accept
it like a lamb when it came. Yet something about this
hypnotic, psychopathic, charismatic killer made all of it
seem natural.

"Take off your shoes," she said.

He did.

She gestured with the pistol. "Stand up. Take off your
pants."

He raised his eyebrows but didn't argue. He dropped
them in a heap in front of his shoes.

She gestured again, in an almost bored way. "Your
shirt."

Zack unbuttoned his shirt, slipped out of it, and let it
drop on his pants.

"Sit down, please."

He sat back down on the couch.

In one quick motion, Mariah scooped up Zack's pants
and shirt and lay them on her stool. Then, turning to face
him, the pistol leveled at his chest, she worked at the
buttons of her dress with the other hand and let it drop to
the ground. She stood, statuesque, a perfect figure
blemished only by a scar on one leg and stitches on the

other. Her hand went to her bra and everything fell to the floor.

Zack stared, shocked. Where her breasts had been was a patch of dark hair on a masculine chest. She tugged at her head and all the long dark tresses came off in her hand. She flipped the wig to the floor. Before Zack could fully comprehend what he was seeing, Mariah slipped on Zack's shirt, then pulled on his pants over her moccasin-like slippers.

Dressed again, she stared at Zack, eyes dark as almonds, black eyebrows on olive skin, teeth white against red lips, as captivatingly beautiful a man as she had been a woman. She gestured again with the pistol and Zack stood up. She came to him, pressed herself against him, placed the suppressed pistol barrel against his temple. Her lips came against his. They were cold as ice. She inhaled, her breath drew the air from his lungs like a vacuum. Her eyes seemed to reach into his soul.

He waited to die.

She removed the gun, turned from him, and walked to the door. "We will meet again someday," she said and was gone.

He heard the truck start, listened to her drive away.

Zack remained unmoving for a very long time. It was not easy to return from the dead. When at last he could move, he walked to the open door and stepped outside. The air was still warm and lapped up against him, warming his cold body, his cold soul. There was the smell of sage, night smells, earthy smells. He looked up. The stars were brilliant in their multitudes across the vast dark bowl. Somewhere a nighthawk cried, a faraway dog barked. Slowly, Zack turned back to the cabin.

Tomorrow, he would go home to his family.

Tomorrow, he would find a way to explain to Janice how he'd lost another FBI vehicle.

Have your read all
R Lawson Gamble's *Zack Tolliver, FBI*, Series?

Prequel: THE DARK ROAD *The Beginning*

THE OTHER

MESTACLOCAN

ZACA

CAT

UNDER DESERT SAND

CANAAN'S SECRET

LAS CRUCES

THE OASIS

OTHER TITLES

PAYU'S JOURNEY

JOHNNY AND THE KID An Old Time Western

Made in the USA
San Bernardino, CA
10 July 2020

75245472R00234